HIGHLANDS CHRISTMAS TRILOGY BOOKS 1-3

HIGHLANDS CHRISTMAS TRILOGY BOOKS 1-3

LOVE. SNOW. HOME.

HIGHLANDS CHRISTMAS ROMANCE

AMY QUICK PARRISH

FLYING CACTUS

Copyright © 2024 by Amy Quick Parrish

All rights reserved.

No part of this book may be reproduced in any form or by any electronic or mechanical means, including information storage and retrieval systems, without written permission from the author, except for the use of brief quotations in a book review. No part of this book may be used or reproduced in any manner for the purpose of training artificial intelligence technologies or systems.

AMY QUICK PARRISH

Highlands Christmas
Books 1-3

THE HIGHLANDS TRILOGY:

LOVE. SNOW. HOME.

For those torn between a cozy Hallmark Christmas movie in July and a documentary on the Loch Ness Monster—this one's for you.

And to my family, who'd probably rather read something else but they still cheer me on anyway—thanks for putting up with me!

AMY QUICK
PARRISH
Highlands
Christmas
Wishes Come True
A
NOVELLA

CHAPTER 1

Snow fell lightly on a cozy upscale home decorated in full Christmas splendor: candles glowed in the windows, icicle lights twinkled on the roof, white lights danced around tall pine trees and sparkled on the bushes. On the front door, a huge balsam wreath with a giant red bow and sparkling lights welcomed visitors.

Through the bay window, a group of guests shared food around a dinner table as laughter filled the air. A fire roared below a mantle covered in greenery, and the rest of the home was decked out to the nines with poinsettias, greenery, and ornaments. A tiny Christmas village with a toy train running through it filled the bay window.

The dining room table was decorated in a festive tablecloth, reindeer napkin rings, and in the center of it all—and quite out of place—a rather garish centerpiece consisting of a tacky toy squirrel holding a bowl of shelled walnuts.

"Who's having another slice of pie?" asked the hostess, Melissa Mackenzie, dressed in a red sweater and a green-and-red plaid skirt. She held up a perfect, tempting slice. Everyone shook their heads no.

"Dave?" Melissa asked her balding husband, who was ignoring her and speaking to a younger, vivacious blond to his right. "Dave? How about another slice of pie?"

Dave looked up, slightly annoyed. "I'm stuffed."

Melissa held out a slice toward the woman Dave was speaking to. She was her brother's ex and a friend. Dave had convinced her that Samantha would be lonely this time of year, and they should invite her since her brother couldn't attend.

"Samantha?"

Samantha plastered on a grin and shook her perfectly-styled blonde hair.

"I'd be so fat I—" She paused and put a hand over her mouth as Melissa frowned and adjusted her sweater over her middle. "I mean, I just couldn't. Right now," finished Samantha.

"I've got a whole other pie in the kitchen. I'll send everyone home with a slice," said Melissa.

The guests, still glassy-eyed from their food comas, reacted somewhere between happy anticipation and overwhelmed guilt.

Melissa began to clear the plates, and two friends followed her into the kitchen to help.

"Oh, really, I can do it," said Melissa.

They insisted, and Melissa accepted their help.

"How about a little Christmas music?" Melissa asked.

"It's still Thanksgiving weekend," Dave complained.

"I'll play the snow-related, family songs, then."

She planted a loving kiss on Dave's cheek, but he brushed past her and turned back to the football game in the living room.

"Oh, that's right. The game."

There was a slight rustling sound in the walls. Melissa froze for a second. Dave banged on the wall, paused, then banged again.

"Those darn squirrels!" muttered Dave.

Melissa shook her head and returned to the kitchen,

cranking up the volume on the music with songs such as "There's No Place Like Home for the Holidays," "Let it Snow," and "Winter Wonderland."

Melissa was in her element, humming and sometimes singing along with the music as guests took part in washing, wiping, and drying. It was a warm, merry vibe, and Melissa loved it.

"Melissa, I love what you've done with this place. I remember the kitchen when you first bought it. And the dining room—what a transformation!" her friend Carol gushed.

"Thanks. Well, with a degree in interior design, I may as well put myself to good use!"

As people began to leave, Melissa handed them beautifully wrapped Martha-Stewart-worthy packages of leftovers, complete with red tartan bows on top.

"Melissa, this is stunning. You shouldn't have," said another guest.

"Oh, it's nothing. I just love Christmas time. Anything to make it last. Luckily, we still have three more weeks."

As the guests left, she noticed Dave hugged Samantha a little longer than necessary. Melissa felt a pit in her stomach, but shook it off and walked over to hug Samantha herself.

"Thanks so much for being here, Samantha. I know it's been such a hard year for you after your breakup with Ted."

Samantha looked up. "What? Oh. Right. Ted." Somehow in the seconds between the hugs, she had managed to tie her scarf in a perfect loose knot. Melissa noticed how together Samantha looked. So odd, considering the garish hostess gift she'd given.

"And thank you for the, uh ... nut basket. It's lovely." Melissa gestured toward the hideous basket filled with shelled nuts and a giant, ugly plush squirrel. It just didn't look like something anyone with Samantha's sense of style would give.

"I just saw it and thought of you," said Samantha as she slipped on stylish black boots.

Melissa snapped back into gracious host mode, plastering on the best smile she could as she helped the guests with their coats.

WITH THE DISHWASHER humming and the last guests driving away, Melissa plopped down on the couch in front of the crackling fire and cozied up under a wool tartan blanket. Dave shuffled in. There was another rustling sound in the walls. He banged on the wall.

"I'll call the squirrel guys again. This is ridiculous," he said.

Melissa was still lost in her thoughts. "What a wonderful party. I'm so glad everyone could make it. Of course, it's nice with just the two of us ..."

Melissa lifted the blanket, an invitation for Dave to join her, which he ignored.

"Lions lost again," said Dave.

"That's too bad. Come. Sit. I really want to snuggle up and talk to you about—"

"I want to talk to you, too," said Dave.

Melissa flushed with excitement. "I was thinking we should take a trip—maybe somewhere really Christmassy, like London, Quebec, Paris, or what about Norway? I've been doing some research, and I think—"

"I want a divorce," said Dave.

Melissa felt like she'd been blindsided by a truck. She couldn't have heard that right.

Dave continued. "I was waiting until the party was over."

Melissa finally found her voice. "But why do you—"

"And I'm seeing Samantha," added Dave.

"Samantha, who was just here? Samantha, who dumped my brother? Samantha, who brought that awful squirrel-nut centerpiece?"

"Yes."

It was silent for a few moments as Melissa tried to process the situation. Dave stood with his mouth pressed into a tight line, waiting.

"What about Christmas?" asked Melissa.

"I'm going to Barbados," said Dave.

"For Christmas? There's no snow."

"Exactly. Melissa, you're the one who likes the snow and the holidays. I'm sick of it. I'm ready to move on. I'm sorry."

"Move on?"

They never traveled anywhere, and all of a sudden, he was going to Barbados? With her brother's ex?

As Dave put on his coat, Melissa remained stunned.

"Where are you going?" she asked.

"To Samantha's. I think it would be a good idea if I'm gone for a few days so you can get your stuff out."

"*My* stuff?!"

"The house is in my name. I'm keeping it."

* * *

As Melissa woke up, she smiled as she saw the snow-lined windowpanes and the cozy Christmas candles in the windows. Then, as she reached for her phone and saw several missed calls, she remembered her reality.

Thank goodness. He's calling back to apologize, Melissa thought. But the call was from a number she didn't recognize. She pressed play.

"Good morning," a lovely Highlands accent chirped. "This is Colin MacGregor from MacGregor, Stewart, and Duncan. I'm phoning about the, uh, matter with your … with Dave. Please ring me at your earliest convenience so that I might know the name of your lawyer."

Melissa sighed. It was real after all. As the tears welled up, Melissa set the phone down and slowly dragged herself out of bed. She pulled on a cozy plaid bathrobe and slippers and lit a fire. Once it was crackling, she plopped herself in the comfy chair beside the fire and made a phone call.

"Hello? Marty? ... Oh, fine. And you? ... I mean, I guess I'm not fine. I need a lawyer, and I wonder if you would ... Tuesday? Sounds good. And I can give them your name as my representative? ... Of course." As she hung up, the tears poured out. She tore into a box of tissues and looked outside.

Yesterday's glorious, shimmering snow had turned to soggy, wet, black grit over wet leaves. Sheets of cold rain fell. Melissa threw a raincoat over her bathrobe and donned some bright red rain boots. She opened the door and shuffled out to the mailbox, unsuccessfully attempting to dodge mud puddles and raindrops. She collected the mail and slogged through the wet leaves and pools of rain back up the walkway to the house.

BACK IN HER COZY CHAIR, Melissa sorted through the mail. Something caught her eye—HUME REAL ESTATE ASSOCIATES. She looked more closely, noticing the return address, *Inverness, Scotland*. Melissa didn't know anyone in Scotland, and it seemed like a long way to send marketing spam. She cracked open a very elaborate seal and opened the letter.

DEAR MS. MACKENZIE,

We are dreadfully sorry to inform you of the passing of Mr. Stuart Mackenzie this past September. After searching through our records, we have discovered that you are his third cousin once removed and the next of kin.

Please ring us at your earliest convenience to discuss plans for receiving your inheritance—among the items are Greenhill, his Inverness estate.

Unfortunately, the estate is in disrepair. We note that you live in the US. Our company can provide the service of liquidating the property and providing you with the proceeds, minus our handling fee.

Please contact us at your earliest convenience to arrange for the liquidation and kindly provide your banking information so we can transfer the funds into your account.

Best wishes,

Archibald Hume, Hume Real Estate Associates

MELISSA SET the letter down and opened her laptop. She searched for *Hume Real Estate Associates.* A respectable looking website appeared. She searched for *Greenhill Inverness estate* and saw a cozy stone home on the banks of what looked like a river. She read the description.

"On Loch Ness! Wow!"

She re-read the letter and glanced back at the photo of the home. She could see what appeared to be a solid foundation. It needed some paint, and the description talked about some other minor updates needed. *I can fix that up myself,* she thought.

Her phone rang. Without looking to see who it was, Melissa answered.

"Did you get a lawyer?" It was Dave. *Ugh.* How had she never noticed that terrible tone of voice he always had?

"Good morning, Dave."

"Did you get a lawyer, Melissa? Or are you incapable?"

In the distance, Melissa could hear Samantha's voice. "Dave, come back to bed."

"In a minute," Dave called to her. Melissa rolled her eyes. "My lawyer will be out of the country for the holidays, so I need to know if—"

Melissa took a deep breath and held her head up, the way she always did right before closing a deal for one of her clients. She smiled. "I have a lawyer. He'll be in touch." She hung up.

Empowered and a bit inspired, Melissa stomped upstairs and into her bedroom.

She pulled a suitcase out of her closet and began to fill it. She heard a squirrelly noise rustling in the walls. She banged on the wall, and the noise stopped. She got dressed, went to her computer, and searched a travel site and a map.

"Inverness. Inverness." She could see an airport there, but all the flights she could find went to Glasgow or Edinburgh. "Edinburgh it is! And I'll have a lovely train ride afterwards."

She clicked *COMPLETE ORDER* and snapped her laptop shut.

She got some notepaper and scrawled a quick note. *Good luck with the house.*

Melissa dragged her suitcase down the stairs and put the note on the dining room table next to the dreadful, obnoxious squirrel-nut centerpiece.

She opened the door. Several squirrels frolicked in the yard, chasing each other and flicking their tails. She grinned, lumbered back inside and grabbed Samantha's garish nut basket, then set it in the doorway.

Melissa made a little squirrel noise to draw their attention. The squirrel closest to her stood up on its hind legs and looked at her. "Yes, you. Come on in!" Then Melissa flung the front door wide open. She waved at her ride share driver and got into the car. As they drove away, Melissa grinned as she watched a stream of squirrels scuttle into the house.

CHAPTER 2

Melissa looked flustered as she dragged her suitcase through the festive terminal. A giant Christmas tree decorated with tinsel and dazzling white lights was in the center of the terminal, and balsam garlands lined the corridors. There were poinsettias at each gate, and some of the airline workers wore elf and Santa hats. As she stood in line at a coffee shop, she noticed a handsome man in a tweed jacket talking on the phone a few feet away.

"Yes, I'm terribly sorry. It's just that I have some personal business to attend to. So she does have a lawyer? ... Lovely. And the name is ... I see. Perhaps I could ring her myself? ... Very good. Thank you. And Happy Christmas." The man hung up.

Melissa mocked his charming accent just the tiniest bit. "And a happy Christmas one and all," she whispered to herself.

The man made another phone call.

Melissa's phone rang, and she answered, "Hello?"

The man in front of her began speaking. "Yes, I'm looking for a Melissa Mackenzie? Terribly sorry, but your husb—er, my client, Dave Foster, needs—*I* need the name of your barrister."

They moved up in line. Still on the phone, he attempted to

whisper his order. "Yes. A short cappuccino with no foam and—"

"Are you ordering coffee?" Melissa asked into her phone.

The man in front of her turned away from the barista and tried to hold his ear as he spoke into the phone. "Terribly sorry. Yes. I beg your pardon—"

Melissa tapped him on his tweed-covered shoulder. He turned around, startled. He was a dream: a young mix of Sean Connery and Colin Firth with a dash of salt and pepper hair.

She was a bit bedazzled. He was just plain confused.

He pulled his phone away from his ear. "Terribly sorry. Have I taken your spot in the queue?"

"No, I'm on the phone—" Melissa tried to explain.

"Didn't mean to interrupt," he responded.

Melissa held up her phone and talked into it, exaggerating for his benefit. "Sir? I believe I'm in line behind you. At the airport," she added.

Mortified, the man hung up the phone and looked at her as the barista stared at him.

"That'll be $5.95. Who's next?" asked the barista.

He fumbled for his wallet and paid as Melissa moved forward.

"I'd like a peppermint mocha, low fat, no whip," said Melissa.

"You want whipped cream on that?" asked the barista.

Melissa blinked. "Uh, no. Thank you."

"Name?"

"Melissa."

The barista wrote on the cup, and Melissa paid.

The man stood silently as Melissa put her wallet away.

"So, you must be Ms. Mackenzie," he said.

"And you must be Colin MacGregor of MacGregor, Stewart, and Duncan," said Melissa.

"I'm sorry."

"It's nothing. It's—" Tears filled Melissa's eyes, and she struggled for a moment.

Colin reached into his jacket pocket and handed her a lovely pressed handkerchief.

"Oh. How nice. Old school." She blew her nose, then looked down at the soiled handkerchief. "I, uh ... I guess I'll be keeping this? I can launder it and get it back—"

"No worries," said Colin.

They stood awkwardly until the coffee arrived. Colin took his and began to wheel away his suitcase. Just then, Melissa's coffee arrived with whipped cream and festive sprinkles on top. Melissa looked at it.

"Didn't you order no whip?" asked Colin.

"Well. Yeah. But this is pretty—"

"Miss? My friend here ordered hers with no whip and—"

"She said *whip*," said the barista, curtly.

"Actually, I distinctly heard her say *no whip*, so since she paid $5.95 for this, you can kindly get her the coffee she requested. Thank you."

Melissa beamed as the barista sighed and made another coffee.

"You're a great lawyer," she said.

"Thank you. I do my best," he said, smiling.

They both paused as they realized they were on opposite sides of the divorce legalities ahead. He held out his hand to shake.

"Lovely meeting you, Ms. Mackenzie."

"And you, Mr. MacGregor. Happy Christmas."

* * *

MELISSA MANEUVERED through the aisle toward her seat. She was loaded down with home design magazines, Scotland guidebooks, an iPad, headphones, snacks, and a neck pillow. She balanced her coffee precariously as she shuffled into her seat. Just as she began to settle, her seatmate arrived.

Melissa stuffed as much as she could under the seat in front of her and tried to suck in her gut so the passenger could get to her seat. Melissa smiled brightly as the passenger awkwardly tried to pass by her but failed. Finally, Melissa hoisted herself up, slid out into the aisle, and knocked into another passenger.

"Sorry," said Melissa.

Melissa had just slid back into her seat when another passenger approached to sit just beyond the first one. Melissa repeated the same slide-and-shuffle.

"Please take your seats and fasten your seat belts," said the flight attendant.

"I'm working on it."

Melissa sat down and began to get organized. Soon all the magazines, books, and iPad were in the seat compartment, her pillow was around her neck, and her carry-on and snacks were under the seat. Just as she was about to put on her headphones, the older woman next to her struck up a conversation.

"First time to Scotland?" she asked.

"Yes," Melissa responded.

"Are you going for business or pleasure?"

"I, uh ..."

"Visiting family?"

"Well, um ... not exactly." Melissa looked ready to cry. She bit her lip, but soldiered on. "I've inherited a home in Inverness."

"Lovely. You're going to check it out, and then your husband will join you?"

Melissa smiled. "You know, I'm so exhausted. Time for a little beauty rest. Talk soon." Melissa put on her headphones and eye mask and pretended to sleep.

* * *

MELISSA PEEKED through her mask as a cheery flight attendant pushed a cart down the aisle.

The attendant smiled down at Melissa. “Good morning. Coffee, tea, orange juice?”

“Coffee, please.”

“Would you like juice as well?”

“Can I?”

“Of course.”

Melissa scrambled to put away her headphones and all her magazines as the flight attendant stood with a frozen smile, holding the drinks. Melissa finally was able to lower the tray table.

“Sorry,” said Melissa, flushing a bit.

“Here you are.” The flight attendant handed her the drinks, and Melissa accepted them.

Melissa glanced up at the map screen and saw they were over Ireland and nearing Scotland. She looked out the window. It was so green. Gradually, she began to relax and shake away her troubles and replace them with excitement. She was going to have a new life.

CHAPTER 3

In the airport baggage claim, Melissa watched as suitcases began to tumble down the conveyor belt. She reached for hers, lifted it onto the ground, and started to walk away, but stopped as a voice called her name.

"Ms. Mackenzie?"

Melissa turned to see Colin MacGregor. He was a bit more rumpled than before, from the flight, but still ruggedly handsome.

"Hi, Mr. MacGregor," she said with a smile.

"I believe you have my bag."

"Um. No, this is mine. See?" Melissa bent down to show him the tag. It read *Colin MacGregor.*

"Oh," she said, feeling her cheeks begin to warm.

"And I have yours." He wheeled an identical suitcase over to her. She took the handle.

"Sorry 'bout that," she said, still flushing.

"No worries. I made the same mistake."

There was an awkward pause.

"I'll, uh, be in touch," Colin said.

"Oh?" Melissa said, confused and a tiny bit hopeful. Then she remembered he was Dave's lawyer and reality came crashing down again. She put on her most neutral, confident smile. "Right. Right. Great. Sure."

Embarrassed, she wheeled her suitcase over toward the taxi lines. Colin trailed right behind her. They stood there as taxis came and went. Melissa took a deep breath and stepped into a taxi, nodding slightly to Colin as they sped away.

* * *

MELISSA LOOKED out the window at the gorgeous city of Edinburgh. She was thrilled.

Beautiful stone buildings, hilly streets, bagpipers playing on the street corners, and Edinburgh Castle overlooking it all from atop a hill—it was just breathtaking. Everything was covered in a glistening layer of new snow. On top of that, the city was in full Christmas spirit: pillars covered in greenery, giant wreaths, markets lined with lights and evergreen garlands.

"Look at this! It's straight out of a fairy tale!"

The taxi driver dropped her off at the train station. "Here we are," he said.

"Thank you so much." Melissa tipped him, and he helped her with her bag.

At the train station, as Melissa stood in line, she noticed another man in front of her had the same bag. He bought his ticket and turned back, nearly knocking into her. It was Colin.

"Small world," said Melissa, just inches away from him. He smelled like soap and wool.

"Indeed," said Colin, trying to step back. They both nodded to each other and walked toward the platform.

MELISSA HOISTED her suitcase onto the train and walked down the aisle to find her seat. As she settled into her seat, she noticed

Colin MacGregor had boarded after her. Melissa held her breath and buried her nose in a novel until he passed her. She breathed a sigh of relief.

Colin came back moments later. "Apparently, I'm 24-A," he said with a nervous grin.

He sat beside her. They both looked uncomfortable, and there was a long silence.

Melissa brightened. "You're on holiday, right? That's what they say in the UK?"

"Aye," said Colin. Melissa felt the warmth returning to her cheeks. What an adorable accent.

"So if you're on holiday, it's okay, right? You're just a guy on a train. You happened to sit next to me, and you can't work on —" A thought occurred to her. "You're not here to spy on me, are you? Do lawyers do that?"

Colin sat up in his chair, offended. "Of course not. We don't do that. It's just a job. I wanted to be a barrister, and family law sounded prosperous, so—"

"Making money from divorces?"

"Well, I …" Colin looked flustered.

"So what brings you here? I see you've got the accent. But you're definitely a New Yorker now, with the—" She saw his reaction and switched course. Good going, Melissa. Way to stereotype a busy lawyer. "Wow, will you look at this countryside? And those sheep? Amazing."

Colin glanced out the window. "I hadn't missed the sheep."

"I'll let you get back to your work," said Melissa, relieved that at least she had changed the topic. Melissa turned her gaze toward the window and tried to focus on the scenery rather than the aroma of Colin's pine-scented soap.

* * *

Melissa was eating a salad and looking out the window at the Scottish countryside. She had made friends with a middle-aged woman across the aisle and was chatting away.

"This is just the most beautiful country in the world. Of course, I haven't traveled much. Dave, my husband—well, he's soon to be my ex-husband—he never wanted to travel," she said.

"I'm so sorry, dear," replied the woman.

"It's okay, though. It's going to be okay. He's taking the house, but—you'll never believe it—I've inherited a home in Inverness."

"Really? What a wonderful surprise."

"You're telling me! I never even knew the guy, but I'm his long-lost relative. So as soon as I got the letter, I bought a ticket out here to come see it. The company wanted to liquidate it for me and just send me the money, but I've done a lot of home renovations. And I needed a … change. So I thought why not?"

Colin looked over at Melissa.

"That's amazing. And what perfect timing," said the woman.

"I know, right?"

Colin began to look suspicious but tried to appear focused on his work.

"And you don't even know the deceased? Incredible," said the woman.

"Quite. Forgive me. Might I see that letter?" asked Colin.

Melissa brightened and rummaged through her bag.

"Here it is," she said.

Colin examined the letterhead. He scanned the letter and frowned. "You didn't give them your account information, did you?"

"No. I thought I should just take the house. I'll go to their office and straighten it out, and then I can just move in."

Melissa was beaming, but Colin looked troubled.

"Would you mind, Melissa, if I researched this a bit?" he asked.

"Why would you want to research it?" Her words hung in the air until a thought occurred to her. "Oh, no. Would I have to split this with Dave?"

Colin took a deep breath. "Not if you wait until you're divorced to accept it. And, actually, you can speak to your barrister and be sure it's only in your name. Or in the name of a child, or even a pet, perhaps."

"Are you allowed to tell me all that?" Melissa asked.

Colin smiled. "I'm on holiday. I'm just chatting with a woman on a train."

Melissa grinned.

"Can you tell me again the name of the company that sent the letter?" asked Colin.

Melissa read from the letter while Colin searched on his laptop. "Hume Real Estate Associates. Inverness, Scotland."

He deftly typed the name and soon found a hit. "Well, they're real," he said.

"Did you think it might not be real?" she asked.

"Sometimes when there's a divorce, scam artists will move in and—"

"Oh, but Dave just asked for the divorce the other night. There's no way a company would have—" She stopped as she saw Colin's face. "What?"

He looked down, then back at her. "I've been employed by your husband for several months. We've been working on divorce proceedings for quite some time," he said. Melissa sat quietly. "I'm so sorry," he said, as her eyes began to fill with tears.

"So … since Halloween? All through November. And he … those late nights at work. And he invited her to Thanksgiving. I babysat her kids when she went on that long weekend at the same time he had a conference." Melissa's face was beginning to flush, and her stomach was in knots.

The woman across the aisle took Melissa's hand. "That's awful."

Even Colin, the callous divorce lawyer, sympathized with Melissa. "I'm so sorry," he said again.

"I'm getting a dog, and I'm gonna put the house in the dog's name until this is over," Melissa said with determination before she buried her nose in her book in hopes of hiding the tears that were threatening to fall.

CHAPTER 4

The train rolled to a stop. A sign on the platform read *INVERNESS*.

Melissa got out of her seat. She felt unsteady and nervous, but determined. "Well, this is my stop. Nice meeting you … Both of you," she added.

"It's my stop as well. We seem to be following each other," said Colin.

Melissa smiled and made a show of checking that she had the correct bag. She let Colin pass before she left the train. As she stepped outside the train station, Melissa looked around. Inverness was a relatively modern-looking city but with old-world charm. The River Ness flowed through the city center surrounding Inverness Castle—a much newer castle than what she'd seen in Edinburgh, built with smooth red sandstone on a small hill. Along the river, the bridges and walkways were decorated with greenery, wreaths, holly, bows, and lights. The sound of bagpipes filled the air as a light snow fell.

"You'll find taxis to your left, or a ride share to your right. Very nice meeting you, Ms. Mackenzie. And best of luck," said Colin.

"Thank you. Uh ... Happy Christmas?" she said.

"To you as well," Colin smiled.

His cell rang, and he answered, waving as Melissa made her way to the taxi stand.

Inside the taxi, Melissa was excited to begin her journey—that is, until the taxi driver spoke in a thick Highland accent.

"Càite?"

"Um, no, I'm Melissa. Nice to meet you," she said.

The taxi driver grinned. *"Aye,* lassie. I said, *'Whaur tae?'"* He still had an accent, but at least he was speaking in English. Or Scots. Still, it took Melissa a moment to process.

"Where to? I'm going to Hume Real Estate Associates. I have the address," she said, handing him a slip of paper, but he dismissed her.

"Never *ye mind, ah ken whaur* that is," he said.

"Oh. Great. Lovely," she said, trying out a new word that seemed more British than *beautiful.*

Melissa looked out at the snowy streets and enticing shops while the taxi driver chatted away in a thick Highland accent, which she had a lot of difficulty following. He pointed toward a large castle.

"This is Caisteal Inbhir Nis, bult` in th' 18th hunner years, bit castles ha' staun 'ere sin th' 11th hunner years, mynd. Th' foremaist wis bult` by Malcom III."

Melissa had no idea what he was saying, so she did what she often did when Dave talked about work. "That's very interesting."

"Aye, and that's *nae th' hauf o'* it," said the taxi driver.

"Oh?"

"Aye. Whin Maìri, Queen o' Scots cam tae Inbhir Nis in 1562, she fun th' gates o' th' castle shut against her. Th' clans Fraser 'n' Munroe teuk Inbhir Nis castle fur th' queen, whilk hud refused her admission. Th' queen efter hanged th' governor, a Gòrdan wha hud refused entry."

"You don't say," said Melissa as she tried to pick out words here and there. She got 'Mary, Queen of Scots,' 'castle,' 'refused admission,' and 'hanged.'

She was relieved to see the real estate office ahead. Melissa's taxi parked. She looked around. The parking lot was empty, and it was dark inside the building. She leaned toward the driver, still in his taxi.

"Would you mind waiting just a bit?" she asked.

"Na kinch," he responded. Melissa was baffled.

"I'm sorry?"

"Dinnae be sorry, na fashes. Ah will hauld yer horses," he said with a twinkle in his eye.

"Well, I'm not in a hurry. I'd just like you to wait a minute, if you wouldn't mind?"

"Aye, Lassie. As I've been telling you, *dinnae fash yersel,"* he repeated.

Taking that as a yes, Melissa walked to the front door and knocked. She knocked again, but given the empty parking lot and the darkness of the windows, she knew she was defeated.

She returned to the taxi.

"They're closed. The house is about twelve miles from here. Maybe I need to rent a car. Do you know any place?"

"O' coorse. Richt by th' train station. I'll tak' ye straightaway," said the driver.

"Oh, thank you," said Melissa.

She sat in silence as the taxi wove through traffic. At the car rental lot, the driver helped her with her luggage.

"Enjoy your time in Scotland, Miss," he said, clear as day and with a grin.

"But you—I couldn't underst—I mean—Thank you," Melissa said, flustered.

"Just a bit of atmosphere I like to provide to the tourists. Safe travels." He waved as he drove off.

* * *

Melissa got into the left side of the car and saw the steering wheel was on the other side. *Oops.* She scooted herself awkwardly over to the driver's side of the car. Melissa tried to get her bearings. She took a deep breath and looked down. The gear shift was on the left-hand side.

"Oh my gosh. It's a stick." *Deep breath,* Melissa thought to herself. Then she took out her letter, plugged the address into the GPS, and turned on the ignition. She took another deep breath. *It's just driving. You can do this.* She slowly backed up. She turned. She started going forward, and there was another car heading right toward her. She panicked and slammed on the breaks. She let the car in front of her go. Then another car. Then another car. And another car. Finally, with an empty street ahead, but a lineup behind her, the car stalled. She started it up again and turned left. But she was still going the wrong way.

Cars leaned on their horns.

"Oh my gosh. Okay. Deep breath."

Melissa turned back into the parking lot and waited. The car stalled again.

Gritting her teeth, she started the car again. She watched the flow of traffic, closed her eyes for a moment, then opened them and made the turn. She was doing it!

"Alba gu brath!" Melissa screamed out the only Scottish phrase she knew: *Scotland Forever.* Beaming, she drove down the correct/wrong side of the street. But now there was a rotary in her path.

"Okay, Mel. You got this," she said, clutching the steering wheel. Gingerly, she turned. For a moment, she was veering straight into oncoming traffic.

"Nope, nope, other way," she told herself as she corrected the car and made her way past the roundabout.

She'd been holding her breath the entire time. She exhaled and continued driving out of Inverness.

* * *

MELISSA CLENCHED the steering wheel as she maneuvered down a narrow little road along the River Ness. River Ness ... something familiar about that. It finally dawned on her when she saw the sign: *Loch Ness*. Of course! Delighted, Melissa pulled over and took a selfie in front of the sign.

As she stood and looked out at the deep, dark waters, she could imagine how the stories must have evolved. This was a dark, long stretch of water in a cold, isolated area. Why not come into the warm pub with a fun story to tell your friends? She found herself gazing at the flat black water, looking for a ripple. Wouldn't it be fun to see something? But it was beginning to snow, and she didn't want to have to add slick roads to the challenge of driving in Scotland.

It was trickier than she expected to pull back onto the *wrong* side of the road. She waited. The snowflakes were big and lovely. Finally, when no other cars were coming, she crept out. She shoved the stick into second gear and finally drove down the road like a regular person.

The snow was beginning to stick, and Melissa's imagination shifted from thoughts of Loch Ness to Christmas. The snow added a sparkling layer of frosting to the hilly countryside and the loch, and she enjoyed the drive, humming Christmas carols along with the radio. The loch had grown wider and the snow was falling heavier when she finally spotted a sign: *Greenhill House*. She was home.

CHAPTER 5

Melissa pulled into the driveway. Greenhill House was made of gray stone, with white-painted wood windows and a bright, cheery front door painted red. The house was two stories, with pointed peaks around several upstairs windows, some lovingly caressed by vines. Holly bushes and a stone fence bordered the outskirts, while the back nestled against the pine-tree-lined banks of Loch Ness.

Melissa couldn't believe it. It was like something out of a movie. She pulled out her phone and was just about to take another selfie when she noticed a real estate sign in front of the house.

"It's not for sale anymore," Melissa said with a grin.

She tugged on the sign and threw it on the side of the driveway. Then Melissa decided to explore her new property. Around the side of the house, Melissa noticed—and appreciated—a stack of firewood on a rack. She'd need more, but that was a start. Directly behind the house was an ancient-looking stone well, its wooden roof covered in snow.

Intrigued, Melissa walked over to it. It looked like a well she had once purchased for her fairy garden, but this one was real and life-sized. The base was made of a circle of stones, there was a wooden roof and a rope with a bucket. The crank looked old, but as Melissa looked down into the well she could see that there was, in fact, water there.

Then a small, iron plaque caught her eye. She dusted off the snow and read:

This sacred well was first discovered in 565. The well soon became known for its healing properties. Locals also believed that a sincere wish made at the well would come true, if one was purse of heart. In 1762 Domhnall MacKenzie came to this well with the wish that his sweetheart, Beitidh Urquhart, would marry him. Upon his proposal, she happily consented. They married December 2, 1762 and build a home here that has stayed in the MacKenzie family for generations.

WHAT A WONDERFUL STORY, Melissa thought. She peered down the well and thought about a young man making a wish for love. She turned back to the house he'd built and appreciated it even more.

"Now it's time to check out the inside!" said Melissa as she hurried back around to the front of the house. She tried the front door. It was locked. She looked under the doormat and spotted a key. She opened the door and went inside.

As she stepped into the wide, spacious foyer, an alarm screamed. Melissa covered her ears as she walked over to a pad of numbers on the wall. Some were dirtier than others. She tried 1234 and the alarm turned off.

"Problem one, solved. You go, girl!"

That's when she noticed the drips coming from the ceiling.

"We'll just get a bucket and then call a handyman—handy person. Fix a little paint. No problem."

She strolled through the kitchen, which had beautiful antique windows. Exposed wood beams and gray stonework gave it a cozy cottage feel. The fridge was probably thirty years old, small and rusted. She opened it, then shut it immediately, holding her nose. *Yeech!*

"Okay, so we'll have to clean that out. Or throw the whole thing out. Immediately."

The adjacent dining room had a wood-burning stove and was stocked with wood. A mouse scurried across the floor.

"Hi there, little fella. We'll be finding you a new home once I get some traps. You can explore the great outdoors. Look at that beautiful loch out there." She opened the side door in hopes it would leave, but it scurried into a hole in the wall.

"Add to list: exterminator and drywall repair."

The living room was spacious with huge bay windows and lovely wood floors, but had serious 70s vibes. She looked at the orange curtains and zebra striped couch and decided to take down the curtains immediately, which she did. "That's better." Right away it was a huge improvement. Melissa paused to look out at the wooded lot and the loch below, now dusted with snow. Down the hill, on the banks of the loch, Melissa spotted two medium-sized spotted brown deer munching on leaves. Their ears pricked up, and they stood very still.

"It's okay, sweetie. We can share this place." The deer looked at her, then relaxed and went back to eating the leaves.

When she returned her gaze to the room, she was jolted again at the sight of the horrible couch. "That's just hideous. Adding slipcovers to the list."

She turned the corner, and her jaw dropped. It was the coziest, most amazing library she'd ever seen. Actually, she'd never seen a library in a home. This place was stacked floor to ceiling with shelves and already stocked with all kinds of wonderful books. There were antique books, poetry, Shakespeare, multiple editions of Robert Burns, mysteries, romances, classics, a foreign language section, history, modern literary fiction, and even a Sci-Fi/horror section. The exposed wood, wall of windows, and stone fireplace was icing on the cake.

"I'm not going to change a thing," Melissa said, settling into a cozy chair and imagining the roaring fire and some tea at her side. Maybe a dog.

"I'm so glad I didn't sell this place. A few curtains, some slip-covers, a coat of paint, and this will be paradise."

She toddled up the stairs. There were three bedrooms, all with gorgeous views of the loch and trees, but all in need of a little TLC.

"New light fixtures, some new bedspreads. You got this, Melissa."

She was heading down the stairs when she heard police sirens roaring down the street.

She looked out the window just in time to see two police cars pull into her driveway.

She opened the door for them.

"What seems to be the problem, officer?" she said before realizing how stupid and American that was going to sound. The taller officer frowned. Were they even called officers here? Bobbies? No. They looked just like the police at home—dark uniform, hat, shiny badge.

"Breaking and entering, ma'am," said the tall one as he reached into his pocket for handcuffs.

"And trespassing," said the shorter one. As they reached for her arm, Melissa wriggled away.

"Oh, no. This is my place. I'm Melissa Mackenzie. I've inherited this from a long-lost relative. I have the letter right here in my bag." she said. She was sure that would clear everything up. But just in case, she rummaged around in her bag. "See?"

They looked at the letter. The shorter police officer looked up first. "So the alarm…?"

"The real estate company that notified me had planned to sell the house and give me the money, but I decided I'd rather keep it. It's beautiful, isn't it? Just needs a little TLC." said

Melissa, beaming despite the fact that there was water actively dripping on her from the ceiling. She stepped aside.

"*Aye,* this was a lovely home at one time. My wife was friends with the owner. Kept to himself. Never took care of it after his wife passed on, God rest his soul."

"See? This is a blessing," said Melissa.

The taller police officer was still suspicious. "How'd you get in?" he asked.

"The key. Under the mat," said Melissa, pointing.

"Might want to change where you keep that," said the tall police officer.

"Right," said Melissa.

Right was like *okay* here in the UK. Melissa decided maybe she shouldn't say *right.* Her thoughts were beginning to drift into a long-winded daydream, but the shorter police officer interrupted her digressive thoughts.

"Could we have a copy of that letter? We'd like to look into this further. I had thought it was for sale—" he began before Melissa cut him off.

"Yes, well, the realtors were going to sell it and give me the money."

"You said that, but—"

"It's fine, I'm sure. But sure, take a picture if you'd like," she said, realizing she'd have to get out of the habit of interrupting, especially in another country and especially with police officers.

They snapped a picture of the letter, tipped their hats, and let her go. Or at least, didn't arrest her. They were the ones who left.

Melissa took a deep breath and waved as they backed out of the driveway. Then she closed the door and looked around. This was her house. Her mice. Her zebra striped couch. Her dripping ceiling. She twirled around like Julie Andrews in *The Sound of Music. Mine. It's all mine,* she thought.

CHAPTER 6

Melissa gingerly drove the narrow, snow-covered road back to Inverness. She pulled up and parked outside a small, independent hardware store. The front door jingled as she opened it. Christmas music played as Melissa filled a cart with cleaning supplies, shades, curtains, buckets, putty, paint … everything. She pushed her cart to the front of the store where the shop owner, a cute older man, stood at the register. He had twinkly eyes, not unlike the Jolly Old Elf himself.

"Hi. I'm just moving here from across the pond, and I could use some recommendations," said Melissa.

"Welcome. How can I help?" he asked.

"I am looking for so many things. I need some help with construction and repairs to start," she said.

"Fergus Dunbar is the best lad in town for that. He lives over by the lumberyard. I'll get you his contact information."

"Great."

"What else can I do for you?" asked the man.

"Well, I'm so new here I barely even know where to start …"

The shop owner pulled out a folder full of town pamphlets, maps, information on local organizations, and lists of activities.

"Of course, you'll want to join the Community website, and you'll want to know about the pipe competition going on this week, and the Highland Games celebration, the Christmas *Ceilidh,* and Hogmanay celebrations."

"What's a *ceilidh*?"

"A party with dancing. You'll love it," he said.

"And Hog- Hogman—"

"Hogmanay. That's our biggest holiday of the year. New Year's celebrations."

"Oh, right. Gotcha. Great." said Melissa, feeling a little silly.

Melissa paid and headed for the door, then stepped back.

"Thanks so much, sir. And I forgot to ask. Is there a place where I can buy a lot of firewood?"

"Sandy MacGregor can help you out. Here's his address," he said, handing her a business card.

CHAPTER 7

As Melissa pulled into the MacGregor's driveway, she couldn't help but notice what a perfect cozy Scottish cottage this was; stone and wood, with well-tended landscaping, and set against a backdrop of rolling green hills, dotted with about a hundred adorable little sheep. A man in the distance, wearing a gray sweater and dark pants, surveyed the sheep. Near the barn, a brawny man in a kilt was chopping wood. Melissa stepped out of the car, holding a thermal mug of coffee and admiring the strong arms of the lumberjack at work. She slammed the door shut, and the brawny kilt man turned. It was Colin MacGregor.

Melissa dropped her coffee to the ground. Colin wiped his brow.

"Ms. Mackenzie. How can I help you?" he asked. She couldn't take her eyes off of him. Who would've known that charming man in tweed from the airport secretly looked like he'd just stepped out of a Scottish lumberjack calendar.

"I'm so sorry. I had no idea. The man at the hardware store sent me here for firewood," Melissa stumbled, trying to avert her eyes.

"Of course. How's Mr. Douglas doing?"

"Very friendly," she managed, trying to sound cool.

He laid down his axe.

"So you need some firewood?" he asked.

"Uh, yeah. Yes. Please."

"It's late in the season. Winters here get quite brisk," he said, putting on a plaid flannel.

Melissa pulled her sweater over her shoulders.

"Okay. How does it work?" she asked.

"We deliver. I can bring it by this afternoon, if that suits you," he said.

"You? I thought you were here on holiday," she asked.

"This is a crofter's holiday. No rest for the wicked," he smiled.

Melissa was desperate to shift her gaze from his still unbuttoned shirt, so she looked out on the hills behind their home.

"I love all the sheep. What's that man doing out there? Is he a shepherd?"

"That's my da. Come. You'll have to see this."

Melissa followed him behind the house toward the sheep-filled hills.

The man walked down the hill to meet them. He was an older man, in his 70s, but not frail. He had gray hair, a tweed cap, and was the spitting image of his son—if his son had remained in Scotland. He extended his hand.

"Alexander MacGregor. Pleasure to meet you. Please call me Sandy."

"Pleasure to meet you. I'm Melissa Mackenzie," she responded.

"An American. Colin, you didn't tell me—" he began, a twinkle in his eye.

"Oh, no. It's just ... we're just—" Melissa fumbled.

"We met at the airport and, by coincidence, Melissa has inherited the old Mackenzie place, Greenhill House," said Colin.

"Good on you. Lovely place, that. Right on the loch, aye?"

"Yes. You know, Colin, it's strange. I stopped by the real estate office, and no one was there. But I have the key and the letter, so everything was just fine when the police—"

"The police?"

"Oh, yeah. Well, they stopped by because I set off the alarm," said Melissa, feeling a little silly.

"I'll continue to look into the matter for you," he said.

"Oh, well, thanks, Colin. You don't have to ..." Melissa couldn't finish speaking because the world's most adorable border collie had trotted up to Alexander. "What a great dog." She bent down, and the dog immediately came to her for pets. "Who's a good dog? What a good doggie."

"He's a work dog," said Alexander. "Let me show you." Alexander whistled and the dog sprang into action. The dog raced up the hill as if his life depended on it. Alexander whistled a different pattern, and the dog turned toward the sheep. He whistled a new pattern, and the dog somehow got the sheep to turn and begin walking down the hill.

"Amazing!" said Melissa.

"That's my da," Colin nodded.

"And the dog knows just how to—"

"Watch," said Colin, pointing.

"Sit!" shouted Alexander. Even though the dog was far away, it heard his master's voice and sat. The sheep stood still.

"Left or right?" Alexander asked Melissa.

"Right?"

He tweeted the whistle, and the dog steered all the sheep to the right and down the hill.

The dog then sat, and the sheep stood still.

"That's amazing! Wow! Bravo!" Melissa applauded.

"Come. Let's get your firewood sorted out," said Colin. They walked back toward the house, passing a barn.

"That reminds me, I was thinking of getting a dog myself. You know, to put the house in its name, so Dave couldn't get it."

Colin grinned. "Come with me," he said, beckoning.

And when a handsome man in a kilt beckons, you follow.

In the warm barn, Colin opened the door to a small stall, revealing a mother and six adorable border collie puppies.

"Oh my gosh. They're adorable," said Melissa, kneeling down.

"Da says they're just the right age for new homes. Which one do you want?"

A little black and white puppy had crawled up on Melissa's leg and was licking her face.

"Hello. Are you my dog? Are you? I love you too. I do. Yes. Yes, I do. You wanna come live with me?"

"I think we have a winner," said Colin.

"How does it work? Do I need to submit adoption papers? How much does it cost?"

"Rubbish. Consider it a gift. Welcome to Scotland," said Colin with a smile.

Melissa teared up. "Oh, thank you. That's the nicest thing ever."

She hugged Colin, then became suddenly aware that he was a hunk of muscular, kilted, brawny… She backed up, and so did he.

"Er, no worries. My pleasure, Ms. Mackenzie," he said.

"Thank you, Mr. MacGregor."

He handed her the puppy, which she immediately cuddled, making it difficult to hold the bag of puppy food he also gave her.

"This will get you started until you can get to a pet supply store. I'll be over this afternoon with the kindling."

"Okay, see you then." Melissa set the frisky little puppy in the back of her car.

CHAPTER 8

As Melissa gripped the steering wheel and concentrated on driving on the left side of the road, the little puppy kept jumping into the front seat from between the seats.

"Baby, I really have to concentrate here." She looked down at the puppy, then looked back up to see a round-about.

She swerved into the wrong lane and nearly crashed into a car. She took a deep breath, finished the round-about, and stopped at a pet supply store.

Melissa carried the puppy inside with her. It kept licking her face. She spotted a clerk.

"What a sweet puppy," said the clerk. "Puppy supplies?"

"How'd you guess?" smiled Melissa.

"Follow me."

Melissa followed the clerk and filled a cart with food and toys. Then they stopped in front of the cages.

"I don't want a cage."

"Some people just find it's nice for the little ones to have a place to sleep while they're, uh … training."

"Oh my gosh. It's been so long since I've had a dog. I'm a cat person, usually, but after my cat died my husband—ex-husband—didn't want a new one. Where do I get a bag of litter?"

"Oh, no. I meant paper training. Dogs don't use—"

"Oh. Of course. I guess I need to learn how to train a dog. Do you know any good trainers?"

"Alexander MacGregor's the best in town. He lives at—"

Melissa nodded. "That's where I got this little guy."

"He does a show at the Christmas Highland Games every year. Are you coming?"

"Sounds like fun. I haven't heard of it," said Melissa.

"Here's a brochure. There's Highland dancing, all the regular games—you know, the caber toss, the hammer throw—then you've got the sheep dog herding shows, the bake-off."

"Bake off? Maybe I could do that," said Melissa.

"Toss your hat in the ring. It's a lot of fun," said the clerk.

"Great. Thanks. I'm Melissa, by the way. Melissa Mackenzie," she said, extending her hand.

"Related to Gerald Mackenzie?"

"Hmmm. I don't think so? I just inherited Stuart Mackenzie's house," said Melissa, feeling a bit awkward.

"Lovely. Nice to meet you," said the clerk.

* * *

BACK AT HER HOME, Melissa carried the supplies from the car as her happy, scampering puppy followed.

"You need a name. What should we call you? Angus? Bobby Burns? Alba? Kenzie?"

She opened the front door, and the puppy followed her inside. She set out a bowl of food and water, which the puppy munched on immediately. She petted him and looked out the windows at the peaceful view of the dark waters of Loch Ness.

"Good dog," she said, patting him on the head.

Melissa went to the fridge. Empty.

"Drat. I keep forgetting to get some groceries."

CHAPTER 9

The car was full of groceries. But it was snowing and Melissa's stomach was growling. She spotted a little sandwich café on the outskirts of town and turned into the car park.

"Just one," Melissa told the hostess, who seated her in a cozy spot by the window.

Melissa looked at all the unfamiliar items on the menu. "Cockamaimie soup? Cootie pudding? No, thanks," said Melissa with a chuckle.

"Cock-a-leekie. Chicken soup with leeks. And the pudding is called Clootie. It gets its name from the cloth it's baked in. If you haven't tried it, I'll get you a sample. Will you be having tea with that?" said the waitress.

Melissa flushed with embarrassment. She always blurted out her thoughts. 'No filter' is what Dave had said.

"She'll have the pudding with tea and the cock-a-leekie. And also a cup of cullen skink. On me," said a woman about Melissa's age.

"Straightaway," said the waitress.

The woman smiled. "If you're having trouble with the menu, you must have come from far away," she said.

"Yes. I'm from Boston," said Melissa. "I'm so sorry you heard me. I don't mean to be an ugly American."

"No worries. I'm Lindsay," she said.

"Melissa. Nice to meet you."

"Likewise." Lindsay gestured to the empty chair beside Melissa. "May I?"

"Please."

"Are you here on holiday?"

"Well, I'm going to live here. I inherited a home, and my marriage … Well, I decided I should try something new."

"Wonderful. We have loads of good adventures here. Do you like hill walking? Or with the holidays coming, you might enjoy the town Christmas baking competition."

"That sounds like fun," said Melissa.

"We start this Saturday. Here's the address." Lindsay handed her a card.

The waitress returned with two different kinds of soup.

"This one is Cullen skink. This is what the Scots brought to New England, and then you Americans used it as the basis for your New England Clam Chowder."

Melissa tried a taste. "It's so smoky. I love it."

Lindsay grinned. "The smoke can be an acquired taste."

"But the rest is so much like clam chowder." Melissa tried the cock-a-leekie soup. "This is good, too."

"Basically standard chicken soup with a Scottish slant, the leeks."

"What's this clootie pudding thing, then?"

"So pudding is always dessert, but it's not necessarily what those of you from across the pond think of as pudding. We have clootie dumplings and clootie pudding. They're basically the same thing. Spiced pudding wrapped in cloth—that's the clootie—and simmered in water."

Melissa took a taste. "Oh. That reminds me of something. Yes, that's wonderful. Maybe something old fashioned from Boston. Not quite Indian pudding. Not quite bread pudding. But something."

They sat and enjoyed their tea.

As Lindsay prepared to leave, Melissa said, "Thanks for sitting here. I don't know anyone in town yet. I mean, just the shop keepers and such. Literally, that's all."

"Well, come to the baking competition this weekend, and I'll introduce you around."

"Thank you. I'd love that. It was so nice to meet you."

"See you soon!" Lindsay waved as she headed toward the door.

CHAPTER 10

Melissa pulled into her snow-covered driveway to find another FOR SALE sign in the yard. She parked the car and immediately went over to the sign and plucked it out of the yard, then threw it into the trash bin just as Colin arrived with his truck.

Colin, now in jeans and a flannel shirt, got out of his truck and began to unload the firewood.

As Melissa opened the front door, her little dog jumped out and scampered behind her.

"He's definitely feeling at home," said Colin.

"Yes. I've got to find him a name."

"Or maybe a friend. Or some sheep. He'll want something to herd soon enough," said Colin.

"You're right. I've heard that about border collies. Maybe I will." Melissa began carrying groceries into the house.

"So have you made an offer on the house?" Colin asked as he picked up a bag of dog food to help her. "Let me know if you need any legal help."

"An offer? No, I'm not taking offers. I've decided not to sell it. I'm going to fix it up."

"Did you buy it from the bank?" asked Colin.

"No, I inherited it. Remember?" Melissa was juggling groceries and the front door, so Colin held it for her, then followed her into the house. He dodged the drip, which was slowing, and looked around.

"Lovely. Really. Loads of possibilities," he said.

"Just a little paint here, fix a leak there ..."

"Where would you like this?" asked Colin, nodding to his bag of dog food.

"I guess the kitchen?"

He followed her into the kitchen and was awestruck by the wall of windows overlooking the loch. He stood gazing out at the dark water and the hills on the other side of the narrow loch.

"Just takes your breath away," he said.

"It really does, doesn't it?" Melissa realized she wasn't referring to the loch and looked away. Colin looked away as well.

"Where would you like me to unload the wood? Some by the fire and some in the stack by the side of the house?"

"That would be wonderful," said Melissa.

Colin went back outside and began to haul in the firewood. He stacked it by the wood-burning stove in the kitchen.

"You should really meet my sister. She's in charge of a lot of the Christmas festival, so she can introduce you to a lot more people in town. I'll be heading back to the States after Hogmanay, so ..."

"That would be great," said Melissa.

"Why don't you come to dinner tonight? I'll introduce you."

"That would be gre—lovely. What time?" She hoped she didn't sound too American, trying to add in words like *lovely* for the benefit of the Scot.

"How about half six?"

"I'll be there," said Melissa.

"Lovely," said Colin. He wasn't talking about her, but she flushed anyway.

CHAPTER 11

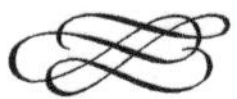

Melissa drove back to the MacGregor farmhouse. In the twilight, the home looked like a perfect cozy dream. It was all lit up in sparkling white lights and greenery. Icicle lights hung from the roof, and the shrubs were covered in white light netting. White lights and red ornaments dotted the large pine tree in front of the house, and a large evergreen wreath hung on the red front door. Melissa knocked the brass door knocker. Colin opened the door.

"Hello!" Melissa handed him a bottle of wine.

Alexander "Sandy" MacGregor came up behind Colin and accepted it. "Colin, so nice to have your girlfriend over for dinner," said Sandy with a grin.

"Oh, I'm here to meet—" began Melissa.

"I just wanted Melissa to meet more people in town, so I thought I'd introduce her to Lindsay."

Sandy nodded, not believing this story in the slightest. As they walked toward the living room, Melissa recognized the woman she'd met at the cafe.

"Lindsay!"

"Melissa! Good to see you," Lindsay said.

"I didn't know you were a MacGregor," said Melissa. Colin looked confused, while Sandy looked amused.

"You already know each other?" asked Colin.

"We met at the café in town," said Melissa.

As Lindsay brought out bowls of Cullen skink, Colin began to explain, "You'll love this. It's a bit like the clam chowder you have in Boston, but this is the original. Smokey and—"

"She's already had it." said Lindsay. "You thought your sister wouldn't teach a newcomer about Cullen skink in this *dreich*?"

Colin grinned.

"Who in this town don't you know?" asked Colin. "I thought you didn't know anyone yet."

"I don't know anyone. Just you, your dad, Lindsay, the people at the hardware store, the people at the pet store, and the people at the grocery store."

They laughed.

"Once you get involved in the Christmas Festival, you'll know the whole town. And you'll meet the rest when you walk the dog," said Lindsay.

Lindsay passed a plate of oat cakes, and they ate their soup and chatted.

While they ate, the snow began falling more intensely.

"We might have to get out the toboggan," said Lindsay, with a twinkle in her eye.

"I'm too old for that," said Colin.

"If I'm able to do it, you can do it," said Sandy.

Melissa watched the family dynamics and enjoyed their banter. "Sounds like fun."

They finished their meal, and Melissa helped Colin and Lindsay with the dishes while Sandy went out to do some chores.

Christmas lights twinkled in the trees and around the yard as the snow fell. It was quiet, except for the sounds of the sheep in the hills.

"Who's first? Melissa and Colin?" asked Sandy as he emerged from the barn with a shiny red toboggan.

"What about the sheep?" asked Melissa.

"They'll move out of the way," said Lindsay.

Melissa wasn't reassured.

Melissa and Colin climbed the steep, snow-covered hill, passing the baaing sheep, and Colin set up the toboggan.

"Ready?" Colin asked.

"This is a bigger hill than it looks," said Melissa, looking down.

"Quite," said Colin.

Colin gave them a running shove, climbed on board, and they were off. Melissa leaned left and right in an attempt to steer away from the sheep, but they were barreling straight toward them. She screamed. Fortunately the sheep scuttled out of the way just in the nick of time. Then they hit a rock and went flying, landing in a heap almost on top of each other. Melissa was covered in snow. Colin gently helped her brush it off. She looked beautiful in the moonlight with the snow in her hair. Colin looked as if he were about to say something, then thought better of it.

"Right. Let me help you up?" He offered his hand. There was an electricity between them that they both noticed.

Sandy, trudging up the hill with Lindsay, grabbed the toboggan. "Our turn now. You hold the chocolate."

* * *

BACK AT THE MACGREGOR HOME, Melissa warmed her hands by the fire as Sandy opened what looked to be a special bottle of Scotch whisky.

"How about a wee dram to warm us up?" he asked, pouring everyone a glass before they could protest.

Colin raised his glass. "To new adventures," he said.

Sandy grinned and looked at Colin and Melissa.

"To new adventures," said Melissa.

"Aye," said Colin.

"*Slàinte,*" said Sandy.

"Say it again?" Melissa asked.

"Slant-yuh. Or maybe Slanch-yuh."

"*Slàinte,*" Melissa tried it out.

"*Slàinte mhath,*" said Lindsay.

"Now what's that one?" asked Melissa.

"It's the response. It means, 'and to you as well' or 'good health to you as well'," explained Colin.

"It's written here on this little wall sign Da has," said Lindsay.

"Wow, you sure don't spell it the way you say it," remarked Melissa.

"That's Gaelic for you," said Lindsay.

"And you pronounce Gaelic like we'd say GAH-lick in Boston. You know, the thing that keeps vampires away," said Melissa. "I always thought it was GAY-lick."

"That's Irish Gaelic. This is Scots Gaelic," said Sandy. Melissa knew enough to know they were very different.

"Well, *Slàinte Mhath* to you as well," she said. They all laughed. "Wait, that's like asking for something with *au juice* sauce, right? Redundant?"

"*Dinnae fash yersel,*" said Lindsay, her Scots accent emerging with the drink.

Colin's eyes were dancing until they locked with Melissa's. He looked away and sipped his scotch.

"THANK you so much for inviting me," said Melissa.

"Our pleasure," said Colin.

"So you'll come over Friday, and we'll bake?" asked Lindsay.

"Or you could come over to my new place. I could definitely

use another set of eyes on it for decorating ideas," suggested Melissa.

"That would be lovely. Then Saturday the Highland Games kick off the festival."

"And the pipe band competition," added Sandy.

"Of course," said Lindsay.

Colin's cell rang. He looked troubled as he glanced at the screen. "Excuse me. I have to take this. It's, er, a client."

Melissa frowned as Colin walked into another room.

Sandy frowned as well. "I'm sorry about that, Melissa. Since he's moved to the States, he's obsessed with work. A regular Yank—er, I mean ..."

"It's okay. He's got a tough client," she said.

"Oh? He's told you of his work?"

"That's how we met. He, uh, represents my husband. Or soon to be ex-husband."

There was a long, awkward silence.

"Lindsay, could you point me in the direction of the powder room? Or the loo?" asked Melissa.

"Just down the hall and to the right," Lindsay said quickly.

Melissa followed Lindsay's directions, leaving Sandy and Lindsay alone while Colin spoke in hushed tones in another room. Though she couldn't hear Colin, she could hear Sandy and Lindsay loud and clear.

"So, is Colin ... the other man?" Melissa heard Sandy ask Lindsay.

"Da, Melissa and Colin are not involved. They're just friends. They met at the airport, and it was just a coincidence that they both ended up in this town."

Sandy sounded truly surprised. "I thought he was just saying that. I was going to invite Caitlin Munro over, but he told me he'd met someone."

Melissa's ears perked up.

"Oh, yeah. There's a lawyer he's been dating. She's spending the holidays with her family."

"Oh. I see. So he does have someone?"

"Yes," said Lindsay.

Melissa took a deep breath and stepped back into the hallway.

"I like Melissa," said Sandy.

"I like her too," said Lindsay with a grin.

Melissa returned. She couldn't see a reason to pretend she hadn't overhead, so she chimed in with the conversation.

"And I like you guys. It was a pleasure, really. I think I'd better get home and see how the little munchkin is doing," she said.

"Have you decided on a name yet?" asked Sandy.

"I was thinking Nick. Or Snowball. Or Belle. Something Christmassy …" answered Melissa.

"Haggis," said Sandy.

Melissa thought for a moment. "Jingles. Maybe Jingles."

"It has a nice ring to it," said Lindsay.

"I see what you did there." Melissa smiled. "Thanks again. I really should head back."

"I apologize for Colin …" said Sandy.

"That's okay, really. Work beckons."

"Are you quite all right to drive?"

"Yes, I'm fine. Thank you." She'd only had a sip. *Scotch must be an acquired taste,* she thought. She had yet to acquire it.

Light snow was falling as Melissa walked to her car. She loved the sound of her boots crunching in the snow and was grateful that it was such light snow she could brush it off of the windshield with her arm.

"Melissa!"

Melissa turned to find Colin running down the driveway to catch up with her.

"Yes?"

"I, uh ... Thank you for coming. This was fun. I'm glad you met Lindsay. Or already had," he said.

"Yeah, thank you. It was fun," said Melissa.

"Your husband—I mean, Dave ..."

"Yes?"

"Do you have a good lawyer? Do you need a recommendation?" Colin looked concerned.

Melissa bit her lip. "I have a lawyer. I hope he's good," she said.

"Me too."

CHAPTER 12

Melissa sang Christmas love songs along with the radio until the Ramones singing "Christmas (Baby Please Come Home)" made her tear up. She switched to another channel and settled on "Sleigh Ride."

When she pulled into her driveway she noticed how very dark it was. "I've gotta get some lights out here."

She opened her notes app and added *lights* to the long list of to-dos. She opened the door and let the puppy outside.

"I'm going to call you Jingles," she said as she cuddled him. He licked her face again and wagged his fluffy little tail. "We'll have to get you some bells for your collar."

He followed her into the kitchen, where she opened her now fully-stocked fridge. She poured a glass of local eggnog, added nutmeg, and sat by the fire. Jingles sat at her feet. Melissa looked at the fire, her new dog, and the snow outside and smiled.

CHAPTER 13

The gingerbread house competition was a much bigger event than Melissa could have imagined. Dozens of teams sat at tables set up with baking materials: bowls of candy, sprinkles, frostings. Judges, dressed as Santa and Mrs. Claus, milled about giving directions, looking at the timer, and munching on cookies.

Melissa and Lindsay were busy building a majestic gingerbread model of Greenhill House. They had little turrets covered in frosting, a spun sugar model of the Loch shimmering behind the home, and powdered sugar snow dusting the roof, the grounds, and the sugary trees. Little gingerbread men stood in the back carrying a gingerbread toboggan.

"What else do we need?" asked Lindsay.

"Santa," said Melissa.

They rolled the dough. Lindsay selected a Santa cutter, and Melissa found a tiny dog cookie cutter. They cut them out and popped the cookies into the oven.

"Fifteen minutes. Fifteen minutes," called the judge, an older woman in a white Mrs. Claus wig, round glasses, and a red apron.

Melissa peeked into the oven. "We've got to let them set, too," said Melissa.

Other teams had created elaborate castles, cozy villages, fairy glen scenes, and more. The timer dinged. Melissa pulled out the cookies.

"They've got to cool. What can we do while we wait?" asked Lindsay.

They began adding red and green candies and spreading white frosting snow around the scene. When the cookies were cool Melissa frosted them like a pro. They arranged the Santa and sleigh on top of the house and used candy as presents.

"Ten ... nine ... eight ..." called the judge.

Melissa frantically set the dog into the sleigh and put a present in his mouth. At the last second, she remembered she'd made a Nessie. She put it into the loch behind the house with a little red bow around its neck. Lindsay put a tiny little candy camera in the hands of the gingerbread people on the banks of the Loch.

"Five ... Four ... three ... two ... one ... Hands off!"

Melissa and Lindsay raised their hands—done. The judges walked around remarking on each gingerbread project. When the woman in the Mrs. Claus outfit arrived, Melissa offered her a gingerbread person.

"What have we here?" she asked, munching on the cookie.

"This is my new home, Greenhill House, on the banks of Loch Ness," said Melissa.

"As you can see, we have Santa landing his sleigh on top of the house, and Melissa's little dog, Jingles, has a present," added Lindsay.

"And in the back, here, we have a Nessie sighting. The little gingerbread people see both Nessie and Santa, and they're not sure which one to take a picture of," Melissa said.

The judge wrinkled her nose. "You take the picture of Santa," she said, then walked away.

Melissa looked crestfallen. "Too much?"

"Don't worry about it. It's adorable," said Lindsay.

The judge tapped a microphone. "And the winner is ... Allison MacDonald, with her replica of Inverness castle as Santa's workshop."

Melissa grabbed a gingerbread Christmas tree from their submission and ate it.

Lindsay giggled. "Let's get out of here."

* * *

MELISSA AND LINDSAY walked down High Street in downtown Inverness carrying shopping bags. Bagpipes played in the distance as happy shoppers filled with Christmas cheer went from one store to the next. They stopped to listen as carolers sang "Ding Dong Merrily on High." Lindsay and Melissa clapped for the carolers and continued walking along the shops.

"Are you excited for the Highland games?" asked Lindsay.

"What are they, exactly?" asked Melissa as she accepted a candy cane from a shopkeeper.

"Just you wait. Do you have a tartan sash?" asked Lindsay.

"A what?" asked Melissa.

Lindsay took her by the arm into a tartan shop. The shopkeeper, dressed in a tartan skirt and wool sweater with what Melissa would soon learn was a tartan sash, greeted them.

"In Scotland, if you go to a formal event, like a wedding, most of the men will be in their dress kilts. Women have some leeway. I like to wear a simple black dress with a tartan sash and maybe matching tartan shoes. Some people go all out and wear a full tartan dress," Lindsay explained, showing Melissa a red-and-green plaid tartan dress.

"I love it," said Melissa, until she looked at the price and blinked.

"That's why I wear a tartan sash. Come on, they're over here," said Lindsay.

They looked at sashes of all kinds of tartan: red Royal Stewart, blue-and-green Gordon, purple Scotland Forever, yellow MacLeod, yellow-red-and-green Buchanan …

"So you'd wear Mackenzie, right? Is that your father's name or your--"

"It's my father's name," said Melissa as she browsed through the racks "In fact, here it is." Melissa held up a blue-and-green plaid sash with white and red stripes.

"Lovely," said Lindsay.

"What else do I need?"

"Do you want the shoes?" asked Lindsay.

Melissa looked at the shoes on display. They were pricey as well. She shook her head.

"No, I think I'm good," she said. She paused at the clan pins. She spotted a Mackenzie pin and read the motto. "'*Luceo Non Uro*—I shine, not burn.' I like it."

"It's a good motto," agreed Lindsay.

Melissa took the pin and sash to the cash register, then looked back at the shoes. *Christmas present to myself,* she thought and set them on the counter along with the rest. "So do I wear all this to the games?"

"Oh, no. You can just wear a sweater and jeans. But some people do like a splash of tartan, so you can wear the sash if you want. I'll pick you up tomorrow morning?"

"Great. Thanks, Lindsay."

CHAPTER 14

Melissa stepped out of Lindsay's car and took in the scene. Tents dotted the frost-covered countryside. Some sold merchandise: tartan sashes, kilts, clan motto T-shirts, etc. Others served as temporary headquarters for each clan. Burly men in kilts—and Santa hats—trudged toward a field where a caber toss was in session. Pipe bands milled about, practicing, twirling drumsticks, and adjusting their kilts. Food trucks sold all kinds of goodies from haggis to shortbread to deep-fried Mars bars, beer, and whisky. A little kiddie train chugged through the whole area, taking kids through a Santa Workshop Wonderland filled with little mechanical elves, reindeer, and Santa and Mrs. Claus.

Mr. MacGregor spotted her and walked over. "Good to have you here, Ms. Mackenzie. And I see you've got your tartan."

Melissa self-consciously adjusted her Mackenzie tartan sash. "Yes. And I see you're in your kilt."

"I never miss an opportunity. We're doing another border collie demonstration on the main field at two. Stop by."

"I will. And by the way, I told Jingles—that's what I named him—to sit and he did!"

"Of course he did."

"But he's so young."

"He's a MacGregor border collie. He knows *sit, stay,* and *down,* as well as some of my training whistles." He patted her on the shoulder and left to greet another friend.

The sound of bagpipes drew Melissa over to a tent where teenage girls dressed in colorful pleated skirts and argyle socks were dancing a traditional Scottish dance over swords.

"If the soldiers could dance without touching the sword, they'd have success in battle, but if a soldier's foot touched the sword, it meant disaster," explained a woman with a microphone. "Some believe the tradition began with Malcom III, who danced over his dead enemy's corpse with his sword on the ground beside the body."

Melissa shuddered and continued along through the shops, buying a beautiful wreath and other decorations for her new house.

She arrived at the pipe band competition and was startled to see Colin dressed to the nines in his kilt with a snare drum strapped to his waist.

"Is there anything you can't do?" she asked with a grin.

The band began to form lines.

"Off we go." Colin waved a drumstick, as he joined the ranks of the rest of the pipe band. Melissa waved, and the band began marching. They played a lot of familiar tunes and quite a few that Melissa didn't know. Lindsay caught up with her.

"Hey. How's it going?" asked Lindsay.

"This is so amazing."

"Right?"

"You know, I think I know this song, but I have no idea what it's called," said Melissa.

"That's 'Scotland the Brave,'" she said.

"Ah. I knew I'd heard it a lot. Do you know the words?"

"I know one verse. My da would be disappointed I don't know the whole thing. Here it comes around …

"High in the misty Highlands,
Out by the purple islands,
Brave are the hearts that beat
Beneath Scottish skies.
Wild are the winds to meet you,
Staunch are the friends that greet you,
Kind as the love that shines
From fair maidens' eyes."

"THAT'S BEAUTIFUL," said Melissa. "Wow, I'm tearing up." She laughed, trying to blink back the tears.

"Let's go see another strength competition."

Men and women alike competed in the stone lifting competition. They all wore utility kilts and clan t-shirts. The women were first. Melissa watched in awe as they bent down, lifted with their knees, and hoisted the giant stones over the mark. The crowd cheered, and the first lifter strutted around in her kilt. Now the next one approached the stone.

"Have you ever done this?" asked Melissa.

"Ach, no. Not me. But it's open to anyone. Did you want to—"

"Absolutely not. I'll stick to baking. Maybe there's a shortbread eating competition?"

"Have you ever had a deep-fried Mars bar?" asked Lindsay.

Before Melissa could ask any questions, Lindsay had steered her into a long line outside a food truck.

"So you really think you're all set to just live here?" asked Lindsay. "What about friends and family from home?'

Melissa thought about it. "You know, a lot of them were friends I had from knowing Dave. I've spent so much time in a relationship I forgot to find out who I am. I think this is a good place to do that."

"I'm sorry. I didn't mean to bring up a sore subject."

"Not at all. It's just something I think about a lot lately."

They moved up in line.

"I wish my brother would move back home."

Melissa didn't know what to say to that. "Maybe he enjoys a new life there the way I enjoy my new life here?"

"Maybe. But I can't help but feel like he's trying to escape."

"We all need some kind of escape sometimes."

The queue behind them had grown to about twenty people. Melissa and Lindsay were next. The food truck was painted blue and white, like the St. Andrew's flag, with a chalkboard menu and a Highland cow on it. Among the many sweet treats were deep-fried Mars bars.

"Two deep-fried Mars bars," said Lindsay. She paid the man for both.

"Thanks."

The clerk handed Melissa a piping hot, lightly fried, ooey, gooey chocolate-and-caramel sensation. "Wow!"

Lindsay laughed. "Right?"

"We'd better find a table."

They walked over to a nearby tent with tables.

"Do I use a fork or a spoon or my hands or ..."

"Just pick it up like you'd eat the candy bar and—down the hatch."

Melissa picked up her deep-fried Mars bar. "It's so warm." She took a bite. "Wow. Someone really knew what they were doing when they invented this."

"It was a man called John Davie, who ran a chippie in Stonehaven," said Lindsay.

"Well, here's to John Davie for taking a break from frying that healthy stuff and giving us warm, gooey chocolate."

They enjoyed their Mars bars in silence, and in the process,

Melissa smeared chocolate on her shirt and her face. "Can't take me anywhere," she joked.

Colin, still in uniform but away from the band, came over to chat.

"So what do you think of the Highland games?" he asked.

He'd caught Melissa with her mouth full. She nodded, gestured, and quickly tried to swallow.

"Mmmph. Mmmph, mmmph," she said, gesturing in a way that she hoped meant she was enjoying herself.

A tall woman with flowing curls of long red hair tapped Colin on the shoulder.

"Colin MacGregor!" she said.

Colin turned and looked shocked. "Fiona. What brings you here?"

"I heard you were in town, and here you are dressed to the nines in your kilt. Did I miss the pipe band?"

"Aye, but we'll be back on again in a wee bit," said Colin.

Melissa noticed he had slipped into Scots. She still had a smudge of chocolate on her face. Lindsay gestured with her napkin, and Melissa quickly wiped her face.

Melissa extended her hand. "Hi, I'm Melissa. Nice to meet you," she said, hoping the chocolate was gone and she had some form of dignity left.

"Oh. An American. I had thought you must be Colin's aunt," Fiona said.

Melissa's eyes narrowed a bit, and Colin covered.

"She does look a wee bit like Catroina, but … she's certainly much younger."

"We met at the airport," explained Melissa.

Fiona raised her eyebrows.

"I'm, uh …" said Colin, flustered.

"He's my husband's divorce lawyer," explained Melissa.

"Oh. I see. So are you two …" Fiona left the question hanging in the air.

Colin and Melissa looked at each other.

"We're friends," said Melissa.

"Lovely," said Fiona. "Colin and I go way back, don't we? We've known each other for donkey's years, as your da would say." Colin looked a little awkward as Fiona wrapped her arm around his shoulders.

Melissa felt her face flush, and she knew she needed to escape. "Great meeting you, Fiona. I'll be heading back to Greenhill House, then. Thanks for looking into things for me, Colin," she said. Melissa quickly blended into the crowd before Colin could say anything.

CHAPTER 15

Landscape workers were busy around the house cutting down dead branches. Inside, painters and drywall workers scurried around the home, avoiding the carpet layers. There was a lot to do, and they were moving quickly, but Melissa was getting overwhelmed with the chaos. Finally, when they brought out the chainsaws to cut down trees outside, Melissa had to retreat upstairs.

Melissa was sitting in her bedroom, trying to center herself, when her phone rang. "Hello?"

"Melissa. I have the final papers, but I don't know where to send them." It was Dave. She hadn't quite forgotten about him, but almost. That's progress, she thought.

"Colin didn't give you my address?" she asked.

"Colin who?" said Dave.

"Your lawyer ..."

"How would my lawyer have your address?" asked Dave in that tone she was glad to have nearly forgotten. Melissa bit her lip.

"Right. Okay. So it's Greenhill House, 18 Victoria Way, Inverness IV1 1LG, United Kingdom."

"United Kingdom?"

"Yes. I've inher—I'm living in Scotland."

"What?"

"Yes. I've moved to Scotland. Feel free to send the divorce pages by post, but it might be faster to fax or email them."

"By post ...?"

"Ta-ta, Dave. *Dinnae fash yersel.* I'll be happy to sign your papers. And a Happy Christmas to you." Melissa hung up and grinned.

She went downstairs. The workers were cleaning up for the day. They'd put up new drywall where the leak had been and had painted the whole first floor. It looked clean and new.

"Time to start decorating," said Melissa with a grin.

She placed her new wreath from the Highland Games on the front door and then looked around, making a list of what to buy.

* * *

In a downtown Christmas shop, Melissa bought an inexpensive box of ornaments, a Christmas tree stand, candles, and lights.

At a farm on the outskirts of town, Melissa picked out a tree, and a young man tied it to her car.

She played Christmas songs on the radio as she drove merrily down the now familiar road along the loch to her home. When she pulled into her driveway, the real estate sign was up again. Was someone playing a prank on her?

Once again, she hoisted the sign out of the snowy yard and into the dustbin. "They must have an awful lot of these signs," Melissa said.

Melissa cut the ropes from the tree and dragged it down from the car, then did her best to drag it into the house. It was slow-going, and she left a trail of pine needles in the snow behind her, but she managed to get it inside the house and into the stand she'd bought. The floor was covered in pine needles. Fortunately, the workers had left a giant broom, so she swept them toward the door easily. As she swept, a car pulled up. Lindsay got out of the car.

"I brought eggnog and some extra ornaments. Do you need any help decorating?"

"I was just about to start. You're a lifesaver."

Melissa put on some Christmas music, and they began to hang the ornaments.

"Thanks so much, Lindsay. I just got a box of these little glass ornaments. All my other ones are back at the house. I don't know why I didn't think to bring them," Melissa said.

"You were packing for an international flight, not decorating for Christmas."

"You're right."

Melissa looked at some cute little painted reindeer made out of clothespins. "These are adorable."

Lindsay flushed. "We made those in school a long time ago."

"But they're special family heirlooms," Melissa protested.

"We made a lot of ornaments over the years. Don't worry. There's more where these came from. And this way it helps the tree feel more homey."

"Definitely." Melissa stood back and surveyed their work.

"It looks great," said Lindsay. "Wow, look at the walls. This place is really coming along."

"They're doing a great job. I'm so excited."

They plunked down in the chairs.

"I can get the eggnog," said Lindsay.

"I wish we had some cookies to go with it."

"Have you bought any cookie sheets or a mixer?"

"Not yet," said Melissa, beginning to feel overwhelmed at all the things she needed to get. "Do you know of a second-hand store where I could get some?"

"Mine are in the car. You can just borrow them. Let's make some cookies!"

Melissa and Lindsay unloaded a giant red Kitchen-Aid mixer, cookie sheets, and a big box of cookie cutters. Lindsay held something behind her back.

"Left or right?" she asked.

"Right?" guessed Melissa.

Lindsay revealed two adorable red-and-green plaid aprons. The one on the right had more red. The one on the left had more green.

They put on their aprons and began to mix cookie dough.

"So. That Fiona … what a knockout. What's the story there?" Melissa tried to sound nonchalant.

"Oh. Well. She and Colin used to date," said Lindsay.

Melissa nodded and dug a scoop into the dough, then plunked it onto the cookie sheet. "And they broke up?" she asked.

"Yeah. When he moved to the states, she couldn't get a visa," said Lindsay.

"Ah. And so now he's coming back for her?" Melissa tried to keep her voice light.

Lindsay grimaced. "No. I sure hope not. No, he's here for Da. I'm not sure you know, but he's got so much joint pain and arthritis now he can barely run the dogs, let alone the croft," said Lindsay.

"Oh. I didn't know that. I'm so sorry. He always seems in good spirits."

"Yeah, he does. I know he wishes Colin would stay and run the croft, but Colin loves his life in America. He loves the big city. Being a lawyer."

Melissa put the last cookie on the tray and put them in the oven. "More?"

"Definitely."

Melissa poured another glass of eggnog for each of them and rolled out more dough.

"So. What's he going to do? I mean, if his girlfriend is here, and his dad needs him."

"I get the idea he's had a change of heart," Lindsay said.

They pressed cookie cutters into the dough in silence for a minute. Melissa didn't know what to make of that, and she didn't want to ask.

"What are you going to do?" she asked Melissa.

"About what?"

"Well. Colin said the house people really want you to sell it."

"Yeah, but I need a place to live," said Melissa. She looked out at the snow falling on the trees outside.

"If you sold it, you could live anywhere. You could go back home, or choose a new place: California. Arizona. Italy. It gets really cold here. And it rains a lot. We're in the middle of nowhere up here. You might not like it."

Melissa looked around at the work in progress: half-painted walls, plaster, and cans of paint. "I love it here. Besides, I've put too much into this house already. I can't leave. When I was a little girl hearing about the Loch Ness Monster, I never imagined I'd live here. I didn't know it was possible."

"Yeah, well. You know the monster was sighted by an owner of an Inverness hotel, right? He's basically just PR," explained Lindsay.

"Don't say that," Melissa teased. "Anyway, I read that there have been stories about something in these waters since Saint Colombo."

"*Columba.* Colombo was the guy on TV in the 70s."

"Yeah. Whatever. Anyway, I've heard there've been stories for thousands of years."

"You're changing the subject. Why don't you want to go home?" Lindsay asked.

Melissa looked around her beautiful home. “It’s like a fairy tale here. The old buildings, the lochs, and the hills. The fairy pools up in Skye—I want to visit those. And I just feel right here. And I haven’t felt *right* in a long time. It’s a really good feeling.”

Lindsay nodded.

“Well, you’re a Mackenzie. It’s in your blood,” she said.

“Maybe it is,” said Melissa.

The timer buzzed, and they took the first tray of cookies out and put the next tray in.

“I brought a bunch of candy decorations, too,” said Lindsay.

Melissa shook her head. “You think of everything.”

“I think we’re just on the same wavelength.”

Lindsay spread out an array of colored candies and peppermint sticks while Melissa made the frosting.

As they decorated cookies and listened to Christmas music, it began to snow again.

CHAPTER 16

Melissa hung new Mackenzie tartan curtains while Jingles slept in his bed. Snow was falling outside, and the sun glistened on it. *See? It can be sunny here,* thought Melissa.

Her cell phone rang. Dave's name and photo lit up the phone screen. She switched her phone to silent and let it go to voicemail.

"You and me, Jingles. We're gonna have a Merry Christmas together." Jingles wagged his tail and sat down at her feet. She wandered into the kitchen for a cookie. She glanced at a flyer she had attached to her fridge: *Highland Barn Dance.*

"Oh my goodness, that's tonight," Melissa said.

She went upstairs to try on her dress. She had chosen a black velvet dress, and the Mackenzie tartan sash and shoes. She spent quite a while trying to get the clan pin on. She looked in the mirror and wondered whether she was dressed like a real local or like a tourist. "Here goes nothing."

When Melissa arrived, she breathed a sigh of relief; it was clear that she was going to blend in. She was one of many women dressed in a black dress with a tartan sash. Other women had tartan dresses, while some had pleated tartan skirts. Others wore nice pants and a blouse. She was fine. Lindsay was right. The men looked dashing in their formal jackets and dress kilts. The barn was decorated in Christmas tartan splendor. Each table had a red velvet tablecloth with red plaid chargers, white china, and silver cutlery. There were bouquets of red and white carnations, roses, and greenery on each table, Christmas lights, mistletoe—the whole place looked jolly and merry. People began to sit as elegant waiters began to bring out the food.

Melissa sat down at a table alone. Her phone buzzed. She silenced it and shoved it into her purse. Colin came in with his father and Lindsay. Mr. MacGregor waved, and they came over to Melissa.

"May we join you, my lady?" asked Sandy with a twinkle in his eye.

"Of course," said Melissa, doing her best to keep eye contact with Sandy and avoid Colin's gaze. He looked spectacular in his Prince Charlie jacket and kilt, with a full dress sporran, clan pin, red plaid MacGregor tartan bow tie, and his sparkling blue eyes.

The music started. Waiters brought plates of oat cakes and *haddie* spread.

"You're going to love the dancing," said Lindsay.

"Oh, I'm not much of a dancer," said Melissa, nervously watching the locals begin to dance.

"We'll teach you," said Colin. He held out his hand. Melissa took his hand and she wondered if he, too, could feel the moment of … something … as they looked into each other's eyes. She flushed red, and he guided her out to the dance floor.

They joined the line dancing. Melissa was soon racing around, breathless, twisting under Colin's arm, moving forward to the next line of dancers, and then the next. The music was fast and fun. When the music stopped, Melissa, flushed, returned to her seat and sipped her water.

"So, what did you think?" asked Sandy.

"It's like square dancing. We did that in elementary school. The Virginia Reel."

"Yes. The pioneers in the US had learned these traditions from their ancestors and other more recent immigrants," said Colin.

Waiters arrived with a giant plate of food.

"Is this the haggis?" asked Melissa, looking at the large lump of mystery meat.

"It is," said Colin.

Melissa nodded, and the waiter served the haggis, *neeps and tatties*.

"Whisky sauce?" asked the waiter.

Melissa looked at Lindsay, who nodded.

"Yes, please," said Melissa.

The waiter poured whisky sauce over her haggis and served the rest of the table.

"So what exactly is haggis?"

"Try it first," said Colin.

Melissa grimaced, picked up her fork, and tried it, bracing herself for the worst. Instead, she was pleasantly surprised.

"This is delicious!"

"Of course it is," said Colin with a laugh.

"And what are these? Potatoes and ..."

"*Neeps and tatties* are turnips and potatoes. Sometimes they serve it with *rumbletythump*, which has rutabaga," said Lindsay.

"And the whisky sauce is really more like gravy?"

"A bit," said Colin.

Melissa took another bite.

"There's a lot of spice," said Melissa. "What is that? Coriander?"

"That's what takes ye back to yer childhood," said Sandy, with his mouth a bit full.

"I like it," said Melissa, now eating with enthusiasm.

They watched and clapped along with the music as teenage girls performed classic dances. As dessert came around, waiters brought an array of choices to the table, served family-style.

"What do we have here?" asked Melissa.

"That's *Cranachan*, our national dessert: raspberries, whisky, oats, and cream," said Colin.

"Wow."

Lindsay pointed to a shortbread covered in caramel. "That's Millionaire Shortbread," she said.

"I can see why it's called that. Look at that caramel!"

Lindsay served everyone a bit of each.

"Delicious. You know, Colin, I can't understand why you live in the States when you have all this. The great food, your fun family..." She trailed off as the Master of Ceremonies tapped on the microphone. He was an older man, dressed in a red Inverness tartan kilt, Prince Charlie jacket, and sporran.

"And now we're ready to announce the winners of the silent auction," he said as the pipe band gave a drum roll.

"The winner of the giant stuffed Santa Nessie is ... Melissa Mackenzie." Melissa clapped her hands together and cheered, then ran up to collect her prize. It was huge. She could barely walk with it. She sat Nessie next to her at the table and patted it.

"Good Nessie. Good girl," she said.

"Only you would love that hideous beast." Lindsay laughed.

"I know. And I do love Nessie. I hope I see it someday."

Colin's eyes twinkled. "Da, you want to tell her, or should I?"

"You tell it best, Da," said Lindsay.

"Aye. Very well. When I was a lad of about twenty, my friend and I were camping out near Drumnadrochit—that's out by Urquhart Castle and the deepest part of the loch." Melissa waited as he took another sip of his single malt. "Well, we were in our tent just about asleep when we heard this weird bubbling sound. We thought someone had taken out a motorboat, but it didn't sound mechanical. So we crept out of the tent and went down to the water and saw a giant fin smack—like a whale does, ken—and then dive under the water."

"And then what happened?"

"Then I woke up," Sandy said with a hearty laugh. Lindsay and Colin shook their heads.

Colin held out his hand to Melissa. "You could use a dance."

"Me?"

"You've got a lot to learn," he smiled.

They made their way out to the crowded dance floor and began dancing.

"Your dad's quite a storyteller," said Melissa.

"That's not quite the way he always tells it. I think he actually did see something," Colin whispered, glancing back at Sandy who was still grinning.

"Well, it makes for a fun story either way," said Melissa.

The song ended, and Melissa and Colin sat back down to have some coffee and after-dinner drinks. Soon, people began gathering their coats, and it was time to leave.

Colin walked Melissa to her car and carried the giant Nessie Santa for her. It wouldn't fit in the back seat, so they tried the trunk. That didn't work either.

"I'll put it in the truck and follow you," said Colin.

"Are you sure?"

"No worries."

"Thank you."

Snow fell as they pulled up outside the house. The lights sparkled, the moon shone on the snow-covered roof, and Melissa felt all warm and happy. Then she spotted the real estate sign.

"Why is this always here?" She hopped out of the car and struggled to pull the sign out of the frozen ground. Colin pulled into the driveway behind her and got out, Santa Nessie in his arms.

Together they tugged the sign out of the ground. They trudged through the deepening snow to the front door and found an eviction notice. Melissa read aloud as Colin read over her shoulder.

"Owned by the bank?" she said. "That makes no sense." Melissa tried the door. It was locked. She inserted her key. It didn't work. She turned to Colin.

"But it's my house. I've put so much work into remodeling it. All my stuff is in there," she said. "JINGLES IS IN THERE!" Melissa frantically peered into the windows.

"Jingles! Jingles! Are you in there?" she called. The little dog barked.

"We've got to go in."

Colin set Nessie down on the front porch. He trudged around the side of the house toward the back door, and Melissa followed.

"Do you think they changed all the locks? How can they do that?" asked Melissa.

"If they think someone is living on their property illegally, they can do it. We'll get it sorted out," said Colin as he tried the back door. It was locked as well.

"The garage!" said Melissa.

They trudged around to the garage, with cold, wet snow slipping into Melissa's tartan shoes as she walked.

Melissa opened the car door, pressed the remote, and the garage door opened. Moments later, Melissa was inside. She looked around and breathed a sigh of relief. Everything was as she had left it—walls partially painted and cookies in a jar on the counter.

"Jingles? Jingles! Come here, Jingles!" she called.

Jingles came trotting into the kitchen. She hugged him. While she hugged her dog, Colin was reading his phone.

"Good boy. Jingles is a good boy. Such a good little—"

Colin put his phone back in his pocket. "I think you should stay with us tonight."

"I'll be fine here," said Melissa, thinking of all the work that still needed to be done before Christmas.

"That eviction notice is real. I'm afraid there's been some sort of scam, Melissa."

Tears welled up in her eyes. "But—"

"We'll work it out. You're tired. Gather up what you need and come stay in our guest room. We can phone the bank tomorrow."

MELISSA PACKED a bag of clothes and dog supplies, then joined Colin, who was waiting at the door. On the way to the car, Melissa took one last glance at her picture-perfect dream home. The pine trees, the hill down to the loch, the deer, the beautiful old wishing well ... *The wishing well!* It was her last hope.

"Colin, can you give me a minute?"

"Of course."

Melissa trudged through the snow toward the enchanting little well and stood before it. She wasn't sure what the best way to do it was, so she took a deep breath and closed her eyes.

I wish that this lovely home was mine to keep forever.

She looked down into the depths of the well and said it again. Three times seemed like a good number.

I wish that this lovely home was mine to keep forever.

I wish that this lovely home was mine to keep forever.

As she spoke the words inside her mind the third time, the wind picked up, and snow from a pine tree above her fell down on her like powdered sugar from a sifter. Her eyelashes were covered in snow, but she felt a warm glow inside her. She wiped her face and, rosy-cheeked, she turned and trudged through the snow back to the sidewalk, where Colin was waiting.

"Are you all right?" Colin asked.

Melissa nodded, despite the knots in her stomach. She put her bags in her car and took one last look at Greenhill House. *Anything too good to be true probably is*, she reminded herself.

"Come, Jingles," she said, patting her leg. Jingles happily ran to the car and hopped into the back seat. Melissa got behind the wheel and followed Colin back to his father's home.

CHAPTER 17

Melissa's bleak mood began to clear as she turned into the driveway of the merrily lit MacGregor home. She was grateful to have made such good friends so quickly.

Colin helped Melissa carry her things as she led Jingles toward the house.

"Oh, wait. Should Jingles stay in the barn?" asked Melissa.

"He's a house dog now. Bring him in," said Colin.

"Are you sure?"

"Aye, of course I'm sure," said Colin. Melissa wondered whether he knew the effect his Scots had on her. She guessed that maybe he did.

They shook off their snowy boots and left them by the door. Colin led Melissa down a hallway toward a spare bedroom. He put her bag down and pulled some fresh towels from a linen closet.

"The comforter's quite good, but if you get cold, there are more blankets in the hall closet," he said.

"Thank you so much," said Melissa. Jingles curled up on a little rug in the corner.

Colin turned to leave, and then turned back.

"Do you want to stay up and have a cuppa?"

"A what?"

Colin grinned. "Tea. Or hot chocolate, maybe?"

The tears were threatening to spill, but Melissa pushed them back. "Colin, you're just too nice."

"Come. Let's get you some biscuits and tea."

Melissa sat on the couch, and Colin handed her his handkerchief. She blew her nose. He smiled at her.

"I'll put on the kettle."

Melissa nodded through her tears.

"Shortbread or gingersnaps?" he called from the kitchen.

Melissa croaked out something garbled. The tears were falling freely now.

"I'll bring both."

Melissa nodded, flipping through her phone. She decided to listen to her voicemails.

"Melissa, this is Dave. I've finalized everything with my lawyer. He'll be in touch soon."

She sniffed and played the next message.

"Ms. Mackenzie, I am a representative from First National Bank of Inverness. It has come to our attention that you have been living in Greenhill House. The home was transferred into our possession after the previous owner's death. We are upholding our possession of the home. You must vacate the premises at once. Please call us at your earliest convenience. Happy Christmas."

Melissa scoffed. "Happy Christmas, indeed."

Colin returned with a pot of tea, a plate of assorted cookies, and a box of tissues under his arm.

"Shall I be mother?" he asked as he reached for the teapot.

"Oh, no. I mean, I'm okay. I'm not that bad."

"It means 'Shall I pour the tea?'" said Colin.

Melissa laughed through her tears. "Oh. Sure. I couldn't figure out what you were talking about."

He poured the tea. Melissa blew her nose again.

"I'm sorry. It's just so much, all at once. At Thanksgiving, I was happy and looking forward to Christmas. Now I'm getting a divorce, and I'm literally homeless."

"No, you're not, you're not, Melissa. You can stay here until you get things straightened out."

"You've already helped so much."

Before she realized what was happening, Melissa leaned in to kiss Colin. Just then Mr. MacGregor padded into the living room, breaking the spell. He saw them, grinned, and then made a show of pouring a glass of water before he returned to his bedroom. Melissa and Colin sat in another awkward silence. Colin's phone rang. He looked at it. It was Dave.

"I'm sorry. I don't know what came over me," said Melissa.

"I think I know what came over me," said Colin. He started to lean in again, but the phone rang again.

"Blast! I'm sorry, Melissa. I really must take this," said Colin.

"I understand. Good night," she said.

He looked forlorn as she walked to her bedroom and shut the door.

In the bedroom, she looked at a framed saying on the wall: *Whit's fur ye'll no go past ye.*

"I wonder if none of this is *fur* me."

She laid in bed, unable to sleep. She looked at the sign again. Then she noticed a MacGregor family tree also hanging on the wall. This sparked an idea. She got out her laptop and began searching. One click led to another and another …

CHAPTER 18

Sunlight streamed through the windows. A tea kettle whistled on the stove. Eggs, square sausage, and tomatoes sizzled in a pan. Melissa came out of the guest room dressed but forlorn.

Colin flipped a fried egg and poured Melissa a cup of tea.

"Good morning," he said as he handed her the tea.

"Thank you. You're all so kind."

Once the breakfast was served, Colin sat down and looked quite serious.

"Melissa, I have some bad news. I looked into the company that sent you that original letter. Although their website is real, and they have a real office and do some legitimate business, I'm afraid their bread and butter is made by scamming Americans. They tell them they've inherited a home abroad and request their bank account information to transfer money after a sale."

"I don't understand," said Melissa.

"It's a scam. This has happened multiple times, and most of the time, it's a recently divorced or widowed woman and—"

"But I'm his long lost—"

"Mackenzie is a very common name. Especially around here.

One could argue that you and the owner come from the same Mackenzie somewhere in the twelfth century. But the fact is, they selected you for your name and your situation. They wanted to scam and then rob you."

"They did. They took my house."

"Well, you see ... it was never yours to begin with."

"What was the owner's name?" asked Melissa.

"Gerald Mackenzie," said Colin.

"The letter said Stuart Mackenzie."

"See? They just make things up," he said.

"Gerald, though. That sounds familiar," she said. Melissa started to open her phone, then realized there was a gorgeous full Scottish breakfast in front of her, and politely put it away. She ate, thinking deeply, trying to puzzle something out.

Lindsay padded into the kitchen in her plaid robe and PJs.

"You're up and at 'em today," she said as she poured herself some tea.

"Gotta be ready for the tree lighting and the big party at the town green," said Melissa, hoping she sounded more cheerful than she felt.

"Definitely don't want to miss that," agreed Lindsay. She paused, then looked from Melissa to Colin and back, as if she was putting two and two together. Melissa flushed, as did Colin.

"I, er—" Melissa stumbled.

"Melissa has a, er, problem with her house. We arrived last night and ... It was best that she stayed here."

"I see." said Lindsay with a smile as she sipped her tea.

"I brought Jingles," offered Melissa, hoping that would change the subject.

"Lovely. Does Da know?"

"About the dog in his house, or about me?"

"Which do you think he'd be more concerned about?" asked Lindsay.

Mr. MacGregor walked into the kitchen. "On the contrary,

I'm thrilled on both counts. I haven't seen Colin with a woman since that—"

"Da!" Colin cut him off.

Melissa blushed.

"I'm just saying, son, you've mourned long enough. It's time to move on," said Sandy.

Colin flushed and went to get more coffee. Melissa looked blankly from Mr. MacGregor to Lindsay and then Colin. What was he talking about? Lindsay looked away.

"His high school sweetheart died ten years ago," explained Sandy. "He left us. Moved to New York to be a big city barrister. He spent months retraining and learning US law. It cost a fortune. Dealing in divorce, no less. Only someone who has lost all belief in love could do that job. And having to learn the laws of a new country ... He was just starting again from scratch. US and Scottish law is just so different."

"I was trying to help people," said Colin.

"By causing pain and finding a dollar amount that will solve it? And you could have helped people in Scotland. You could have moved to Glasgow, not the other side of the world."

Melissa looked away now.

"Da. I came back. I'm here. Stop punishing me," said Colin.

"I'm not punishing you. I want you here. I miss my son. You've been more yourself this past week than you have been in years. And I think—" He looked at Melissa and winked. "I think you should put your barrister skills to good use and help Ms. Mackenzie with her house situation."

Melissa wanted to crawl under the table and hide. She stood instead. "Thank you for breakfast. And for letting me stay here. I'm going to go back to the house and get the rest of my stuff. Do you know a good place for storage?"

"There's no need for that. You can store everything in our barns," said Sandy. Melissa smiled, and Sandy took her hand.

"What about the animals?" asked Melissa.

"I have a feeling it'll be temporary. Colin will straighten things out," said Sandy.

CHAPTER 19

The repairs at Greenhill House had made all the difference. Melissa's Christmas decorations were picture perfect, the new paint job sparkled, and the landscaping blended well with the woods and loch.

Melissa wiped away a tear as she opened the garage door and went inside. The kitchen was Scottish farmhouse chic. She walked through the living room. Fresh paint, new rugs. She went into the den—still in process, but looking better. Then into the library. She took one long look out the window with its stunning view of Loch Ness, then turned to the wall of bookshelves. Something caught her eye. She climbed up the short stepladder to retrieve it. She looked at the cover: *The History of the Mackenzie Family.* She looked at the long line of MacKenzies, dating back to the fifteenth century.

As she was about to put the book back on the shelf, a piece of paper fell out. She opened it, took a good look, and traced her finger down the line. She was stunned.

Carefully, she snapped a picture of it with her phone, then she made a phone call.

"Hello? Yes. I'd like to request a birth certificate."

CHAPTER 20

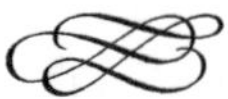

Melissa, festively dressed in a Santa hat, red sweater, and red jacket, joined the crowd gathering in the center of the town where the tree lighting was about to take place. Lindsay spotted her from across the street. She waved, and Melissa waved back.

"How are you holding up?" Lindsay asked as she crossed over to her.

"Pretty well, actually. I've found—"

The mayor interrupted with the beginning of the ceremony. "Welcome to the annual Inverness tree lighting ceremony. We'll begin with the local pipe band, led by Sandy MacGregor."

The drumbeat started, and soon anything Melissa had wanted to say was drowned out by bagpipes. Lindsay grinned at Melissa and mouthed the word *later*.

Colin was a part of the procession of pipers. Melissa couldn't take her eyes off of him in his kilt. But just as Melissa was about to say hi, Fiona—the woman who'd gone to high school with Colin—made a beeline for Colin. Melissa noticed how Fiona kept reaching out to touch Colin.

"And now the moment we've been waiting for ... the lighting

of the tree," said the mayor. There was a drumroll from the pipe band. "Join me! Ten, nine ..."

The crowd joined in. "Eight, seven, six ..."

At the end of the countdown, the mayor flipped a switch, and the tree's lights dazzled. At the same time, the whole town lit up: the stores, the street lamps, decorations over the streets and Inverness Castle.

"It's breathtaking," said Melissa.

"Right?" said Lindsay.

Melissa continued to admire the lights. "Wow."

Carolers began singing, and the crowd joined in. The Christmas parade marched by. Families marched together, wearing matching costumes, ugly Christmas sweaters, light up hats, and more.

"Why didn't we think of that?" said Melissa.

"Next year."

Melissa looked away. Lindsay put her arm around her. "Even if we can't work things out with your house, you can get another one," said Lindsay.

Melissa blinked back tears. She had already spent too much of her own money on the renovations. If she couldn't get the house back, she was sunk.

"Let's just live in the moment, shall we? *Carpe* Christmas," she said.

"*Carpe* Christmas," said Lindsay.

They walked down the street, which glistened with colorful lights, greenery, and bows. Lindsay bought light-up antlers and Christmas light necklaces, and they both put them on and laughed. Some of the stores served wassail, cookies, mince pies, and other treats. They gobbled them down and shopped till they dropped. Lindsay emerged with lots of packages, and Melissa had a small bag of dog biscuits.

"Want to stop by my place and drop your bags, and we can get ready for the party?" asked Lindsay.

"Sure."

* * *

IN THE GUEST room of the MacGregor home, Melissa's phone buzzed. Then it buzzed again. She sat up in bed and reached for her phone. It was 2 am. She had about ten text notifications.

Wanted to invite you to our New Year's Eve party. Where are you? We can't reach you.

Sending out Christmas cards. What's your new address?

Heard about you and Dave. So sorry. Call me.

Melissa smiled. Of course her friends from home hadn't forgotten her. And what seemed like a lifetime to her had, in reality, only been a few weeks. She had left without telling anyone of her plans, and they were probably just finding out. It was still evening in Boston. If they didn't know where she was, they didn't know how late it was.

She began texting back emojis and pictures of Scotland. She felt a warmth she hadn't felt in a while. After about a half hour, she set her phone down. But now she was awake, so she turned on her computer. Soon she was deeply absorbed in a family tree website.

* * *

MORNING SUNLIGHT SPARKLED on the snowy hills behind the MacGregor home. A flurry of baking was underway in the kitchen as Melissa and Lindsay filled trays with shortbread, bannock, and other treats. Colin and his father came in, dressed in their lumberjack finest, carrying a huge pine tree that they'd slayed.

"Cutting it a little close?" Melissa joked. "I mean, you've got hours left until Christmas."

"Just because you yanks start decking the halls in October ..." bantered Colin back at her.

"Ooch. Enough. It's Christmas," said Lindsay.

"Still just Christmas Eve. Plenty of merriment ahead," said Sandy.

Colin and his father set up the tree and began checking the lights. Lindsay carried a box of ornaments into the living room. She held up the angel.

"Remember when Mum always put this up?"

"It was Gran's," said Colin.

"It was?"

"Of course. I remember it on her tree. She gave it to Mum for Christmas one year."

"And someday I'll give it to one of you," said Sandy. They were sober for a minute as Sandy placed the angel on the top of the tree.

"Remember these birds?" asked Colin.

"Your mother was a loon for birds," said Sandy.

As Colin and Lindsay began to decorate the tree, Melissa stepped away. Sandy put his arm around her. "Don't be shy, lass. We need your help."

"I just feel like everything I touch turns to—"

"Nonsense. Life is impermanent. Take a candy cane. Eat it. Enjoy. It's gone. But there will be other treats to be had." He handed her a red glass ornament. "Colin made this when he was in school."

"It's beautiful," said Melissa.

"You should see my work in the mediums of macaroni and popsicle sticks," said Colin.

Melissa laughed. "I bet it's superb."

"Oh, yes. I was gifted from an early age. See?" He held up a Christmas tree made from popsicle sticks, pasta, and paint.

"Lovely."

Soon the tree was decorated, and they all sat by the fire to admire it.

"Anyone for tea and biscuits?" asked Lindsay, already heading into the kitchen.

Melissa sat there, feeling awkward. "Thank you again for taking me into your home, especially on a major holiday when I just met you."

"Lass, you're always welcome here. Now. We have a tradition in this family of opening one gift on Christmas Eve and the rest on Christmas morning."

Lindsay returned with a tray of tea and shortbread. "Mum started it. Her grandmother was from Iceland, where they receive books on Christmas Eve and spend the evening reading books and eating chocolate."

Colin smiled and handed Melissa a gift.

"For me?" Melissa opened it. *The History of the Mackenzie Family of Inverness.*

"Oh my goodness. This is perfect." Melissa examined it. It was a more specific history than the book she'd found in the library at Greenhill House.

"I've seen you looking at those genealogy sites, and I thought this would help fill in the gaps you can't find online."

"Thank you so much." She handed Colin a package. "It's not a book, but it's something you can use right away," she said.

"Should I wait till tomorrow?"

"You'll want it before Christmas," said Melissa with a grin.

He opened it. It was an Ugly Christmas Jumper—complete with lights.

"For the party."

"Of course," said Colin as he held it up. "Thank you. I feel so very Americanized."

"It's you, Colin," said Lindsay.

Melissa handed Lindsay a package. It was a much cuter Ugly Christmas Jumper. And for Sandy, a light up hat. They all exchanged books and opened a box of chocolates. Soon they were all settled into their armchairs, reading and eating chocolates while the fire crackled and the snow fell.

Melissa sat up straight and gasped.

"What?" asked Colin, looking up from his book.

"You won't believe this." She opened her phone genealogy app and showed Colin her tree. "I had a hunch, so I started digging—this was back when you said Mr. Mackenzie's name was Gerald. And I dug and I dug, but I couldn't find anything. But I did find this." She handed him a slip of paper. Colin blinked. "And I thought maybe it was a coincidence. So I was trying to find proof online. But now between that, this, and my own family tree ..."

"What is it?" asked Lindsay.

"You really are Gerald Mackenzie's relative," said Colin.

"You are?" asked Lindsay.

"Good on you, lass," said Sandy.

"Let's ring the bank straightaway," said Colin.

"Now?"

"I'll do you one better. The owner of the bank is throwing a Christmas party tonight. Let's go," said Sandy, standing up and slipping on his shoes.

They pulled on their Christmas jumpers and hats and headed out the door.

* * *

When they approached the home, cars were parked on both sides of the street, and festive Scottish music spilled out of the house.

"Are you sure this is okay?" asked Melissa.

"We went to grade school together," said Sandy as he walked up the sidewalk to the front door.

Inside, everyone was dressed in tartan, festive Christmas

jumpers, and light up hats. They fit right in. As a *ceilidh* band played, people danced and munched on mincemeat pies, cookies, and punch.

Sandy set down a large, hastily wrapped gift—clearly a bottle of Scotch whisky—and they all joined the party.

Colin went up to an older man in a suit, shook hands, and spoke to him in a corner. The man looked over at Melissa and then came over.

"Hello, Ms. Mackenzie. Pleasure to meet you. I understand you believe you do have a claim on the Mackenzie home," he said.

"I do. If you look here, and in this book, and with these birth certificates ..." she said, showing him images on her phone.

He looked at her notes and nodded. Melissa handed him the eviction notice.

"I can print everything up and get it all to you. And I can get a lawyer to—"

"No need, lass. It's Christmas," said the banker. He tore up the eviction notice and grinned. "I'll still need to put things straight with our lawyers, but if your family tree works out, there will be no problems."

"I think we're in need of a toast," he said.

Sandy poured them all a dram, and they raised their glasses.

"*Slàinte Mhath*!" they all said as they clinked their glasses and drank.

"To family," said Sandy.

Colin's eyes twinkled at the way his father looked at him and Melissa.

"*Alba gu bràth*," said Melissa. They all clinked glasses. "I live in Scotland now."

"Aye, you do, lass."

And for the first time in a long, long time, Melissa felt like she belonged. And it felt wonderful.

As the party ended, and they put on their coats, Colin and

Melissa found themselves standing in the moonlight. There was a faint green shimmer in the night sky.

"Is that the aurora borealis?"

Colin looked up. "Aye, I believe it is."

"It's incredible."

They gazed at it for a long moment and then Colin pointed to the porch ceiling above—mistletoe.

"Where I come from, it's good luck to kiss under the mistletoe," he said.

"It is?"

"I just made it up. But I'm a lawyer. Want to argue with me about it?"

"Did you know that book you gave me would have the evidence I needed to keep the house?"

"I suspected that's what you were going after, but I didn't have all your family names and dates to make the connection for certain," he said.

He looked up at the mistletoe again. "But your stall tactics won't hold up in my courtroom, Ms. Mackenzie. Are we going to do something about this mistletoe situation? I think good luck would be helpful in the new year."

"I agree, barrister," Melissa said as Colin leaned in and kissed her. "I think I'm already pretty lucky."

He took her hand. "Let's get you to your new home."

Snow was falling steadily, and the Northern Lights shimmered. It was a perfect, magical winter wonderland as they drove along the loch toward Greenhill House. When they arrived, they each got out of the truck and stood awkwardly for a moment.

Melissa broke the silence. "Well, thank you so much, Colin. For everything."

"I hope you'll come over for Christmas Day. Or we could come here?"

"I'd love that. Let's do both."

They heard a strange noise: a bubbling followed by a splash. They looked at each other. It was coming from behind the house. They ran through the snow to the backyard. As the Christmas star shone overhead, snow fell. The Northern Lights glowed a mysterious, beautiful greenish-blue, and a long rippling shape emerged from the loch. A fin shimmered in the moonlight. There was a loud splash, like a whale breaching. The ripples followed a long line in the moonlight, stretching deeper and deeper, down toward the end of the loch.

Colin raised his eyebrows.

"Was that what I think it was?" asked Melissa.

"Apparently you've got Nessie's seal of approval. You're a real Scot now. At least a real Inversnecky."

"Inversnecky? Really? Is that what they call us?"

"It's that or *Clann Na Cloiche,* 'Children of the Stone,' in Gaelic," said Colin, taking her hand. He leaned in.

"I haven't put up any mistletoe yet," said Melissa, still a little nervous.

"I brought my own," said Colin, holding up a sprig. Melissa laughed. "May I?"

Melissa leaned in and kissed him.

"Happy Christmas, Melissa," he said.

"Merry Christmas."

Melissa stood looking at the peaceful snowy loch. "I hate for the holidays to be over so soon," she said wistfully.

"Hogmanay's next week—the biggest, best New Year's celebration you've ever seen," said Colin.

Arm in arm, they watched as … whatever it was … dove back into the water, swimming further and further down the lock, the moonlight glistening on its back.

AMY QUICK PARRISH

Highlands New Year

A HIGHLANDS CHRISTMAS ROMANCE

CHAPTER 1

Caitlin cradled her hot chocolate in her hands as she watched the snow fall on the streets of Boston outside her Back Bay apartment. On the table next to her sat a postcard from Inverness, Scotland, with a cheery message from her best friend, Melissa. Caitlin shook her head, picked up her phone, and dialed Melissa.

"Hello?" answered Melissa. "Caitlin?"

"What were you thinking?" Caitlin cut to the chase, her directness a hallmark of their friendship.

"Hi, Caitlin. How are you?" said Melissa. She sat next to a picture window in the living room, looking out upon a snowy hill that led down toward the banks of Loch Ness.

"Well, I'm hurt and shocked that my best friend moved to Scotland without even giving me a heads up. What. Were. You. Thinking?!"

"I wasn't. Dave left me and took the house—it was in his name, even though I had poured my heart and soul into renovations."

"Not to mention you were his wife!"

"Yeah. I should've paid more attention. Who doesn't put the house in both names?"

"A cheater." Caitlin had disliked Dave for quite a while but hadn't thought he'd actually cheat on her best friend.

"Apparently so."

"I'm so sorry. What a jerk. And at Christmas! Who does that?"

Melissa sighed.

Caitlin pressed on. "What about all your stuff?"

"Well, right now it's still in the house. I'm going to get it moved to storage."

"Don't you want it there with you?"

"It's mostly furniture. My sister went through and got the photos, family items, personal things. She's coming out next month. The rest of it I don't care about. This place came somewhat furnished, and little by little I'm replacing things."

"With what money, if I dare ask?"

"It turns out there was a little money included with the house that I inherited."

"Enough to live on?" asked Caitlin.

"Well, I'll need to get back to work again soon," said Melissa.

"Can you be an interior designer in another country?"

"Of course. I mean, it's not like you need a local license or anything."

"But what about a visa?" asked Caitlin.

"Oh, yeah. I've been putting a lot on the credit card, but no worries. I'll pay it off," said Melissa.

"Mel, I mean a travel visa. Are you even allowed to just move to another country and live there indefinitely?"

Melissa was silent. *Hmmm. Probably not. Of course not.* She was embarrassed, but it hadn't even occurred to her.

"I mean, people do it," said Melissa.

"Have you looked into how to do it? Other than buying a plane ticket and just doing it?"

"Not yet."

"How long have you been there?" asked Caitlin.

"Just about three weeks,"said Melissa.

Caitlin typed into her laptop and did a quick search. When she found the information she was looking for, she read it aloud. "A US citizen can stay in Scotland for as long as six months without a visa, but they must have a valid US passport, a return ticket home, and proof of financial means to support themselves."

"My passport's good for another five years."

"Okay ..." said Caitlin.

"I can get a flight home."

"And ..."

"And I'll get a job," said Melissa.

"Self-employment as an interior designer in a rural area isn't proof of means to support yourself."

"It's not that rural. I'm just a few miles outside of Inverness. That's a big city. There's an airport," said Melissa.

"Well, I'm just trying to help," said Caitlin.

"I know."

"And I'm sorry I've been hard on you. You must be hurting. I'm so sorry."

"You know, it was terrible when it happened, but I think the change of scenery has really helped. And I've met ..." Melissa trailed off.

Caitlin perked up. "You've met ...?"

"Well, I've met someone. We're not serious or anything, but his family has taken me in and—"

"You've met his family! This *sounds* serious," said Caitlin.

"Well, it's ... we're mostly ... well, it's ... he ... It started out that we just met by coincidence. He was at the airport, then he was on my flight, then he was on my train."

"Stalker?" asked Caitlin.

"No, coincidence. We were just flying to the same town. But then he turned out to be Dave's lawyer," explained Melissa.

"No!"

"Yeah."

"So he's American?"

"Well, he'd been living and working in the States to avoid some painful memories here. Now he's feeling ready to embrace his homeland again."

"Because he met you?" Caitlin sipped her hot chocolate with delight.

"I think he just realized how nice it is here, what a great family he has, and how … I mean, I don't know. I can't speak for him."

Caitlin sighed. "So you're all right."

"I am."

"I was just so worried to hear you left so suddenly. And it's such a change. I mean, just a few weeks ago I was at your dinner party …" Caitlin's voice trailed off as she made a realization. "So the Samantha who was at your party, the awful woman who brought that terrible squirrel centerpiece thing—she was the other woman?"

"Yeah. Turns out Dave had been seeing her for a while."

"I'm so sorry. That's terrible."

"Yeah. Well. It's over now. I'm glad we're done. And it really is wonderful here." Melissa stood and looked out at the snow falling on the pine trees and the loch below. "You really should see it. I'm right on Loch Ness. I see deer just about every day. And I have a dog."

"You're on Loch Ness!"

"Yeah. Inverness is the town at the north end, and the loch stretches a long way toward the southwest. It kind of looks like a river in some places and a lake in others."

"Have you seen anything?"

"I mean, there are all kinds of things: birds, eels, occasionally a seal will swim up from the North Sea. It could've been anything."

"You *have* seen something, haven't you?!"

"Well, something. But—"

"That's it," said Caitlin suddenly.

"What's it?"

"I didn't want to leave my friend all alone during the holidays. I see you've found a whole family to spend Christmas with, but I think it's time for me to come visit you for the new year."

"That would be great! I have so much room. When can you come?"

Caitlin was tapping on her computer again, searching flights. She scrolled down. *Boom.* "There's a plane with one seat on it leaving tomorrow night. Gets in the next morning at 7 a.m."

"Fantastic. How long can you stay?"

Caitlin looked at her phone calendar. "I have the week off."

"That's perfect. Colin says New Year's is the big holiday around here anyway. They call it ..." Melissa had to think. She hated when she misspoke or mispronounced words, so she'd been working on this one. "Hogmanay."

"Hogmanay?"

"A big New Year's celebration. It'll be so much fun. I can't wait to see you!"

"Same! I'll talk to your sister and bring some stuff you might want or need."

"Perfect. And I'll see what kinds of reservations we might want and—Hey, maybe we can have a party at Greenhill!"

"What's Greenhill?"

"That's the name of the estate."

"Estate? Is it some kind of a—"

"You'll see. I can't wait. I'll be at the airport at 7:15."

"Great. See you soon!" Caitlin hung up and looked around

her apartment. What should she bring to Scotland for a week in the winter, and for New Year's Eve?

She grabbed a suitcase and set it on the bed, then went to her closet. Turtlenecks, jeans, sweaters ... something dressy. She tossed in a plaid dress, a neutral black dress, and some cute boots. A scarf. Long johns. Mittens. Gloves. Hats. Warm socks.

She looked around her apartment wondering what Melissa might be missing from the US. Peanut Butter? Something Boston-specific? She couldn't think of anything but decided to send her a care package upon her return once she knew what Melissa could and couldn't get in the UK. Still, she couldn't come empty-handed.

In the end she ended up packing a small jar of peanut butter, a bag of Dunkin' coffee, a Boston Strong Christmas ornament, and a little photo ornament of the two of them in their college years.

CHAPTER 2

Melissa filled her cart at the local grocery store. She was an excellent cook, and Caitlin loved her cooking. It was just a matter of figuring out what to make. Something local—but she'd never made haggis and had no idea where to even get it. Might have to go to a restaurant for that. She picked up shortbread, tea, scones, clotted cream, jam—all the basics for a nice tea— and finger sandwiches. She picked up a Cadbury cake, looked at it, then set it down. Nothing pre-made. She'd make something. But what would Caitlin like? What was authentic besides haggis?

She turned a corner and found the answer: salmon! Salmon was something she knew how to make. She wheeled up to the fish counter and looked at all the choices. Smoked haddie spread sounded good, too. And something to put it on ... Toast? Crackers? What did they call crackers here? She knew cookies were biscuits. Chips were crisps. French fries were chips. She knew they had Christmas crackers, foil wrapped banging devices with a toy inside and usually a joke—not edible. She'd have to just wander the aisles and see.

Just as she found her way to the crackers, she bumped into a beautiful, thin, striking woman with gorgeous cascades of long red hair.

The woman smiled shallowly. "Melissa! Are you still in town?"

"Hello, Fiona. So nice to see you. Yes. I inherited a place and—"

"Oh, I thought you were selling it so you could move back to the States."

"Nope. Nope. I've moved in! It's mine. I just have to finalize the paperwork, and I'm a true Scots … woman." She bit her lip, realizing the only time she really heard people say "true Scotsman" was to verify what the man was wearing—or not wearing—under his kilt.

"I see. Well, how lovely for you."

Melissa knew Fiona wasn't trying to be condescending, but she couldn't help but feel small, chubby, and inelegant next to her. And ineloquent, if that was even a word.

Fiona eyed Melissa's groceries. "Looks like you're filling your cart for a party!"

"Oh. Well, I'm having a friend visit from out of town."

"Wonderful. I hope you have a wonderful time with him!"

"It's actually … Nevermind." Fiona had dated Colin in the past and—*fret not, Melissa. He likes you.*

"Well, good to see you."

* * *

KNOWING CAITLIN AS SHE DID, Melissa stopped by a shop where she could stock her bar. She emerged with a lovely bottle of Talisker Skye single malt, some Scottish gin, good elderberry tonic water, and a case of Malbec. She decided to get the rest of the Scotch once Caitlin was there and had tasted some. That way they could get what they liked.

As she overheard various chatter from the other shoppers,

she became aware that she really didn't have any concrete plans for this holiday. She had assumed she'd do something with Colin, but ... Why had she assumed that? It was a big-deal holiday. He probably had already made plans for Hogmany before she'd first encountered him in the airport. Of course he did. That was likely half of the reason he was visiting this time of year. All his friends from university would be in town. She was more and more grateful every second that she had a friend—a good friend, an old friend—coming to spend the week with her. Because even at home, it had to be a pretty serious relationship to make plans for New Year's Eve, didn't it?

She was in line at the checkout when she saw Colin's sister Lindsay walk in. Lindsay spotted her and waved, then continued to the back of the store. When Melissa had paid, she wasn't sure what to do. Waving was enough, right? She shouldn't follow Lindsay to the back of the store. That would be weird. But standing around, loitering outside a liquor store was also weird. While she was standing there wondering what to do, she spotted a flyer advertising a town Hogmanay celebration. Just as she'd noted the date and time and decided she'd check out their website when she got home, Colin walked through the door.

"Melissa!"

"Hi, Colin! I just saw Lindsay come in!"

"Oh? I need to be sure she adds something to her list. Come back with me?"

"I've already checked out."

"Okay, then come to my house tonight for dinner, and we'll talk," said Colin.

"I've got a friend coming to town tomorrow, and I need to be up early," replied Melissa.

"Really? Lovely."

Colin was in a hurry, and Melissa was torn. She wanted to see him, but she had so much to do tonight.

He took her hand warmly and paused. "When can I see you, then?"

Melissa breathed a sigh of relief. She hadn't wanted to be the result of some pity party. She had started to imagine he was just a barrister with a heart of gold who'd helped her win back her house, nothing more. "You could come by my house this afternoon? Or we could get lunch somewhere?" she suggested.

"I'll grab lunch from the cafe next door and then pop down to your place." He gave her hand a quick squeeze and then dashed to the back of the store to find Lindsay.

As she drove home to Greenhill House, she was surprised that the Christmas radio channel she'd found was already back to playing regular music. There was still snow everywhere, and people still had their decorations up. But just like at home, that was it—a hard switch off to the holiday season.

But Hogmanay was coming, and she couldn't wait.

She pulled into Greenhill House half expecting to see yet another real estate sign. She'd gone around and around with them—it turned out they were a scam organization—but those times were gone. This was officially her house now. And once she could find a steady job and income, she could stay.

CHAPTER 3

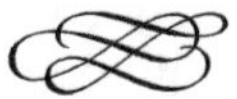

Caitlin sat in the back seat of the cab watching as the driver sped down the Massachusetts turnpike toward Logan airport. She worried about what her friend may have gotten herself into. Melissa was always so trusting, and that was usually her downfall. She loved people and always saw the best in them. But sometimes they took advantage of her. Caitlin didn't like the idea of Melissa sounding so smitten with her husband's divorce lawyer. It just sounded fishy. And to suddenly inherit a home in the same town where this guy lived? Coincidence? Caitlin didn't believe in coincidences.

MELISSA WAS WAITING in her car at passenger pickup when she spotted Caitlin wheeling out her small suitcase. She waved and popped open the trunk—or the boot, as she was learning to call it. When Caitlin finally weaved her way through the waiting cars, Melissa pulled her into a tight hug.

"How are you? How was your flight? Are you hungry? You look great!"

Caitlin laughed. "One thing at a time! Flight was fine, I'm

kinda hungry ... It feels like morning. Is there any place to get coffee?"

"You bet!" Melissa stuffed the suitcase into her trunk and popped the lid closed. Caitlin opened the car door and proceeded to get into the driver's seat. In the UK, just as cars drove on the other side of the road, the driver's seat was also on a different side. Melissa was thrilled to finally be able to be the person who made the joke: "Oh, that's okay. I'll drive."

Caitlin looked at Melissa then at the steering wheel on the right side of the car. "Oh yeah!"

Melissa giggled. "Happens all the time. You won't believe how many times I've gotten into the car as if I expected Jingles to drive or something. Oh, by the way, this is Jingles."

Caitlin followed Melissa's wave toward the backseat and instantly fell in love with the black-and-white Border Collie puppy. She couldn't resist scratching his soft ears. "What a good dog. Hi, Jingles. Hello!"

Caitlin continued to make dog-conversation as Melissa rather expertly maneuvered the car into the correct lane to exit the airport. Soon they were driving along at a good speed as if she were a native. Even the formerly white-knuckle roundabouts were getting easier.

"So, welcome to Inverness," Melissa said as she gestured toward the city center.

"It's beautiful," Caitlin said, looking out at the snowy Ness River and the impressive Inverness castle made of rosy pink stone. "Like a fairytale."

"That's what I said. Especially about Edinburgh, but really, everywhere. I'm so glad you're here."

"Me too."

"So do you want to stop at a coffee shop or go straight to the house?"

"Are you kidding? I've gotta see this house that has sent you moving across continents!"

Melissa smiled and began to relax. It was so good to be around someone easy and familiar. It had only been a few weeks, but it felt like ages since Caitlin had been at her dinner party back in the states. It was the night Dave had asked for a divorce. She couldn't believe she hadn't seen any of her friends or family since then. What had she been thinking?

Somehow that was becoming a refrain. But of course, when you face sudden trauma no one can expect you to think clearly and act objectively. Of course she was going to go full force, making rash decisions solely on pure adrenaline and emotion. *That's got to be in a psychology textbook or something,* Melissa thought.

"Okay. So I'll show you the house and get you settled in. We'll have tea—"

"Coffee?"

"Yeah, but we're going to say we're having tea."

Caitlin laughed.

They drove past the outskirts of Inverness along the narrow, snowy, tree-lined road beside a dark body of water. It looked like a river, but soon Caitlin spotted a sign for Loch Ness.

"This is it?"

"This is it."

"We gotta get out and get a selfie."

Melissa had anticipated this and had already slowed down. She parked alongside the road and got out. They stood under the sign with the loch behind them. "I think your arms are longer," she said.

Caitlin nodded and pulled out her phone. "Ready?"

"Say 'whisky.'"

"Whisky."

They did a few more in different poses-Charlie's Angels gun pose, surprised Home Alone faces, and startled OMG-what's-that-in-the-water poses.

"We can photoshop some kind of monster into that one," said Caitlin.

"Or maybe one of these days we'll see something again."

"Again! You saw something already?"

"Well, there was bubbling, and something was moving in the water. Could've been anything—they say the loch is full of eels, occasionally a seal will swim in or even a whale."

"But you saw something."

Melissa shrugged and smiled mysteriously.

"Shall we see Greenhill?"

"Why of course, my lady."

Caitlin got back into the driver's seat, looked at the steering wheel in front of her, and slid over to the other side.

"It's good for the core," said Melissa with a laugh as she plopped herself into the driver's seat. They drove just about a mile further down the road and then pulled up to a large stone fence with an iron gate. Beyond it, the lovely Greenhill House was nestled in the woods with Loch Ness in the back.

Caitlin's jaw dropped. "This is amazing," she said, looking up at the gorgeous stone home. Snow and greenery made it look like a fairy cottage or something out of a Hallmark Christmas movie.

"Yeah! I mean, thanks." Melissa drove through the gates and parked the car.

Caitlin was lost in thought as Melissa parked the car, popped the trunk, and grabbed her suitcase. She got out and stared at the house while Jingles scampered up the walkway.

"It's like … it's just … amazing," said Caitlin, at a loss for words.

"Come see the inside," said Melissa. Bells jingled as she flung open her wreath-adorned cherry wood door.

"Wow!" said Caitlin as she stepped into the foyer.

"It was a mess. The old man had lived alone and let things go. Lots of avocado green appliances, an orange couch, that kind of thing. But the woodwork is amazing, and the glass and windows are all original."

"When was this built?"

"Still trying to work that out. Likely the mid-to-late 1800s."

"So it's not that old."

"Not for around here. But there's an ancient well in the backyard that has been around for centuries. Once you've had the tour, remind me to show you."

As they walked into the kitchen, Caitlin turned to Melissa. "Amazing."

Melissa hadn't needed to do much with the kitchen. It had classic white cabinetry, wood floors, stonework, and lots of bright light shining through a wall of windows. She'd added a few touches here and there—thistle tea towels, a new white backsplash, and new appliances.

Melissa put the kettle on. "Not much of a breakfast on the airplane, I bet?"

Caitlin laughed. "We settled in, had dinner, slept an hour, and all of a sudden I was hearing a cheery 'Good morning.' I think I managed a sip or two of coffee before we packed up and landed."

"That's the good and bad of the Boston flight—very short. Let's get you upstairs. You can unpack and settle a little, and I'll be mother."

"What?"

"That means 'I'll pour the tea.' Except, I think maybe I'm supposed to say that right when I pour the tea. Still learning the lingo."

"Apparently," Caitlin laughed and put her arm around Melissa. "But I can see why you wanted to stay here. What a place!"

"Come see the library."

"The library? Is that near the drawing room, Madam?"

"C'mon!" Melissa said, rolling her eyes. She led Caitlin down the hall to a large, cozy room lined floor to ceiling with warm cherry wood bookshelves. Twin armchairs nestled by a warm fire looked out another wall of windows. A bird feeder packed with blue tits and siskins sat on a snowy hill leading down toward the loch. But Caitlin's eyes kept returning to the books. The place was packed with everything from fairly recent best-sellers to antique classics.

"Wow, so many beautiful antique books!"

"Yeah! This 'MacKenzie Family History' helped me prove that this house was meant to be mine, despite the scam."

"So, wait, explain that again."

"Somehow these predators got a hold of my name—they prey on Americans who might love to inherit a home in the UK. They sent me a letter saying this home had belonged to my long-lost uncle, and I had inherited it."

"But, it was."

"Well, yes, it was. But they had used the name of some guy I definitely wasn't related to. They wanted to sell the house for me, then give me the money."

"Well, that sounds like a good deal."

"Of course it does. Except, I didn't want the money; I wanted the house. So I took their for sale signs down and moved in. They didn't like that."

"I can imagine."

"So how'd you figure it all out?"

"Colin—my friend I was telling you about—is a lawyer. Right away, it didn't seem right to him that they wanted my bank account information before they'd even received an offer. It seemed weird, and it was. But, it turns out this place was owned by a Mackenzie, and through sheer Christmas magic—or their bad luck—they happened to randomly select the one MacKenzie in Boston who was actually related to the previous owner. We established a family tree and documentation, and the place is mine now."

Caitlin shook her head in disbelief. "That's incredible."

"Yeah."

"Can't make this stuff up. If it were a movie, no one would ever believe it!"

"Truth is stranger than fiction, I guess! Anyway, let's get you upstairs so you can see your room. We can have our tea in the library."

"Jolly good," said Caitlin.

"I think that's England. And probably from a hundred years ago?"

"I Googled it earlier, and apparently, posh people still say it. I'll have to watch more Ted Lasso so I don't sound like a wanker."

"That might make you sound more like a wanker." Melissa grabbed Caitlin's suitcase and headed toward the stairs at the end of the hallway.

Caitlin's room was large enough to be comfortable but still cozy. There was a bed, a dresser, a chair, and two windows with views of the loch.

"Amazing! I can lie in bed, turn my head to the side, and try to spot Nessie!"

Melissa laughed. "I'll leave you to get freshened up. There are towels in the dresser, bathroom's just across the hall, and be sure to try the heated towel rack. It's fabulous!"

"Good on you!"

Melissa rolled her eyes at Caitlin, who laughed.

CHAPTER 4

Showered and settled in, Caitlin came down the stairs dressed in a plaid blazer, turtleneck sweater, and jeans and carrying an adorable pair of red wellies. She looked as if she'd stepped straight out of a Scottish mystery show. "Is it tea time?"

"Sure. Which room do you think, the library or the living room?"

"Oh, the library! I just love all the books, and that view!"

"I'll go make a fire. Kettle's on and scones are about to pop out of the oven. Let me know if you hear a ding."

"You've really got this all sorted out!"

Melissa shrugged but was secretly pleased. She had always been a follower in her marriage with Dave. Here, she could carve her own path, and she was. She was making her own decisions on everything—from decorations to food to her car—and she finally even had a dog.

Expertly building the fire, Melissa struck a match and lit it. Once it was crackling, she went back to the kitchen to find that Caitlin had found the oven mitts and removed the scones from the oven but was now rummaging around in the fridge.

"What can I help you find?" asked Melissa.

"I found some different jams, but maybe butter?"

Melissa grinned. "You want clotted cream."

"Clotted?" asked Caitlin, aghast. "It sounds like a heart attack waiting to happen."

Melissa found the container she was looking for and set it out on a tray with the scones, jams, and tea.

"Try it before you deny it," Melissa said with a grin.

They went into the cozy library. Melissa set down the tray, and Caitlin set down the teapot. Melissa spread clotted cream onto a scone, then added strawberry jam and some sliced strawberries. "Try that," she said, handing it to Caitlin.

"Mmmmph!"

"I know, right?"

"Wow. A lot better than those dry hockey pucks we get in the coffee shops at home!"

"Yeah," Melisssa said, sipping her tea.

"So I guess the 'why' is obvious—right opportunity at the right time. But still, what an impulsive decision to decide to move here instead of just taking the cash."

"It just seemed like the thing I should do."

Caitlin looked around. "I mean, it's really awesome!"

"Right?"

"So what should we do this week?" asked Caitlin.

"Well, today's the 28th. We have some time till Hogmanay. Apparently it's three days of celebrations. The 31st, 1st and 2nd, I think?" said Melissa.

"And you can find me a man in a kilt?"

"There will be plenty of men in kilts!"

Caitlin grinned.

"So from today on, we can get tickets to various events on the 31st and maybe get ready for a party on the first. In between, we can do some sightseeing. Sound good?" asked Melissa.

"Sounds perfect. What should we see?"

"Well, there's obviously Loch Ness in the back, here. But the best place to go is Urquhart Castle. It's a few miles down—it's a really long loch—in Drumnadrochit. It's a really cool old castle, and it's also where the Nessie museum is. It's worth seeing."

"I'm in," said Caitlin.

"And then there are the sights to see around Inverness. But we'll be there for Hogmanay. Oh, and another place to visit is Culloden. The site of a sad battle," said Melissa.

"That sounds kinda depressing."

"Well, it is an important monument to a lot of people. We should at least see if it's open this week," said Melissa.

"Okay."

"Balmoral isn't too terribly far, a little over two hours' drive."

"We can do that," said Caitlin.

"Depending on the weather. These roads are tiny and full of sheep on a good day. I'd worry about ice," said Melissa.

"What's there?"

"Oh! Well, it was Queen Victoria's favorite castle. Her Majesty Queen Elizabeth loved it. It's where they'd go to get away from it all: to go on hikes or ride horses or hunt—ducks or foxes or deer or whatever it is they hunt," said Melissa.

"Will it be open?"

"We'll check it out."

Caitlin thought for a second. "Will they *be* there?"

"I don't think so. I think they go in the summer. Remember, they were there when Diana died," said Melissa.

"So terrible," said Caitlin as memories flashed in her mind—thousands of flower bouquets lying outside Buckingham Palace and the heartbreaking sight of young Harry and William trudging along behind their mother's coffin in the funeral procession.

"Awful," said Melissa.

They were quiet for a while, sipping their tea.

"So where else?" asked Caitlin, trying to break the gloom.

"There are distilleries. And there's the Isle of Skye."

"That sounds promising!" said Caitlin.

"And there are distilleries on the Isle of Skye. Well, distillery. I've been wanting to go there. I don't know if we have time for all of these, but I think we can definitely manage to do Urquhart Castle, Eilean Donan castle, Isle of Skye, some hill walking, and distilleries. What do you think?" asked Melissa.

"Let's do it!" said Caitlin enthusiastically.

As they finished their tea, a car pulled up in the driveway. Melissa looked out to see her friend Lindsay getting out of her red Mini.

Lindsay saw Melissa at the window and waved. Melissa opened the door and called to her. "Hey! You've gotta come meet my friend Caitlin!"

Behind her, Caitlin shook her head. "So American."

"Well, we *are* American."

Lindsay navigated the walkway dressed in jeans, a sweater, and a plaid scarf while carefully balancing a plate of food and a bag.

When Lindsay reached the door, Melissa stepped out in her slippers. The snow was cold on her feet, but she didn't mind. "Lindsay! Thanks for popping over. Lindsay, this is Caitlin, my best friend from home. Caitlin, this is Lindsay, the first friend I made in Inverness!"

They exchanged "nice to meet yous," and Lindsay came inside.

"I brought some of the leftovers from Christmas—not just what we had, but my Da has a lot of friends who like to bring mincemeat pies, shortbread, tablet, and such," said Lindsay.

"Wonderful! Thank you!" Melissa took the food into the kitchen and set some pieces of sugary tablet onto a little plaid plate. She put on a kettle of tea, and the three sat by the window.

Caitlin picked up a piece of tablet. It looked like fudge. She took a bite. "This is delicious!"

"Yeah! It's so great. It's like fudge, but it's–"

"Infinitely better!" said Lindsay.

Melissa smiled and bit into a piece of tablet as well.

"So what have you planned for your visit?" asked Lindsay. "Can I take you around, show you some sights?"

"Well, we were thinking of seeing Urquhart Castle and then driving west toward the Isle of Skye."

"Wow! Most people sleep in, wear their pajamas, and eat tablet and mincemeat pies over the holidays, but you've got some proper plans in place!" said Lindsay.

"Too ambitious?" asked Melissa.

"I expect not, depending on the weather. In fact, my uncle has a summer cottage in Skye. He's on holiday with his in-laws, so I bet I could ring him and see if it's available," said Lindsay.

"That would be amazing! And, of course, you're invited!" said Melissa.

"And shall we bring Colin?" asked Lindsay.

"If he's free," said Melissa. "I wouldn't want to—"

"Melissa, he wants to. I'm sure of it."

"I can't wait to meet him," said Caitlin, who then looked like she wanted to bite her tongue after Melissa gave her a look.

"He's just ... a friend," said Melissa carefully.

Lindsay laughed. "If he's just a friend, then that's just an eel that people keep seeing in the loch out back."

Melissa laughed and felt more settled. It was so hard to know where a new relationship was headed, and given that Colin was only in town for the holidays, Melissa couldn't help but try to keep her thoughts of him at a distance. And, speaking of distance, a long distance relationship wasn't something she'd considered until now.

Lindsay was watching Melissa's face. "Melissa, stop worrying. I haven't seen him this way in years."

Blushing, Melissa nodded.

Hoping to clear the air, Caitlin asked, "So what do we pack for the Isle of Skye?"

CHAPTER 5

Lindsay drove, while Melissa rode shotgun. Caitlin sat in the back, admiring the passing scenery.

Melissa held up a map and showed it to Caitlin. "So we're here, just past Inverness. We're going to drive down this road along the Loch and stop at Urquhart Castle. Then we'll go on through Drumnadrochit and up toward Eilean Donan. That's the famous castle from ... well, from everything. It's in calendars, and it was in the movie Highlander."

"What's Urquhart?" asked Caitlin.

"Um. It's old ... It's where most of the Nessie sightings tend to happen." Melissa looked to Lindsay for help.

Lindsay laughed. "I'm Scottish, but I'm not the Encyclopedia Britannica! We'll get a leaflet when we arrive. It's old. It exploded once, I think. And ... yeah, we'll get the history there."

"And then this infamous Colin will meet us?"

"Aye. Leave it to him to have business meetings during the holidays." Lindsay was the one biting her tongue now, because Colin was Melissa's ex's divorce lawyer.

"No rest for the wicked, and Dave certainly ... well, he'll keep Colin busy," said Melissa.

. . .

As they drove down the narrow road along the loch, Melissa fiddled with the radio.

"No more Christmas music," said Melissa.

"I've got a Hogmanay playlist. Wanna try that?" Lindsay suggested.

"Absolutely!"

They sang along to everything from modern classic dance and party songs to funny little Scottish songs like "Donald, Where's Your Trousers?" This they sang with gusto. It was a fun song about a man who came from the Isle of Skye and had to deal with teasing from the lassies about the wind blowing his kilt.

It was a short drive down the narrow, wooded road, and they soon arrived at Urquhart castle. It was completely different from the relatively modern Inverness Castle. Urquhart was a ruined castle made of gray stone; nevertheless, it had an impressive, imposing facade. Sitting right on the banks of Loch Ness, the castle was a favorite vantage point for Nessie hunters.

As Caitlin walked through the doors of the visitor center and down the glistening snowy path toward the ruined castle, she couldn't help but imagine what it must've been like in its heyday.

She looked through the pamphlet and read aloud, "The last soldiers to march out of the castle blew it up!"

"So that it couldn't be used by the enemy," said Lindsay.

"Who was the enemy at the time?" asked Caitlin.

"Sounds like the Jacobites, but I thought they were the good guys?" asked Melissa.

"Depends on who's writing the history, doesn't it?" replied Lindsay.

Melissa nodded. "Or which historical series we've watched, more likely!"

"For me, it's all … well, a long time ago. What happened happened, and here we are," said Lindsay.

They snapped photos against the crumbling gray stone walls with Loch Ness in the background. Then they climbed a tower to look out at the loch.

Melissa's cell rang, but she silenced it.

Caitlin looked out over the dark water. "I wish we could do the boat tour."

"I guess you'll just have to come back this summer!" Melissa suggested.

"Or move here, like Melissa did," teased Lindsay.

Melissa laughed. "Hey, you never know. Life is full of surprises."

"I'm not moving away from a good supply of peanut butter, Hershey products, and the Bruins."

Melissa laughed. "You might find you have a taste for oatcakes, deep fried Mars Bars, and football."

Caitlin looked confused.

"You know, soccer!"

Melissa's phone rang again. This time she looked at it. It was a second call from Colin. "Just a sec, I'd better get this."

"Hey, Colin … Yeah, we're down here by the castle … You're here? … Okay, I'll come on up!"

Melissa hurried up the stone steps toward the visitor center. Inside, she made her way through all the postcards, guide books, and sweatshirts toward the front door, where she found Colin. He looked dashing in a long gray coat and gray plaid scarf.

"Hey!"

"Hey, yourself! Sorry I took so long."

"No worries, we've been having fun. We've been learning

about the castle's history. We're just bummed we can't take a cruise because it's winter."

"There are cruises in the winter," replied Colin.

"There are?"

"Of course. In fact, they're probably easier to book in the winter."

"Oh my gosh, I've got to tell Caitlin!"

Melissa grabbed Colin by the hand and guided him through the gift shop and then outside. She hurried ahead of him down the steps as he raced behind her.

Lindsay looked up to see Melissa racing down the icy stairs. She gasped as Melissa's feet shot out from under her and she landed hard on the concrete.

"Melissa!" Lindsay and Caitlin both rushed to her side, as Colin raced down the steps. They arrived just in time to see him lurch and fall, landing inches away from Melissa.

"Well, aren't you two a pair?" said Lindsay.

Melissa used both arms to push herself up, but her knee gave out, causing her to fall back down.

Colin was able to get up, but he was limping and wincing as he did so.

"*Et tu*, Colin?" asked Melissa.

"Apparently so. I don't think I've broken anything. Just a sprain. But you should see a doctor."

"You should both see a doctor," said Caitlin.

"But the nearest hospital is back in Inverness!" said Melissa.

"And back you'll go. I'll take Caitlin to Skye, and you can catch up tomorrow once you're mended. We can't have you exploring the Fairy Glen or climbing around the Old Man of Storr with twisted ankles, or whatever it is you have," said Lindsay.

"But—"

"We'll be fine, Melissa. You two drive back and get yourselves fixed up. We'll leave the light on for you," said Caitlin.

Reluctantly, Melissa and Colin hobbled back up the stairs, through the Visitor Center, then to his car.

"Are you going to be able to drive?" asked Melissa.

"Sure. It's an automatic. It'll be fine."

"I forgot to tell them the cruises are open!"

"Luckily you have a magical little device in your purse that will allow you to tell them from here."

"Wish I'd thought of that ten minutes ago," sighed Melissa. She reached into her pocket to pull out her phone only to find the glass completely shattered.

"Oh no!" Melissa wailed.

"Does it still work?" asked Colin. "I had to ship some packages for Da, and there's some clear packing tape in the glove compartment. Try covering it with that. It won't look good, but at least you won't cut your finger."

Melissa found the tape, covered her phone, and texted Caitlin and Lindsay.

Colin started the car, and they turned out of the parking lot.

"I'm sorry, I didn't even introduce myself to Caitlin," said Colin.

"Well, you sure *fell* for her," said Melissa.

Colin shook his head. "Ha ha."

Melissa laughed as he turned the car onto the road back toward Inverness.

Light snow began falling, and Melissa couldn't take her eyes off the Loch.

"So what's the plan for tonight?" asked Colin.

"I mean, shouldn't we stop by a hospital?"

"Correction: what's *their* plan for tonight?" he said.

"Well, I assume now they're going to do the Loch cruise. Then they'll go on to Eilean Donan castle."

"Lovely. We can drive up and meet them in Skye."

"Okay."

* * *

As Caitlin and Lindsay climbed down the stairs of the lookout tower in the castle, Caitlin paused to take a photo. She spotted Melissa's text. "Guess what! The cruises are open!"

"Oh, great! I've never done it," said Lindsay.

"Never? How is that possible?"

"When you live nearby, it just doesn't seem like a priority?"

"Do you mind going?"

"Not at all! My da famously—or infamously—saw something in that Loch once. Maybe Nessie will recognize me as his kin and give me the honor of showing her face?"

"I'd be happy to spot even a ripple! Let's book this cruise!"

* * *

In the hospital, Melissa sat in the waiting room as Colin retrieved the clipboard of forms for her to fill out. "I don't have a primary care doctor here. And what about insurance?"

"Your American insurance probably won't work. You can try, but I'd be surprised if they take it. Let me do a little research."

Colin searched his phone and soon read aloud, "Anyone in the UK can access emergency services, but non-emergency services may not be free for visitors to the UK."

"So they can fix me, but I'll have to pay for it."

"Probably."

"Ms. MacKenzie?" a nurse called out.

"Yes?" replied Melissa.

"Can you please follow me?"

A few X-rays later, Melissa was hobbling back to the waiting room on some new crutches. There, she found Colin sitting with his leg up, wrapped in an elastic bandage.

"Mine was just a sprain," said Colin. "I'll bring the car up to the door in a few minutes."

Melissa checked her phone while she waited. Caitlin had sent her a text with a selfie of Caitlin and Lindsay in front of a giant replica of Nessie. Melissa had just clicked a little heart on the photo when Colin texted.

"I'm out front."

She tucked the phone into her purse. Gingerly, she pulled herself to standing with the crutches and slowly made her way toward the door. It opened automatically. Outside, the sidewalk was covered with salt. She hadn't thought about snow and ice and crutches. She inched her way toward the car. Colin helped her in, tucked her crutches in the back, and closed the door.

"Your place or mine?" joked Melissa.

"Let's go to yours. Do you need any groceries?"

"No, I stocked up because Caitlin was coming. That was before we decided to go to Skye."

"Okay. I'll make you dinner. We can sit by the fire and plan our Hogmanay celebrations."

As THEY PULLED into Melissa's driveway, the snow was coming down heavily. Colin tried to take her arm, but the crutches were in the way. "You all right?" he asked.

"I got this," Melissa responded. She looked up toward her house and saw lights on. "Oh my gosh, I forgot about the dog sitter."

"We can tip her and pay her for the days she didn't work. I'll chip in."

"No, I've got it."

They entered, and Jingles came running and barking to greet

them. The dog sitter, a young college student named Aoife, came to the door, surprised.

"So sorry about this. We've had a slight change of plans," said Melissa.

"Are you all right?" asked Aoife, looking at Melissa's crutches and Colin's wrapped ankle.

"We'll live. We're going to rest up here, and then meet our friends in Skye for New Year's."

Aoife blinked. "You're still going to Skye?"

"Sure. Our friends will drive out tomorrow, and we'll join them later on. It's not that far."

"But the storm!"

"What storm?" asked Melissa.

"They're predicting three feet of snow over the next three days. You might get to Skye, but you will have a heck of a time getting back," Aoife explained.

"Oh no!"

Melissa handed Aoife some cash. "Thanks so much for agreeing to watch Jingles. I'm sorry we couldn't stay gone."

"Let me know if you decide to go, but from what they said on the news, it doesn't sound like a great idea. Well, I'm off to get the messages."

Melissa looked to Colin.

"Groceries," whispered Colin, as Aoife walked toward her car.

"Why do you call getting groceries 'getting the messages'?"

"Something to do with messenger boys delivering food, maybe?" guessed Colin.

"Should we get the messages?" asked Melissa.

Colin looked around the kitchen. The firewood was stacked beside the wood stove; there was a second stack next to the pantry and more outside. The pantry was brimming with canned goods. The liquor cabinet was coming along, as was her wine stash, thanks to her friend's arrival. "Doesn't hurt to go out and get a few last minute essentials, but I think you've got the basics covered. We can buy something to roast at home since we won't be going out."

"I think I'll text Caitlin."

"Good idea. I'll bring in some more wood from outside, and then we can drive into town."

Melissa opened her phone.

"Have you seen the weather forecast? It's supposed to snow like crazy! We're going to stay here. Feel free to come back."

Melissa pushed the send button just as Colin came to the door with a load of firewood.

As Melissa walked to the door to open it for Colin, her phone flashed:

"Message Send Error."

She didn't notice.

CHAPTER 6

Caitlin was thrilled as they stood on the dock waiting to board the boat. "I can't believe I'm about to get on a boat and ride down Loch Ness in search of Nessie!" said Caitlin.

Lindsay laughed. "Yeah, you and several thousand other people every day. And no good sightings since that one where the guy admitted on his deathbed it was a hoax?"

"C'mon, don't you believe just a little?" asked Caitlin.

"Like I told you, my Da definitely thinks he saw something. And he's not associated with any hotels or restaurants around here, so there must be something to it. It's just hard to believe so few people get photographs," said Lindsay.

"I'll open my camera now and be ready!"

Lindsay laughed.

Soon the Captain—a handsome, bearded man with dark hair and blue eyes—greeted them. He took Caitlin's hand and helped her onto the boat. "Good afternoon! Hope you all had a happy Christmas. I'm Captain Drew, and this is my first mate, Angus. He also happens to be my best mate."

"Nice to meet you," said Caitlin, unable to pull her eyes away from Angus. His long, wavy dark brown hair, combined with his beard and mustache, nearly hid his playful warm brown eyes. His strong arms held the boat steady as they boarded. To Caitlin, he looked like a time-traveling Celtic warrior, who probably played flaming bagpipes into battle.

As Angus handed them each life jackets, Caitlin tore her gaze from him to put it on. Despite the cold breeze and light snowfall, Caitlin was thrilled as the boat left the dock and motored out onto the smooth black waters of Loch Ness.

"So where are you from?" asked Drew.

"Inverness," said Lindsay, grinning.

"All the way from Inverness? What a long, epic journey," said Drew with a laugh. "And might you be from Drumnadrochit?" he asked, turning to Caitlin.

"I'm from Boston," said Caitlin.

"No!" said Angus.

"Yes ..."

"I am too!"

Caitlin looked Angus up and down. He was a burly guy, muscular with long, dark hair, a beard, and twinkling brown eyes—and, at least to Caitlin, a heavy Highlands accent. "Really?"

"Well, I'm from here, but I live in Boston now. I'm here for the holidays just now."

"Oh! That's cool. I live in the Back Bay," replied Caitlin.

"Jamaica Plain."

Caitlin nodded. Lindsay noticed a little spark between them and smiled.

Drew narrated the history of the loch. "The first sighting of 'the creature' on record occurred in the sixth century AD, and there have been sightings of something in the water ever since. We've got teams doing studies; but even with the best equipment and modern technology, we run into trouble. For one thing, the loch is 745 feet deep. Imagine a 50 story building. That's as high as the loch is deep. Also, it's very dark and murky down there due to all the peat. Recently, we've had DNA experts analyze what's in the water. Their answer? Eels."

"I heard some other theories are about seals," said Lindsay.

"Yes, as well as whales that swim in through the ocean. And, of course, the plesiosaurus. Hugh Gray was the first to photograph something in the water. You can see his photo in the museum when we're done."

"That's not the famous one deemed a hoax?" asked Caitlin.

"No, that one was done by a lad called Chris Spruling, who admitted to shenanigans on his deathbed. The Gray photograph hasn't been proven a hoax. Many studies, abstracts, scientists, and photographers have examined these photos. You never know," said Drew with a wink.

Caitlin liked him. "Have *you* seen it?"

"Aye. I saw something. Unfortunately, my phone was charging, and by the time I got it open, the creature had dipped back into the loch," replied Drew.

"That's what they all say," Caitlin said with a grin. She followed Drew's gaze to the other side of the loch where dark clouds were gathering.

"I think we're going to have to cut out early," he said. "I'll be happy to get you a refund for the lost time."

"What's wrong?"

"Looks like the storm's arriving early."

"Oh. I hadn't looked at the weather. Sure, we should probably get back anyway. We're headed to Skye for the holiday."

Drew and Angus looked at each other. "You're planning more travel?" asked Drew.

"Aye, we've planned to meet our friends in Skye. They slipped and had to drive back to Inverness, but they'll be joining us soon," said Lindsay.

Angus shook his head. "I think you'd better tell them to stay put. Look at the radar." He passed his phone to Lindsay.

Lindsay took a look at his weather app. A giant blue splotch of snow was centered over the Highlands.

"Wow!"

As they neared the dock, the snow began falling faster. "Waterproofs, anyone?" asked Angus.

"We'll be okay in our winter coats, but thanks," said Caitlin.

Angus tied up the boat, and Drew helped them onto the dock. "Be careful, it's slippery."

"We definitely don't want to end up in the hospital like my brother and Melissa," said Lindsay. "What do you think, Caitlin?"

"I don't know. You're the local. I mean, what kind of snow removal and salt trucks do they have here?" asked Caitin.

"The bigger issue might be the wind on the bridge or other accidents. If you get a truck stuck, the whole road can be backed up for hours. I really wouldn't recommend it," said Drew.

"Skye's lovely, but you can always visit in the summer," said Angus.

The snow was coming down harder now. They walked toward the cars, and Angus helped remove the snow from Lindsay's windows. "Why don't you come get a cuppa with us and warm up. There's a little shop in Drumnadrochit that you'll like. It's just a five minute drive."

"Sounds good! Then we can decide what to do."

CAITLIN ACCIDENTALLY WALKED to the driver's side of the car. Lindsay laughed. "You want to take a turn driving?"

Caitlin smiled. "Thanks, but I'm good. It's hard enough to drive on the opposite side without adding in low visibility and slippery roads!" She slid over to the passenger's side of the car, and Lindsay got in and started the car.

Angus waved for them to follow him, so they did.

* * *

THE LITTLE CAFE WAS COZY, with brick walls, exposed wood overhead, and a fireplace in the corner. Caitlin ordered Lady Gray, a black tea containing orange and lemon peel. She paired it with a lemon scone. Lindsay had Chamomile with shortbread. Angus had a cup of cockaleekie soup, and Drew had a toastie, a type of grilled cheese sandwich. They sat between a cozy fire and a window that framed a view of the beautiful little town gradually getting coated in fluffy white snow.

The owner went outside every few minutes to shovel the walkways.

"I think we'd better see if there's an inn with a room," Lindsay said as she pulled out her phone and started to search.

Before she got very far, Angus spoke up. "I hate to bring bad news, but I looked for housing a few days ago when I arrived. All the hotels and inns were booked. You're welcome to try. Maybe there's been a cancellation. But I don't think you're going to find anything."

Lindsay looked out at the snow. "I guess we'd better head back to Inverness, then."

Caitlin turned to Angus. "It was really nice meeting you."

"We should get in touch back in Boston," said Angus.

"Definitely! Here, let me give you my number."

He handed her his phone, and she entered her number. He immediately texted her so that she would have his as well.

"Maybe we can get together for Burns Night."

Caitlin stared at him blankly.

"It's a holiday for Robert Burns. We eat haggis, read his poems."

"What an amazing idea to have a whole holiday around a poet!"

"Aye."

The snow was falling more heavily now, and the owner of the cafe turned the sign around from OPEN to CLOSED. The group stood and put on their coats.

"Thanks for the boat tour and the conversation," said Caitlin.

Angus replied, "Till we meet again." Caitlin smiled.

CHAPTER 7

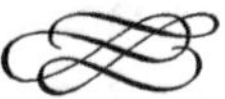

The trees blew in the wind, and snow made visibility near impossible. Lindsay was a brave, steady driver, gripping the steering wheel in the near white-out conditions. She kept the car at a slow and steady pace as they turned back toward Inverness. "Fortunately, it's just 15 miles," said Lindsay. "Can you text Melissa that we'll be home soon?"

"Of course." Caitlin pulled her phone out of her pocket and sent the text.

"The wintry west extends its blast, and hail and rain does blaw; or, the stormy north sends driving forth the blinding sleet and snaw," said Lindsay.

"What's that?"

"Robert Burns. He knew a thing or two about Scottish winters."

Caitlin's phone buzzed. She looked down and read the text. "Melissa says they're fine. They've got plenty of food and drinks, and they'll have the fire stoked for us."

"Lovely," said Lindsay.

Suddenly, Lindsay slammed on the brakes and screamed "Hold on!"

As the car spun precariously close to the loch, Caitlin screamed. Lindsay swerved to the left, then veered back to the right and onto the grass to avoid the cars behind them.

The car behind them stopped inches away from their bumper, and a huge tree lay across the road in front of them.

As they sat in the car, dazed and with hearts racing, they turned back to look at the car behind them. It was Drew.

He got out. He wore a big furry red-and-black plaid trapper hat and a black down coat. In his hand was Lindsay's handbag.

"Are you all right?" he asked.

"I think we were very lucky!" said Lindsay, her heart still pounding with anxiety.

"I was trying to catch up with you. You left your handbag in the cafe." Drew handed it to Lindsay. "I didn't have your number, so I thought I'd try to catch you."

"In this weather! Oh, you definitely shouldn't have."

"Angus had my number," said Caitlin.

"Aye, but he went to the store."

"Well, thank you so much. It was an awful lot of trouble to go to," said Lindsay. She looked at the giant tree. "Think we can move it?"

"Not without a crane. That'll be there until someone can saw it apart, and my saw's not in my truck at the moment." Drew looked at his weather app. "They're saying 3 inches an hour, zero visibility, and possibility of ice."

"How can there be ice and three inches of snow an hour?" asked Caitlin.

Drew shrugged. "Welcome to Scotland."

Lindsay looked close to tears. "Caitlin, I'm so sorry. We're not going to the Isle of Skye. Now we may not be able to get back to Melissa, and you came all this way to spend time with her."

"No worries, Lindsay. This is an adventure! I'm snowed in at

Loch Ness. Ten year old Caitlin is beyond thrilled, and I'm pretty stoked as well!"

"I don't want to sound too forward, but I really wouldn't recommend waiting for someone to remove this tree. Angus and I are staying at a lovely inn at Drumnadrochit. You can't miss it. There's a huge fireplace and epic views of the Loch. And, as Angus mentioned, there aren't any rooms left in the area. With this storm, there might be a cancellation," said Drew.

Caitlin and Lindsay looked at each other. The snow was falling like crazy, and they had no way back to Inverness. It was time for a new adventure!

* * *

MELISSA BUILT A FIRE, and Colin brought in more firewood.

Melissa asked, "Does the power often go out when there's a storm?"

"Aye, sometimes."

"Maybe we should cook the chicken now, so that if we lose power, we have something to eat?"

Colin nodded. "Good idea. And we can pull out the dutch ovens I saw in the pantry. With those, we could cook in the fire."

The fire sparked and soon roared. The tea kettle whistled, and Melissa poured a pot of Earl Gray. She and Colin sat together on the couch and turned on the TV.

"Should we watch a marathon? I don't even know ... What kinds of movies do you like? You do like movies, don't you?"

Colin laughed. "Aye. Of course."

Melissa realized she didn't know a lot of Colin's favorites and was reminded that she hadn't known him long at all. There really was no possibility of this—whatever it was—evolving into a bigger relationship. Was there?

"At home I owned all kinds of DVDs, but now ..." Her voice trailed off as she realized Dave would take all the DVDs. "Actually, it's fine if Dave takes them. That's much less clutter. We can just stream something."

After some searching, they finally settled on *An Affair to Remember*.

"Do you really like classics?" Melissa asked. "Dave's idea of a good movie involves football or explosions."

"American football bores me to tears, and I like how quaint a black and white movie feels."

"Great!"

Melissa pushed play and nestled up against Colin under a cozy blanket. She felt safe and relaxed.

* * *

CAITLIN AND LINDSAY stood before the huge stone inn located on the banks of the loch. With its ancient-looking gray stone facade, turrets, and chimneys, it reminded Caitlin of something out of a movie. But rather than imposing and ominous, the inn appeared cheery, warm, and cozy. Snow clung to the turrets and dusted the festive holly wreaths. A sign above the door read "McAlister Inn - Established 1934." The smell of a peat fire beckoned.

"What do you think, Caitlin?" asked Lindsay.

"It looks fabulous!"

"How do you feel about Angus and Drew?"

"Well, it's a large inn, and there'll be lots of others around. If they wanted to kill us, it would've been a lot easier to just dump us in the loch while we were on the boat," said Caitlin.

Lindsay laughed, and they grabbed their bags and trudged toward the front door.

The interior felt like a giant ski lodge, only cozier. Wood floors, exposed wood and stone, lots of windows and a huge stone fireplace with a roaring fire made the space feel warm and inviting. To the left of the entrance was a lively pub. To the right was a large library and sitting area. A wheeled ladder provided access to floor-to-ceiling shelves filled with anything someone could want during a snowstorm—books, DVDs, and board games.

"This is amazing!" said Caitlin.

They went to the desk.

"Hi. There's a tree blocking the road to Inverness, so we're stuck. Is there any chance you have any rooms left?" Lindsay asked.

The receptionist shook his head. "I'm sorry, we're all full." He saw their faces drop and looked at the heavy snow outside the window, then quickly added, "But it's after 5:00, and check in is usually at 4:00. I have some guests who have yet to arrive. If they're blocked by that same tree, it might be your lucky day."

Caitlin and Lindsay nodded.

Caitlin asked, "How long can you hold the room?"

"Technically, I'm supposed to hold it until the next morning. However, our cancellation policy says that if a guest experiences unforeseen circumstances—such as a snowstorm—they can cancel before 6 pm and get a refund. So why not take a seat in the pub, have a drink, play some darts, and relax. I often find that when I simply enjoy my time, things work out." He winked at them. "I'll hold your bags behind the reception desk."

CAITLIN AND LINDSAY dropped their bags and walked down the hall—still adorned with all the Christmas greenery and lights—to the cozy pub. There was a roaring peat fire, music, and loads of customers.

"Are you up for a wee dram?" asked Lindsay.

"Always. What do you recommend?" said Caitlin.

Lindsay studied the bottles behind the bar. "Well, Talisker is from the Isle of Skye. If we can't be there in person, we can at least try their Scotch. They've got the 10 year, a blend called

Storm—which I like even better than the ten year—and Talisker Skye."

Caitlin thought for a moment. "I'll try the Talisker Skye."

"I'll try the ten year. Maybe my tastes have changed."

They ordered, and the friendly bartender served them two drams and a plate of oat cakes with butter.

"*Slàinte* mhath," said Lindsay, raising her glass.

"Slanty what?"

Lindsay laughed. "Means 'good health, cheers ... drink up me hearties.'"

"Slàinte mhath," said Caitlin. She wasn't too far off in her pronunciation. She and Lindsay clinked glasses.

"And the response is 'do dheagh shlàinte.'"

"Do dheagh shlàinte!"

"You're getting the hang of it!" said Lindsay.

They were only a few sips in when Lindsay's phone rang. "Ms. MacGregor, I'm happy to say that we do have a room for you," said the receptionist.

"Wonderful! We're in the pub at the moment. Is it all right if we check in after we finish?"

"Take your time. If you'd like to pop over and give us a credit card so we can reserve it, that would be lovely."

"Will do."

Lindsay hung up her phone. "We got the room. I'm just going to run up to the desk and pay the deposit."

"Should I do it? I don't have much local currency to pay you back with."

"We'll work it out. You can buy the next round."

As Lindsay went to secure the room, Caitlin looked around the pub. There was an old cherry bar with blue-and-white plaid barstools, antler chandeliers that somehow felt very tasteful and appropriate, a buck on the wall, a picture of Scottish poet Robert Burns, and art featuring sheep, Highland coos, Eilean Donan Castle, Urquhart Castle, and Inverness Castle. The pub was filled with people of all ages cheerfully chatting away. Caitlin took a bite of oat cake and sipped her scotch. The Talisker tasted like the sea. Smoky, briney, with a touch of sweetness—was it honey? She felt like she was imbibing a sense of place. The roaring peat fire complimented the smokiness in the scotch.

"Can I get you anything else, Lass?" asked the bartender.

"When my friend returns, we'll probably order dinner."

"If you'd like a table, I can put you on the waitlist. But as you can see, no one's going out on a night like this. Your perch here at the bar may be your best bet."

"It's on the top floor. Lovely room. You'll enjoy it," said the bellhop. Lindsey followed him down a narrow hall and up two flights of stairs to the room.

When he sat down the bags and opened the room, Lindsay could scarcely believe her eyes. It was a corner room with its own fireplace, a couch, several large chairs, a coffee table, and a wall of windows with a magnificent view of the loch. "This is amazing!"

"It's our suite. You'll find two beds on one side and two on the other. Normally it's for families, but in a storm like this, we sell it at the regular rate."

"Thank you so much!"

Lindsay tipped the bellhop, and he left.

She stood at the window watching the wind blow snow across the road. She loved storms, and this was a beauty. She shivered and decided to grab a sweater from her bag. Then she started back down the stairs. As she neared the ground floor, she could overhear the receptionist saying, "I'm sorry, but our policy is that if a customer doesn't check in by six p.m., we reserve the right to let the room to another customer."

A man replied angrily, "But there's a blasted storm out there, and we were delayed!"

"I'm sorry. We received no phone calls, and there was another party on the waitlist."

Lindsay shrunk back and wished she were invisible.

"So you're telling me you've rented out our room, and it was the last room in the place?"

"Terribly sorry, sir."

Lindsay decided to make a dash for the pub and rejoin Caitlin, but as she stepped off the last stair, the floorboards squeaked. Lindsay grimaced and tried stepping back up into the stairwell, but the customer turned. It was Drew, and beside him was Angus. Her stomach lurched. Had she and Caitlin taken their room?

"Hello!" she said.

"Lindsay? Lovely to see you," said Drew "How did you manage to ..." He trailed off as it dawned on him. Lindsay flushed dark red.

"You take the room," she said quickly. "You were only late because you returned my handbag."

Drew looked down at his shoes. Fair was fair, but he was also a gentleman. The receptionist quickly began arranging some brochures behind the desk.

Angus laughed. "Haud yer wheesht, Drew. Let's have a dram, and I'm sure we'll come up with a solution."

Drew and Angus followed Lindsay into the pub where Caitlin was finishing her first Talisker.

"Angus! Drew! Hello!" said Caitlin.

"It seems that you've bested us. We thought we could be gentlemanly and return your handbag—with all the money still in it, mind—and here you go and beat us to our room," said Angus with a grin.

Caitlin was horrified. "Oh no! We got your room? Well, you can have it back. We'll wait for another."

"There are no other rooms."

"Even with the storm? You'd said there could be cancellations."

"This was the last outstanding reservation. When Drew and Angus didn't show up and then didn't call, they gave their room away," Lindsay explained.

"Well, you should have it back. Maybe they'll let us stay in the pub or in the lobby until the storm's over, and then we can drive back to Inverness. It isn't far."

"We'll see. In the meantime, you can buy us a round of drams to drown our sorrows," said Angus.

They joined Caitlin at the bar, and she handed them menus.

"It's a good night for Cullen Skink," said Drew.

"Their oat cakes are amazing. Homemade. Warm," said Caitlin.

"Considering you took our room, I think we'll be having the steak and lobster dinner," said Drew with a grin.

"Anything for you two," said Lindsay.

"What are we drinking?" asked Angus.

"This was Talisker Storm," Caitlin said as she raised her empty dram glass.

"Nice," said Drew.

Angus opened his menu. "Either way it shakes out, no one's going to be driving for a day or two. I think it might be a good night to introduce this American lass to some of our best single malts."

Caitlin grinned. "What shall we try?"

They looked at the list. There were all kinds of flights. They had a Bruichladdich flight with Classic Laddie, Port Charlotte, Islay Barley, and Octomore. There was a Talisker flight with Talisker Storm, 10 Year, 18 Year, and Dark Storm. There was an Ardbeg flight with a 10 Year, the Wee Beastie, and something called Corryvreckan.

"Why don't we each get a flight, and then we can try them all?" said Caitlin.

"Excellent choice," said Lindsay.

The bartender overheard them and grinned. "What can I get you?"

"I'd like the Talisker flight," replied Lindsay. "My friend Angus would like ..."

"The Ardbeg flight," Angus said quickly.

"Drew?"

"Bruichladdich," answered Drew.

"Caitlin?"

"What about this Arran flight?" Caitlin asked.

"That will be a lovely one. I love Arran," said Lindsay.

"Excellent. And are you ready to order a few starters?" asked the bartender.

"We'll have two Scotch eggs and four bowls of Cullen Skink," said Lindsay.

"Thank you. I'll get that put in right away."

A table opened, and Drew quickly snagged it, then helped everyone move their drinks.

"So how did it happen that you two had this room reserved? I thought you were from around here?" asked Caitlin.

Drew nodded. "I'm from Inverness, and—I think he told you this already—Angus is as well, but he lives in Boston now. We knew we'd be working and that the roads might be bad, so we thought it would be fun to stay here. It's got the best pub in town and a great view of the loch. Plus we'd have a fun Hogmanay celebration."

Lindsay nodded. "So you booked it in advance?"

"Well, in advance is a loaded term. I'm always a last minute guy, so I booked it this morning after I took a look at the forecast."

"So this actually could be someone *else's* cancellation?" asked Caitlin.

"Ha. Nice try. Let's take a look at that menu. I've been craving lobster thermidor," said Angus.

Lindsay laughed and swatted Drew with the menu as she handed it to him.

"Caviar and the best champagne? The oldest single malts? Here's one ... Highland Park 30 year, or maybe Jura 18 year?"

The waiter came over and placed the flights and the Scotch eggs on the table. "Cullen Skink will be up soon. Can I tell you about the Jura or Highland Park?"

Lindsay flushed. "We'll stick with our flights for now."

"They're in order from sweet/honey to smokey/peated. Try them in that order. Here's a dropper—you may want to see how it tastes with a drop of water in it. Also, I do recommend taking a bite of oat cake to cleanse the palate between sips."

"Thank you," replied Lindsay.

"If you're new to Scotch, I recommend starting with this Bruichladdich Classic Laddie first. There's no smoke, and it's quite smooth."

Caitlin nodded and eyed it.

"And if we like it heavily peated, with the salty air of a bonfire at sea with a dead mermaid thrown on the fire?" asked Angus.

"Talisker or perhaps one of the Ardbegs," answered the waiter.

"Talisker Storm," said Lindsay with a nod.

"Why does the mermaid have to be dead?" asked Caitlin.

"You wouldn't want to burn her alive, would you?" asked Angus.

"Maybe she's a sorceress," said Drew.

"She probably is, but that's no reason to burn her alive," said Lindsay.

"This is getting way too serious, folks. Slàinte Mhath!" said Angus, and everyone clinked glasses.

"Do they have mermaids in Scotland, or do they just have selkies?" asked Caitlin.

"*Just* selkies?" asked Angus with a laugh.

"We have everything. Selkies, Kelpies, Waterhorses …" said Lindsay.

"What's the difference?" asked Caitlin.

"Shouldn't we be discussing the flights?"

Caitlin sipped her first dram. She had the Arran flight.

"What do you think?" asked Lindsay.

"It's good. Light," replied Caitlin.

"Which is it?"

"The ten year."

Lindsay smelled it. "Mmm. Vanilla?"

"I think so. It's light and sweet but has a depth to it."

"I love that one," said Angus.

"No dead mermaids there," said Drew with a laugh.

"So what's the difference between a kelpie and a selkie?"

"Kelpies are water horses. Not necessarily Nessie, although there is a film that implies it—aptly named *The Water Horse*. They're from around here. Selkies are from the islands, aren't they?" asked Lindsay.

"They'd have to be," said Drew.

"They're women—usually women." said Angus.

"Sometimes men," said Lindsay.

"Women who shapeshift," said Angus.

"More like women who are actually seals that can morph into women and live on land," said Lindsay.

"And they marry men and … I dunno. But they're different from mermaids and different from Kelpies, for sure," said Angus.

"Thanks. I'll have to get a book on Scottish myths and legends," said Caitlin.

"We've got loads of them. And some don't feel they're just myths," said Angus.

"Well, considering what you two do for a living, I can see why you'd say that."

Drew replied, "Angus actually isn't—"

"How's the Bruichladdich flight?" Angus asked, cutting Drew off.

Drew sipped his first dram. "Caitlin, be sure to try this one early on. It's the Classic Laddie. If you're new to single malts and not sure where you stand on smoke and peat and that sort of thing, this is a classic, clean, clear Scotch."

She took a sip. It was smooth and bright but with a nice depth. "I like it," she said.

"Now this next one is 'heavily peated.' It's the Port Charlotte. Give it a try."

"I don't want to drink all your Scotch!" said Caitlin.

"Never ye mind. Yer the one footin' the bill, lass," said Angus with a wink.

Caitlin reached for the glass like she was Marion Ravenwood and took a hearty sip. Her eyes widened in surprise. "Wow."

"That's right!" said Drew.

She handed the dram glass back. "So that's peat."

He nodded.

"There isn't always a lot of firewood around here, so we burn peat moss. Grows everywhere, burns well, has a glorious smell of the highlands," said Angus.

"All of Scotland, really," said Drew.

"But for me, it's home, distilled into a bottle," said Angus.

Caitlin smiled. "You miss it here," she said.

"Aye," said Angus. "I come back whenever I can."

Lindsay sipped her dram. "Wow!"

"Which is that?" Caitlin asked.

"Ardbeg. Wee Beastie. Try it!"

Caitlin took a whiff before she drank.

"That's cheating! C'mon, now, down the hatch!" said Angus.

She took a sip, and her eyes widened in shock.

"You okay?" asked Lindsay.

"It's like a hot sauce eating contest, but for Scotch!" Caitlin said, taking a sip of water.

"Do you like it?" asked Angus.

"Maybe."

Angus cut up the Scotch eggs and passed them around on plates with oatcakes. "Cleanse your palate," he said gently.

Caitlin took a bite of Scotch egg. It was a hard boiled egg covered with a mildly spicy sausage, rolled in breadcrumbs, and fried. She dipped it in mustard and had some oatcake.

"They sure go well with Scotch," Caitlin remarked.

Lindsay nodded.

"That Wee Beastie sure has a kick!" said Caitlin.

"And the surprising thing is it was only in the barrels for about five years. It's quite young, but when they tried it, it was ready!" said Angus.

"You get excited about Scotch," said Caitlin.

"Aye. My da had a collection of about two hundred single malts given to him by friends over the years. Every Hogmanay, he'd bring some out, and we'd all try them, like this, with flights," said Angus.

"Nice," said Caitlin as she took another sip and noticed Angus's warm brown eyes.

The waiter approached their table. "How are those flights going? Would you like any more drinks, or are you ready to order?"

Lindsay looked around the table. They'd only begun sipping. "I mean, we're here for the night."

"At least you are!" laughed Drew.

"I know the lads are interested in your specials today. They've got lobster thermidor on the brain!" said Lindsay.

"Our specials tonight include a hearty venison with an elderberry sauce and autumn squash. We also have a steamed halibut with asparagus and risotto as well as a seafood cioppino with crusty fresh-baked bread. Then on our menu, we have some small bites—a haggis turnover with whisky sauce, a foraged mushroom tart, and a shrimp and bacon skewer."

"That all sounds amazing," said Lindsay

"We'll take the lot!" said Caitlin, trying out a phrase she'd heard in a movie and feeling silly for repeating it.

"You really don't have to ..." said Drew.

"It's the least we can do. You braved the snow to return my handbag, and I'm grateful to be able to repay you," replied Lindsay.

"We've been a tae o' shits, playing with you over this," said Angus. Caitlin assumed he meant a couple of shits but wasn't certain. She couldn't help but notice how his accent came and went depending on who he was talking to and what about.

"No you haven't. And we insist," said Lindsay.

Angus grinned. The waiter took down the order and was off.

Outside it was dark, and they could only see the snow falling where it hit the street lights.

"I suppose we could sleep in our car," said Drew, working hard to look pitiful.

"Maybe the manager would let us sleep in the coat room," said Angus.

Caitlin's gaze drifted toward a dart board near the bar. The people playing had just finished and handed the darts back to the bartender.

"We could play you for it," said Caitlin.

"For what?" asked Lindsay, concerned.

"Darts. Winner gets the room."

"No deal," Lindsay said immediately.

"We could share the room if we win," said Drew.

Lindsay looked skeptical.

"Well, the venison will take a while. I challenge you to a duel, Ms. … What's your last name, Caitlin?" asked Angus.

"Montgomery," answered Caitlin.

"So you're Scottish."

"By ancestry, anyway."

"Ms. Montgomery, I challenge ye to a battle of skill and marksmanship in the field of … dartery."

"Dartery?" Caitlin laughed.

"It's like archery, but with darts."

"Very well, I accept," she said with a bow.

"And the winner gets … " said Angus, a hopeful look on his face.

"A spot on the floor of our room," said Caitlin playfully.

"The floor? Come now. At least a sofa. Is there a sofa?"

Lindsay knew very well there were, in fact, four beds and a sofa. And a coffee machine. And a microwave. And a fireplace.

"I hereby proclaimeth that whosoever can score a triple 20 thrice may sleep upon the sofa," said Caitlin in her best Cinderella's footman voice.

Angus nodded. "Okay. So what's a triple 20?"

Lindsay studied him. Was he a dart shark? He seemed like one.

"This green part here, numpty," said Drew, pointing to the inner ring under the 20.

Were they playing a version of Good Cop/Bad Cop but with darts? Lindsay took a big sip of her dram and nodded. "Caitlin vs. Angus? Or are we playing doubles?" After all, it had been Caitlin's idea.

"Double or nothing?" asked Drew.

"No!" both women said immediately.

"But we can play doubles. If you don't think Angus can win it on his own," said Caitlin.

"I can throw a dart onto a little circle across the room," said Angus.

"Alrighty then. I'll get some darts." Caitlin walked over to the bartender, left a deposit, and returned with two sets of darts.

"Who's up first?" she asked.

"Lassies first," said Drew.

Caitlin looked at Lindsay.

"Go ahead," said Lindsay.

Caitlin stood in front of the dart board, focused on the red dot in the center, and held up the dart. She aimed and tossed it gently—straight into the inner red ring under the 20. She smiled and turned, waving her hand to a flabbergasted Angus.

He took his dart, aimed, and got an 18.

"Lindsay, you're up," said Caitlin.

Lindsay threw and got a triple 17. "That should count for something!"

Caitlin was keeping score with a piece of chalk. "Definitely. But it's the triple 20 that wins the bet!"

"Thrice," Lindsay reminded her..

Drew rolled up his sleeves and steadied his arm as he locked eyes with the dart board. He threw, and the dart sailed straight into the triple 20.

"Beginner's luck," he said with a shrug.

Caitlin narrowed her eyes at him, then stepped up to take her turn. She took aim and deftly tossed the dart right next to Drew's.

Angus's fist went up in the air. Drew scowled at him, and he lowered it.

A crowd was gathering. Lindsay and Caitlin only needed one more triple 20 to win.

Lindsay took the dart and closed her eyes. She threw it, and it landed in the 19.

"Tough luck," said Drew with a gleam in his eye.

Angus took his dart, planted his feet like he was ready for a caber toss, and twisted up his face in concentration until Caitlin was giggling uncontrollably. He threw the dart. It landed right between the black background and the wire rim of the inner triple 20.

There was a hush from the crowd, but Caitlin was already shaking her head. The bartender walked up and confirmed: "Close, but no cigar," he said.

"Too bad about your tip," said Angus.

"Angus, you've been in the States too long. We don't work for tips over here. I'm salaried, and my boss—"

Drew shot him a look, and the bartender turned and began taking drink orders. Lindsay noticed, but didn't know what to make of it.

"Come here often?" asked Lindsay.

"Aye. It's a pub in the town where I work," said Drew with a shrug. "And Angus grew up here."

"Even in Inverness, most folks know each other … and their business," said Lindsay.

"Our food's going to be here soon. We'd better get this settled," said Caitlin. She held the dart up, concentrated, and tossed it effortlessly, landing it just shy of the triple 20.

Angus raised his fist in the air, and this time Drew didn't correct him.

Drew took his dart and tossed it straight at the triple 20. It hit, then bounced to the ground. The crowd went wild.

Lindsay grinned and took the dart. She took aim and closed her eyes, then gently tossed the dart. It hit the triple 20, and the crowd cheered.

A waiter arrived with their food, and they settled down to eat.

"I guess dinner's on us, then?" said Lindsay.

"We'd better get some warm food in us before we're kicked out to the streets," said Angus.

The food was delicious. Haggis, neeps and tatties with whisky sauce, roast chicken, Wee Beastie soaked steak with potatoes, and a cozy seafood stew. They all shared bites and sipped their drams. Caitlin looked around the pub—what a cozy, comfortable place.

She couldn't help but say, "I wish they had more places like this back home."

"They're there, if you know where to look," said Angus.

"Boston has some great Irish pubs," agreed Caitlin.

"Aye. But there are some Scottish pubs as well. Good *craic* and fun banter."

"Oh?"

"I'll take ye to one sometime ... if you're interested," said Angus.

Caitlin smiled. "Of course I am."

"Excuse me," said Drew as he folded his napkin and stood. "Be right back."

Lindsay's eyes followed him as he walked toward the lobby.

"Can I get anyone more to drink?" asked the waiter, blocking Lindsay's view.

"I'm still working on the flight," said Caitlin.

"Angus?"

Angus shook his head. "I'm good."

"And you, lass?"

"No, thank you," said Lindsay.

Drew returned. "Good news. I talked with the Innkeeper. They've got some room in the servant's quarters, so we can stay there tonight."

"Really?" said Lindsay.

"Aye, they say they keep rooms for occasions like this. There might be some sacks of oats and cases of whisky, but it'll do."

"Are you going to sleep on the floor?" asked Caitlin.

"No, they said they've got cots or air mattresses or something. It sounds just fine," said Drew.

As the waiter began to take their plates, Lindsay asked for the check.

"Thank you, Lindsay," said Angus.

"Well, I'm sorry about the room."

"You won it, fair and square."

Lindsay nodded. "Well, it was great meeting you two."

"We'd better get to bed so we can get an early start if we want to get to Skye tomorrow. We've got a lovely Airbnb in Portree, right on the water. We're going to tour the Talisker distillery, see the Old Man of Storr, and maybe see what the Fairy Glen looks like in the snow," Caitlin said, brimming with excitement.

Drew shook his head. "I don't know how to tell you this, Caitlin."

Drew pulled up his weather app and handed her his phone. "Winter storm warning until 2 pm … Monday."

Lindsay's jaw dropped. "Monday?! You're kidding."

Drew shook his head. "I got a text."

Lindsay opened her phone. "I got one too. Didn't hear it."

"Isn't today Friday?" asked Caitlin.

"All day," said Angus.

"I'm sorry to say, but I don't think you'd be able to get to the Isle of Skye without a proper snow plow or a helicopter," said Drew.

"So we're stuck here with you lads tonight, tomorrow, and Sunday?" said Caitlin with a grin.

"Well. There are other people staying here, so you could beat them in darts too. But we'll be in the pub watching you play," said Angus.

"So I guess we'll see you two for a full Scottish breakfast down here tomorrow morning?" asked Lindsay.

"Are you still footing the bill?" asked Drew playfully.

"We'll see how you slept in the supply room," said Lindsay.

CHAPTER 8

Back at Greenhill House, Melissa and Colin sat by the fire drinking hot toddies and watching the snow drift outside the window.

"I'm lucky the previous owner had such an array of board games," said Melissa.

"Scottish winters are good weather for that," said Colin. He put his arm around Melissa. "But maybe they can wait until tomorrow?" he whispered and began to kiss her neck.

"Absolutely!" said Melissa, as she snuggled against his warm sweater.

* * *

THE NEXT MORNING, Caitlin rolled over as she heard a clunk at the door. She opened her eyes—four-poster bed, antique furniture, snow pelting against the windows. She stretched and turned to see Lindsay in a red-and-black flannel robe and slippers, sitting by a fire drinking her morning tea.

"Morning," Caitlin croaked.

"Good morning!" said Lindsay. "They left us a pot of tea and some scones."

"Wow!"

"Yeah! And there's jam and clotted cream."

"Nice."

"There's also a note—full Scottish breakfast is included with the room. However, it won't be ready until nine because the cook is still shoveling his car out."

"That's too bad. But we're fine with scones and tea."

"Look at it out there!" Lindsay gestured toward the window.

They stood at the window. Cars were buried in snow. The road was nowhere to be seen amid the drifts of snow. And the only way they could make out the loch was that it was a flat space with no trees.

"Brutal!"

"I hope the guys were okay."

"I'm sure they were. Somehow I think they were exaggerating about the sacks of oats and casks of whisky to make us feel bad."

"You think?" said Lindsay with a laugh. "They're definitely a couple of characters."

Caitlin hopped out of bed, grabbed a cup of tea and a scone, and crawled right back under the covers. "What a nice robe. So smart of you to bring it," she said to Lindsay.

"I didn't bring it. There's one here for you as well. It's in the closet."

"Wow!"

"Yeah."

Caitlin sipped her tea. "I think I'm a little too cozy to venture out of bed just yet, but maybe later in the day," she said with a stretch.

"I understand. You must still be jet-lagged too!"

"Maybe. I think the cold weather and snow just make me want to hibernate."

Caitlin opened her phone. "I wonder how Melissa and Colin are holding up."

She texted Melissa,

"Hey! How's it going? We're snowed in!"

Melissa replied,

"We are too. Going sledding this afternoon!"

Caitlin read the text aloud and chuckled. "Nothing stops her."

"She's a powerhouse," Lindsay agreed.

"Join us?"

"Melissa wants to know if we'll join her," said Caitlin.

Lindsay looked skeptical. "We can try. But look out at the parking lot. It hasn't been plowed, and the roads in front haven't been plowed either."

"Is that unusual?"

"Yeah. Usually they're able to keep up with it. I think this storm caught everyone by surprise, and so many people are already away for the holidays … Tell her we'll try."

Caitlin typed on her phone, then set it down. "I'll have to see if I can even get out of bed," she said.

"Same. Those flights …"

"We probably should've started with flights of beer or cider." Caitlin gingerly hoisted herself out of bed and stood at the window, taking in the view. "Oh, look! There's a balcony."

"How nice. I bet that's lovely in the summer. Caitlin, you'll really have to come back in better weather."

"This is fun! I'm actually loving it. And, I'm getting to know you."

"And getting to know Angus," said Lindsay.

"Aye," said Caitlin, trying out the expression. "I mean, yeah. And you're getting to know Drew."

"They're nice lads."

"Nice lads! They're rugged lumberjacks with gorgeous accents. They're warm and cozy, and I just want to—"

Just then, there was a knock at the door. Lindsay threw Caitlin the other red-and-black flannel robe, then called out, "Just a second!"

Lindsay opened the door, and there stood Angus and Drew, looking surprisingly bright-eyed and bushy-tailed.

"Speak of the devil," muttered Caitlin.

"Morning, lassies. I see you've got some tea and scones. Breakfast will be ready at nine if you want to meet us down in the dining room," said Angus.

"The cooks were able to get here? But how? The roads are still drifting, and the parking lot hasn't been touched," asked Lindsay.

"They were able to scrounge up a couple of under-qualified lads who have to sing for their supper," said Drew.

"Well, I'm qualified. I run a restaurant in Boston," said Angus.

"Anyone can make oats," said Drew.

"But only a real chef can cook square sausage, tattie scones, and the like," countered Angus.

Caitlin found herself studying his long, dark hair and beard and imagined kissing him. She tried to keep her face as blank and neutral as she could.

"Anyway, we need to pop back downstairs and get cooking but wanted to be sure you had a personal invite," said Angus, looking directly at Caitlin. She blushed as she realized how disheveled she must look first thing in the morning. As if he could read her mind, he winked at her. "Later?" he asked.

"See you," said Caitlin.

* * *

OUTSIDE, the snow continued to drift and blow. Inside, a fire in the stone fireplace created a cozy atmosphere for the customers as they trickled into the dining room for self-serve tea and coffee. Caitlin and Lindsay each filled a cup, then they found a table near the fireplace. Soon Drew, Angus, and the bartender began bringing out food for a buffet.

"THANK YOU FOR YOUR PATIENCE, FOLKS," said the bartender from last night. "We normally serve a full Scottish breakfast and special orders, but we're short-staffed today because of the storm. Our friends Drew and Angus have stepped up to help, and we have what we hope you'll find to be an adequate buffet for breaky."

As the crowd stood and began to queue up, Lindsay and Caitlin followed. The assortment of foods was impressive—tattie scones, regular scones, oatmeal, oranges, raspberries, scrambled eggs, toast, muffins, black pudding, square sausage, and bacon.

A customer asked for HP sauce, and Drew deftly grabbed a bottle from under the bar. Someone else asked for jam, and he went into the kitchen and returned with several varieties.

"Do you need any help?" asked Lindsay.

Angus opened his mouth, but Drew elbowed him.

"We're just helping out in exchange for our room and board," said Drew.

Lindsay noticed a little grin on the bartender's face as Drew said that. Drew shot him a look, and the grin quickly disappeared.

As Lindsay and Caitlin carried their heaping plates to their table, Lindsay whispered, "I think there's something funny going on."

"What do you mean?"

"I mean, everyone in a small town knows everyone.That's a given. But Drew seems especially familiar with this place."

"Hmm."

They ate their breakfast and looked out at the snow. "Any word from Colin and Melissa?" asked Lindsay.

"They're going to stay put. Melissa's baking."

As they finished, Angus came over to sit with them. "What are your plans for today?"

Caitlin looked outside at the blowing snow. "I dunno. Maybe read by the fire? Cards?"

Angus shook his head. "You came all the way to Scotland to see the Highlands."

"I can see them. Kind of," said Caitlin with a grin.

"We'll give you a proper tour. Ever been on a snowmobile?"

"Years ago, in Wisconsin."

Angus nodded. "Lindsay?"

Lindsey shook her head. "Never."

"We'll have to remedy that," said Angus in his best Braveheart accent. "Meet us downstairs at eleven, and dress in warm layers."

"Okay then," said Caitlin.

"Here are some snow pants from the lost and found."

"What?" asked Caitlin.

"They've got all kinds of things in that storage room where we stay."

"Angus, I'm not sure you're—" said Caitlin.

"See you in a few!" said Angus with a wave.

CHAPTER 9

Lindsay and Caitlin arrived in the lobby dressed in multiple layers and warm hats. Drew, dressed in a warm black coat with a furry hood, handed them each a helmet.

Caitlin smashed her hat down and tried on the helmet.

"Looking good!" said Angus.

At that moment, the lights flickered. Lindsay and Drew looked up at the lights. They turned off, then snapped back on.

"That was close," said Drew.

"Yeah. Imagine being snowed in *and* not having any power," said Caitlin.

"Best not to imagine it at all. We don't want to create a Stay-Puft marshmallow situation," said Angus.

Caitlin laughed. "Can't have that."

Angus winked and said, "I knew you were a woman of excellent taste."

Lindsay, puzzled, looked from Angus to Caitlin.

"Ghostbusters," explained Caitlin.

"Ah. Before my time."

"Required viewing," said Angus. "I think we may have our evening plans set now!"

Then the lights flickered again, and went out. The crowd in the pub was silent, then everyone began talking at once.

"I wonder if they have a backup generator?" said Lindsay.

"Aye. I'll go see," said Drew.

He slipped into a room behind the concierge's desk.

"He seems awfully helpful and concerned for a mere guest trying to sing for his supper," said Lindsay.

"Aye. Uh, I'm gonna go see if he needs help," Angus said as he followed Drew.

Caitlin and Lindsay pulled off their helmets and unzipped their coats as they watched the staff scurry around. After a few minutes, the lights snapped back on. Soon Drew and Angus slipped out the staff room door and back into the lobby.

"What's up?" asked Caitlin.

"We now have a mission. We need to fill the petrol canisters to keep the generator running," replied Drew.

"Yikes. How much does it take to keep a whole inn up and running?"

"That's the trick. We're going to hand out torches and the like—can't have candles in an old inn—and we'll only use the generators for the kitchens to keep the food from spoiling and so we can cook."

"We?" asked Lindsay, looking at Drew with a smile. "Shouldn't the owners or the manager be involved in this?"

"Aye," said Drew. "They are. But since we're already outfitted for a snowmobile ride, I said we'd go out to fetch the petrol."

Lindsay nodded knowingly. "That's very kind of you," she said sarcastically.

Caitlin wasn't getting it, but Drew and Angus could see that Lindsay was realizing the truth: Drew wasn't just a helpless customer sleeping in the work room.

"Okay, you got me. But will you still come with us? It'll be something to do, and we will show you the sights ... that is, if there are any to be seen."

"Of course," said Caitlin.

As they began to bundle up, the concierge came up to Drew. "Mr. McAlister, they say roads are still blocked by fallen trees, so it may be several days until they can restore power."

"I'll take care of it," said Drew.

"Mr. McAlister?" said Caitlin, finally understanding. She was embarrassed it had taken her so long to realize that Drew owned the inn.

Drew smiled apologetically. "All right. I may not have been up front about the room."

Caitlin narrowed her eyes. "But it *was* your room?"

"Aye. I had booked it for Angus and me. But you lasses are welcome to it."

"So the storage room or servants' quarters ..."

"I do have a private suite on the top floor: fireplace, four-poster bed, lovely views of the loch ... in good weather. And a nice couch for Angus."

"We'd better get the petrol canisters and hitch up the trailer," said Angus.

"Meet us out front in about fifteen minutes—if you're still interested," said Drew.

"We are," replied Lindsay.

* * *

"YOU'LL NEED to put your arms around me," said Angus as Caitlin hopped on the back of the snowmobile. "Hope that's okay."

"That's fine," said Caitlin. She put her arms around him and noticed how secure she felt.

Lindsay slipped onto the back of Drew's snowmobile and

fastened her helmet tight. "How fast are these things going to go?" she asked.

"They're pretty fast. And you'd better put the visor down, or snow will fly in your face," answered Drew.

Drew revved the engine, and they were off. Lindsay had never been on a snowmobile before. It was fast and loud, but she felt like she was gliding over the snow. They plowed through giant drifts like waves on the ocean and raced across the countryside, past snowy pine trees, snow-covered houses, smoky chimneys, and sledding children.

Caitlin held on to Angus, leaning left and right with him as they swerved around pine trees. The snow showered down on them, and the white powder drifted into peaks like meringue pie. She could feel his strong arms and the warmth of his core as he maneuvered the machine through the snow.

Caitlin was relieved to see lights inside the building and someone behind the counter when they finally reached the petrol station on the outskirts of town.

"Thank goodness," she said.

"They're always open, even in the worst conditions," said Angus.

Lindsay and Drew arrived behind them, and they all took off their helmets. While Angus and Drew bought the gas, Lindsay and Caitlin went inside to warm up.

"Should we get snacks in case the cooks never make it?" asked Caitlin.

They browsed the aisles. It was mostly snack food, a few instant cake mixes, and cans of soup. As they looked around, underwhelmed, Angus came in and snatched up several packages of batteries, some loaves of bread, and some milk. "Slim pickings," he said, "If you see anything you like, best to get it now. There's more snow scheduled for tonight, and they've extended the storm warning until tomorrow."

Lindsay couldn't hide her frustration, and Drew put his arm

around her. "We could try taking you back to Inverness on the snowmobiles."

"The town Facebook page says there are loads of trees still down," Lindsay said.

"That's why we would take the snowmobiles."

"In white-out conditions and with the cold? I'm happy to stay at the inn. I just feel terrible for Caitlin."

"I was the one who made the last-minute decision to come rescue my impulsive friend who came to Scotland without a plan," said Caitlin with a wry chuckle.

"This is true," said Lindsay, smiling. "I can see why you're friends."

"Yep. She's safe at home with stacks of firewood and electricity, and here I am in the middle of a town I can't pronounce with some … admittedly ruggedly handsome Scots."

Just then, Angus snuck up behind them. "Did I overhear someone calling me 'ruggedly handsome'?" He slipped an arm around Caitlin's waist.

"Uh, we were talking about a wild haggis we saw out back," said Caitlin quickly.

"Wild haggis," said Angus, grinning. "An accurate nickname. I accept."

Drew opened the door. "Time to go. Can't have you getting too used to this lovely heating and electricity. At least not until we get the generators up and running."

"Do you have enough?" asked Lindsay. "It must take a huge amount of fuel to heat the whole inn."

"We have enough for today, and Sean will bring the rest tomorrow. We've got plenty of wood for the fireplaces, as well," said Drew.

Donning their helmets, they braved the cold and wind.

* * *

Melissa sat at her kitchen table, staring at her laptop. Multiple tabs about immigration and visas filled the screen. She sipped her coffee and looked over her reading glasses at Colin, who was working on some briefs.

"I think if I fill out this form and tell them that I'm an interior designer and own property …"

"Best if you can set up an actual business in town," replied Colin.

"Can't I have a home office?"

"That's true. Yeah, you don't want to get into more real estate before you're even legal."

"You do think I'll be able to stay, don't you?" Melissa hadn't really considered the possibility she couldn't remain in Scotland. "I mean, people move to different countries all the time."

"They do. But there are a lot more that try and can't. It's complicated. People are starting to have some strong feelings about immigration around here. Americans are less popular than they once were," Colin said, staring at his computer screen and sipping tea. He didn't notice the effect his words were having on Melissa.

She got up and went to the window. "Caitlin was right. What was I thinking? I never should've come here. I never should've tried to fix up this house and live here, and … Colin, you should be home taking care of your father. What about all the sheep? And the dogs? How can he get out to feed them?"

Colin saw that Melissa was on the verge of tears and hopped up to put his arm around her. "That stubborn old crabbit could take care of that croft in a raging ice storm."

"No, he can't. He fell and hurt his hip."

"And with my leg, how much help could I really be?" said Colin, brushing her brown hair out of her tear-stained blue eyes.

"What about the animals?" asked Melissa.

"Melissa, I was kidding. He has help. Jaime Ferguson comes

out every morning. Don't worry. It's all going to be okay," said Colin, kissing the top of her head.

"Caitlin's trapped in—"

"She's not trapped. She said they were having fun and playing darts with the lads they met on the Nessie tour."

"It's all my fault. Everything's all my fault," she said, collapsing into a chair at the kitchen table.

"Melissa, you're talking mince."

Melissa raised an eyebrow. "What?"

"Nonsense. If anyone's at fault, it's your ex-husband."

"Talking mince," Melissa repeated. "Teach me more."

"More what? Scottish insults?"

"Yeah!"

Colin thought about it. "My favorite might be 'awa' n' bile yer heid.' I can't think of anything else right now."

Melissa opened a new tab and did an internet search. Soon she was giggling.

"He's a scabby, howlin' numpty!" she said.

"Aye."

"He's a boggin' bampot!" she giggled.

Colin read over her shoulder. "A doaty dobber."

"A hackit howlin' feartie," she said.

"That he is."

Colin kissed the top of her head again. "It's going to be all right. Let's fill out these forms and send them in before the end of the year. You'll start the new year with a clean slate. And maybe a little Hogmanay luck."

They set to work.

CHAPTER 10

When Caitlin and Lindsay returned to the inn, the lights were still out. Many lodgers were playing games: chess, checkers, cards, and darts. Some sat at the bar bantering with the bartender. But there was anxiety in the air. People kept looking out at the wind and the drifting snow and searching for bars on their dying phones.

"This isn't going to last long," whispered Drew. "People are going to get bored."

Angus slipped into the storage room—which Lindsay had long suspected was Drew's private apartment—and emerged with two guitars.

He began tuning one and gestured for Drew to pick up the other.

Standing on the stone platform of the fireplace, Angus began strumming his guitar. The crowd quieted. And then he belted out Bob Dylan's "Shelter From the Storm." Caitlin's jaw dropped. He didn't do a classic Dylan voice. It was his own, strong and warm. Drew sang backup vocals and accompanied him on guitar. The crowd gave their rapt attention.

"What a voice!" said Caitlin.

"Absolutely," said Lindsay.

The crowd applauded enthusiastically, and Angus grinned. Then he launched into The Proclaimers' "Oh Jean." The crowd sang along with the chorus. It was magical.

They continued with other sing-along songs like "No, Nay, Never" and "Loch Lomond"; but sprinkled in songs by The Pogues, Flogging Molly, and a quiet rendition of "Blackbird" by the Beatles.

Just as he hit the final note of the song, the lights snapped back on. The crowd erupted into cheers.

"Hot beverages for everyone and maybe even some mics and amps for the guitars!" Angus yelled to the crowd.

"You're great acoustic!" shouted Caitlin.

Angus launched into "Sweet Caroline," a song that made Caitlin think of Boston and Red Socks games—they always played it after the 7th inning. She loudly added the "BAM BAM BAM!" in the chorus, and he winked at her.

"We're gonna take a break so we can get you folks some dinner. But we'll be back tonight!"

As they sat down next to Lindsay and Caitlin, Lindsay said, "I don't know about Caitlin, but I definitely know my way around the kitchen. You two can't be cooking breakfast, fetching gas, entertaining the masses, making lunch and dinner, and then playing another set—and I really want to hear another set. So I'm going to get dinner up and running. I make a mean Cullen Skink. What ingredients do you have back there?"

"Everything in the fridge needs to be cooked tonight. I'll loan you an apron and a chef's hat, and we can get cooking … literally," said Drew.

"Need an assistant? I can slice and dice," offered Caitlin.

"You can be our sous chef," said Drew.

THE KITCHEN WAS HUGE, white, and fully stocked.

"How long were we out of power?" asked Lindsay.

Drew replied, "The fridge is on the backup generator, but the freezer isn't. Let's get all the meat out and see what we can do."

While Lindsay and Drew cleaned out the walk-in freezer, Caitlin and Angus sorted through the large refrigerator. Caitlin began chopping onions, celery, and leeks. Angus peeled potatoes. It would've felt like drudgery except Angus and Drew kept making playful banter and telling jokes, so the time passed quickly. Soon everything was ready to go in the pot. Just then, the door opened and in came a couple dressed from head to toe in heavy snow pants, coats, and accessories.

"Myrtle! You made it!" said Drew, greeting her with a hug.

"Aye! We never would've gotten here in that old minivan. We heard you took out the snowmobiles, so we went over to the neighbors and borrowed theirs. Patrick and I will take over from here."

"Don't you want to warm up first?"

"Nonsense!"

Myrtle had already rolled up her sleeves, and her elderly husband, Patrick, was getting out pots and pans and butter.

"Never ye mind, we've got this. Go on and run the show, boss."

Drew flushed and Lindsay laughed. "There's no denying it now!" she said.

"Okay, you got me. I'm head chef."

"Not from what I saw back there. True, you are capable of a basic breakfast, but I think you missed out on culinary school," said Lindsay.

"What makes you say that?" asked Drew.

"Because *I* went to culinary school," Lindsay said quietly.

Drew had no response.

Then Caitlin realized, "So you actually *wanted* to be cooking back here today?"

"Well, I thought it would be fun."

"Why didn't you. ... why aren't you ... " Caitlin was torn between her manners and her curiosity.

Lindsay bit her lip. She wasn't one to bare her soul. Only a few people knew that opening a restaurant had been her dream. She hated the thought of anyone thinking that her life hadn't gone the way she'd planned. So in her most businesslike, pish-posh voice, she repeated, "I thought it would be fun."

"It *is* fun. Never had as much fun in my life as when I opened a Scottish pub in Boston. You find a cozy space, you fill it with memories of home—paintings of Highland coos, Robert Burns, tartan cushions, and loads of amazing Scottish music. You create the menu, with your own take on your grandma's classics. And then the people find you, and it's home for them too. It's kind of like creating your own country. Your own Neverland. Your own kingdom," said Angus.

Caitlin took in the fierce pride and love he showed for his bar and vowed to go there as soon as she got home.

"By all means, Lindsay, please work back here today if you'd like," said Drew.

"I really would," said Lindsay. "I mean, you're obviously going to be short-staffed, even with these lovely people who made it in."

"It's settled. You'll work back here. Perhaps the innkeeper will forgive your tab in exchange?"

"Oh? Think you can arrange that, can you?" replied Lindsay with a smirk.

"And I'll ask him to match the wages he pays Myrtle and Patrick."

Lindsay nodded, and Drew winked at her.

"Angus. Start planning out your next set. You go on at 5, then again at 9. We're having a *ceilidh* tonight that folks will talk about for years."

Caitlin looked at Drew expectantly.

"And Caitlin. What do you do back home?" Drew asked.

"Marketing. Market research. That kind of thing."

"Okay, then. Learn about the customers. Learn who Angus's audience is. Age ranges. Favorite types of music. What songs they'll sing along to and which *ceilidh* dances they know."

Caitlin nodded. "Got it."

"Ready group? Break!"

As everyone scattered, Angus called after Drew. "What are you gonna do?"

"I'm going to help with the snow removal crew, so we don't lose power again. Then the townspeople can get to their jobs, so they can have a proper Hogmanay celebration when the time comes!"

THE AFTERNOON WAS FUN. Caitlin chatted up the customers in the lobby and dining room. Angus kept the coffee, tea, and biscuit stations full while he contemplated his setlist. And Drew recruited a group of burly customers to join him in the snow and tree removal quest.

Lindsay was in her element: planning menus for dinner before the *ceilidh*; making soups; and roasting chicken, venison, and vegetables.

CHAPTER 11

The sun burned a brilliant orange low on the western side of the loch by the time Drew and his team returned, tired and hungry but chuffed with their progress. Angus and the bartender set out snacks: oatcakes, cheese, and a selection of charcuterie Lindsay had organized, along with crisps, barbecue wings, and buckets of beer. Caitlin had made friends with everyone in the room and had a long list of possibilities for Angus's setlist.

"Ready for a break? I think it's five o'clock somewhere," said Angus.

Caitlin poured herself a cup of tea and reached for a biscuit. Angus took two biscuits and a large cup of coffee.

"Coffee? Really?" Caitlin asked.

"Drumnadrochit runs on Dunkin'," he said with a grin.

"Drum-na-dunkin?"

"Sure. We'll open a franchise," said Angus.

"Not here!" said Caitlin with such force that even she was blown away.

"No?"

"No! That's fine for Boston, but this place runs on charm and cozy little inns and peat moss fires and rugged lumberjacks who play guitar," said Caitlin.

"You fancy rugged lumberjacks who play guitar?" Angus asked playfully.

"Sometimes," answered Caitlin.

"Just sometimes?"

"Only during a snowstorm," said Caitlin.

"Oh?"

"When they're charming and named Angus."

"Oh!"

Angus pulled her closer and brushed his lips against hers. "That okay?"

"More than okay," said Caitlin, pressing her lips into his.

Drew walked past and muttered, "Get a room."

They laughed and separated. Angus noted the antique clock on the wall. "It's nearly time for my set. Rain check?"

"We'll see," said Caitlin with a grin. But she knew as soon as he started strumming his guitar and singing in that silky, gravelly voice she'd be a goner.

CAITLIN SAT at a table halfway between the stage and the bar. There, she could help replenish snacks and deliver drinks but still get a good view of Angus as he played. His fingers danced across the frets as his gentle voice crooned and the crowd sang along.

"And now we have something fun for happy hour. We're doing acoustic karaoke. First up, Caitlin!" The crowd cheered—they were all some of her closest friends after this afternoon—and Caitlin flushed red.

"Have you got a song?" he asked.

"You know, we have a real karaoke machine behind the bar, complete with songs and a mic," said the bartender.

"Bring it," said Caitlin.

She flipped through the songs and settled on one to answer Angus's version of "Better Man." Soon Salt-N-Pepa's "Whatta Man" began playing. Caitlin was surprisingly good, and several of her new friends sang backup.

"Who's next?" asked Caitlin.The crowd was quiet, so she flipped through the songs. "Shall I do another?"

"Freebird!" someone yelled.

Caitlin pressed go, and "In the Cold, Cold Night" by the White Stripes began playing. It was a quiet, contemplative song. As she sang, the bartender lowered the lights, leaving Caitlin in front of the Christmas lights, against the backdrop of the fireplace as the snow blew and drifted outside the windows. Angus soon joined her, singing backup, and adding his own guitar. As Caitlin sang and looked into his dark brown eyes—so wise and warm— she felt transported to another time. He seemed so familiar for someone she'd just met. She took a deep breath and tried to ground herself, to clear her head, but it wasn't working. She was so drawn to him, and she just wanted to press up against him and—

"Thank you! We'll be back after dinner! See you soon!" Angus called out to the crowd.

Nearly breathless, Caitlin was reassured by his showmanship and poise. Maybe it was part of the act, right? Show the Yank a good time, sing songs, and pretend to be in love?

She sat at her table and looked at her phone. She had three text messages from Melissa.

"Still planning on a Hogmanay party here at Greenhill. Are you okay?"

"Lindsay says you've got an amazing room at a beautiful old inn. PICTURES PLEASE!"

Followed by a photo of her singing with Angus.

"Caitlin!! Who is this??"

Angus set his guitar in the seat next to Caitlin. His long, dark hair fell in front of his face as he grinned at her and applauded. "I didn't know you were a singer."

"I didn't know you were either," replied Caitlin..

"I have a lot of guest musicians play at my pub back in Boston. You should come."

"I should," she nodded.

He held out his hand. "I'd ask you to coffee, but we're already here. What about a moonlit walk through the forest on snowshoes?"

Caitlin had never walked on snowshoes before, but there was no way she was going to turn down an opportunity to be alone with this luscious hunk of pheromones in the moonlight. "Sounds like a plan."

"Meet you in the lobby in fifteen minutes?"

Caitlin nodded.

* * *

TRYING to navigate through the drifting snow on the giant snow shoes, Caitlin felt like she was walking like a duck. Angus barreled through the snow confidently. She watched and did her best to follow him.

He noticed her struggling and turned back. "Try this. Literally kick your foot into the snow," he said.

She kicked her foot and planted it, then kicked the other. It worked well enough.

"Good! Now just try to follow in my footsteps. It's easier if someone has already blazed a trail."

Walking through the glistening, snow-covered forest, Caitlin couldn't believe that just a few days ago she was sitting in her apartment in Boston, thinking her friend was insane for moving to Scotland. It was a beautiful country, and she'd only seen a tiny bit of it so far. Excitement filled her as she imagined hiking on the Isle of Skye, visiting Edinburgh castle, or seeing a puffin. She couldn't wait to come back in better weather, but her winter trip was already beyond belief.

"Then you also want to use your poles, like this," he demonstrated keeping his balance with the poles. "After that, it's just one foot in front of the other."

Soon they were both traversing the deep snow with ease as their breath formed white clouds in the frigid air. The towering trees coated in fresh snow formed a sort of tunnel over them. Caitlin imagined they were living hundreds of years ago. The shimmer of moonlight on the snow added to the magical feeling of the night. Reaching a clearing in the woods, Angus took her hand and pulled her close. As his lips brushed against hers, she felt her pulse quicken. The world around her faded away as she let herself melt into the warmth of his body.

As the snow began falling harder, Angus pulled away. "You must be freezing. We should get you inside."

"I'm good."

He grinned. "Me too. But I can't have you getting frostbite. We've got another set to play."

She swatted him playfully, and as he attempted to run away, she tackled him. Soon they were both flat on their backs, watching the snow falling down on them as they looked up to the stars. Angus inched over to her and kissed her. As she kissed him back, she suddenly felt a cascade of snow fall onto the back of her neck. Looking up, she saw two squirrels chasing each other through the trees. Angus laughed and held his arm out to help her up.

"Let's plan on a rain check. Or snow check," he said.

Navigating the snow more easily now, Caitlin felt an electricity between them as they walked hand in hand through the snowy forest toward the inn. She would be happy to be snowed in with this man forever.

CHAPTER 12

Back at the brightly lit Inn, the scent of freshly baked oatcakes and Balmoral chicken mixed with the smokey fire and a tinge of pine still in the air from Christmas. In the kitchen, Lindsay was in her element, plating beautiful dishes as fast as the wait staff could carry them. Caitlin and Angus blew through the front door, shaking snow from their coats and snow pants. Drew greeted them with a floor mat and a towel.

He eyed the pair. "How was the snowshoe experience?"

"Gorgeous," said Caitlin, her cheeks red and her blue eyes bright.

"Breathtaking," said Angus, looking at Caitlin, who flushed a deeper red.

"Let's get those clothes into a dryer now that we've got the electricity up and running. Would you two like a table for dinner, or should we just send something up to your room?"

Angus and Caitlin looked at each other. They were both exhausted and needed rest before they played another set.

"Come on up," said Caitlin. "We can warm up by the fireplace and maybe practice the next set."

"Practice? Blasphemy!" laughed Angus.

"There's a crowd gathering, and I'm afraid we may have over-hyped the fact that there's a band playing tonight," said Drew.

"A *band*?! We're not a band. We're just a couple of—" Caitlin winced as she realized she'd used the words "we" and "couple" together. There was no walking it back, so she stumbled onward.

"People who'd better at least create a setlist based on the few chords we know," said Angus.

"I'll send up some room service," said Drew with a laugh. "And Caitlin, you can use my guitar if you'd like.." He handed it to her, and she nodded in thanks.

Angus followed Caitlin to the room, carrying both guitars along with his boots and hat. "I think you're gonna need a bell-hop," said Caitlin.

"Unfortunately, I think I am the bellhop at the moment," said Angus.

Caitlin opened the door and set her stuff on the bed. The logs and tinder were already stacked in the fireplace. All she had to do was light a match, and it was soon roaring. They sat in the large, comfortable chairs by the fire and felt the warmth wash over them.

Caitlin went to the small tea kettle on the dresser and flipped the switch. She poured packets of hot chocolate into the mugs, and soon the water was bubbling and gurgling. She poured and stirred.

"Thanks," said Angus. "Though we might need coffee for this set."

"Do you play often?" asked Caitlin.

"I've got a band back in Boston, and we play in my pub sometimes. I mean, it's an easy venue and audience."

"What do you usually play?"

"Anything that works well acoustically. I like alternative rock and Scottish ballads, Irish drinking songs and the like."

Caitlin nodded.

"What about you?" he asked.

"I haven't touched a guitar since college. My friends in high school wanted to start a band, so I bought a guitar and took lessons and ... they found other things to do, and we never did it."

He nodded. Once his hands were warmed sufficiently, he began to strum his guitar. Caitlin watched as his fingers danced over the frets. She worked hard to shut down her inner-teenager swoon as his dark, wavy hair fell in waves around his chiseled face, framing brown eyes that held a hint of mischief.

"You definitely know more than three chords," she said as she watched him play.

Angus grinned, "I think we should keep it simple though. Songs that not only we know, but that everyone in the audience will know. People are shut in, it's Hogmanay, and not everyone had planned to spend the holiday at a tourist-trap in a tiny town."

Caitlin looked through her playlists on her phone, and Angus jotted down songs he liked. She played songs that she liked, and he listened. Then he shared some of his favorites. Soon there was a knock on the door.

"Room service," called a voice from the hall.

Caitlin opened the door to find Drew standing there with a little room service cart.

"How's it going?" he asked. "Can I bring this in?"

"Thanks. Come on in," said Caitlin, moving to create a path for Drew as he wheeled the cart into the room.

"We've got a good list started," said Caitlin.

"Though we're just getting warmed up, literally and figuratively," said Angus.

"Well, this will be sure to warm you up. Lindsay made

Balmoral chicken with neeps and tatties. Whisky sauce on the side. And here's a bottle of Malbec. Unless you'd rather have Scotch?"

"Malbec is perfect. Thank you, Drew!" said Caitlin.

He nodded. "Looking forward to your set."

They lifted the silver lid on the food, which smelled delicious. Caitlin looked at her plate. The chicken was wrapped in bacon and covered in a sauce. She cut into it and found it was stuffed with something.

"What's that?" she asked.

"That'll be the haggis."

Caitlin took a big bite. "This is amazing!"

"Aye. Be sure to add a lot of sauce on the chicken and the tatties," said Angus, demonstrating by adding a heavy dollop of whisky sauce.

They talked music as they ate and watched the snow fall and the fire crackle. Soon they had built up a list of ten songs that they both knew, thought the audience would like, and that would work for two guitarists who hadn't planned to hold a show.

Caitlin finished the last bites and watched as the fire began to die out.

"Shall we?" asked Angus.

"I guess we shall," she said, taking his hand.

Downstairs, the inn was buzzing with customers ordering pints.Waitstaff rushed around, serving and clearing tables. The dartboards were all busy, and the pool table had a crowd around it.

Caitlin raised her eyebrow at Angus.

"It'll be fine," he assured her.

They sat down on the two chairs Drew had placed next to the fireplace and adjusted the mics. The bartender turned on a small spotlight, and Caitlin looked out at the crowd. How did she get into this? She hadn't played for an audience in years.

Nervously, she strummed the first chord, and soon they were playing.

The crowd quieted and listened to Angus's silky yet gravelly voice as he crooned classic rock, alternative, and grunge, along with classic Scottish and Irish songs. Caitlin sang backup until they reached her songs, then Angus sang backup for her.

When they finished, the crowd erupted into applause. Caitlin looked at Angus. They stood and did an awkward bow.

"Good set!" said Caitlin.

"Right back at you. Should we go find Drew and Lindsay and a pint?"

Just as Caitlin was about to respond, a woman pushed her way through the crowd.

"Angus! So good to see you!" she said. She swung her long blonde hair over her shoulder and touched his arm.

"Hey ..." Angus said, reaching for her name. "Elspeth!"

"You can't forget me! Can you, Angus?"

"Not a chance," he said, looking rather trapped.

"What brings you to town?" Elspeth asked, her hand still resting on Angus's arm.

"Hogmanay celebrations. Hanging with Drew," Angus said, then realized he should have mentioned Caitlin.

Elspeth looked at Caitlin. "Did they have trouble getting the usual musicians? Your set seemed ... whimsically improvised."

Caitlin tried to smile sweetly, but if she'd been a cartoon, her ears would be spouting steam. She was embarrassed to realize that Angus could see it.

Angus quickly stepped in.

"Caitlin's an amazing musician that graciously agreed to play a set with me tonight when everyone—line cooks, wait staff, housekeeping—found themselves snowed in these past few days. How'd you manage to get here?"

"A friend texted and said you were in town. I can't believe you didn't call," said Elspeth.

"You came here in a snowstorm?" Caitlin blurted out without thinking.

Elspeth just looked at Caitlin like she was in her way. "I'm used to snow. I live here."

"I live in Boston. We're pretty used to it as well."

Caitlin enjoyed watching the metaphorical wheels spin in Elspeth's head as she began to put together that Caitlin and Angus *both* lived in Boston. Fortunately for all of them, Lindsay arrived.

Lindsay peeled off her apron. "Great set, you guys! Any plans for tomorrow?"

"I was actually just about to ask if I could steal you away so we could strategize about how to get us back together," Elspeth said to Angus in a low voice.

But Caitlin heard. As shock and hurt washed over her, Lindsay quickly took matters into her own hands.

"Caitlin, can you help me with some ideas I've got for the breakfast menu?" Lindsay asked.

Caitlin narrowed her eyes, then nodded. "Sure. And I've got ideas for a new setlist, too," she said, leaving Angus standing with a bemused Elspeth. "Solos."

CHAPTER 13

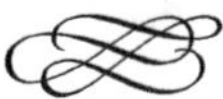

As Caitlin snapped green beans, she imagined she was tearing off their heads. "We've gotta get out of here," said Caitlin as she ripped another bean in half.

"Why the sudden change?" Lindsay asked.

"He's obviously got a girlfriend, and here I was, taken in with his long hair and charm and guitar playing ..."

"We don't know what the situation is. It just seemed like it would be best to step away and let them talk."

"I'm not a step away kind of person," said Caitlin.

"I can see that. But rather than get into a cat fight or throw your drink in Angus's face, let's take a breath and get a clear head."

Caitlin sighed. Lindsay was right.

"You came here to have fun and catch up with Melissa," said Lindsay. "Instead, you're trapped in an Inn with a rugged lumberjack who ..."

"Who I don't know."

"Solution? We get back to Inverness and celebrate Hogmanay with Melissa as planned."

"How?" asked Caitlin. "They say most of the road crew are out of town for the holiday."

"We've got all these lumberjack types up here with nothing to do. Let's organize our own Highland Games and get them to compete in moving fallen trees. Then we can get out."

"Great idea!"

"And they'll all wear their kilts," said Lindsay with a smile.

* * *

THE NEXT MORNING, Lindsay and Drew organized everyone into teams as they gathered for a full Scottish breakfast. Guests piled their plates with square sausage, eggs, beans, potatoes, bacon, white pudding, black pudding, tattie scones, and toast. Excitement filled the air as burly men in kilts wolfed down their hearty breakfasts.

"How did they all have kilts with them? Is it like how Americans always pack a pair of jeans?" Caitlin asked.

"They may have had them for Hogmanay parties. Or maybe had a spare utility kilt in the boot of the car," said Lindsay. She was joking, of course. Still, Caitlin couldn't believe the sea of muscular men forming what looked like an army to clear the roads.

Drew stood on the stone base of the fireplace and addressed the crowd. "We've had a good time with you all, but I know many of us had plans for Hogmanay that didn't center on being snowed in. You've made plans. You have friends you want to see. It's an important time of year. And with the road crew workers on holiday, it's up to us to make a difference."

"FREEDOM!" yelled one burly, kilted man, who had somehow managed to find blue and white makeup to paint his face like the Scottish Saltire flag.

Everyone laughed, but his shout charged the already energized crowd.

"We're going to treat this like a reality show competition. You start out on snowmobiles, then snowshoes, then you find the downed trees. Get into teams and lift—just like a caber toss—and then go to the next one. First team to move the tree on the main highway gets this bottle of single malt. First team to remove all the trees gets a coupon for a week stay here ... and all the Belhaven you can drink for a year."

"Freedom!" they cried again, clamoring toward the door.

Laughing, Lindsay and Caitlin filled their own plates and sat in the corner by the fire.

"Didn't see Angus this morning," said Lindsay.

"Probably still in bed with that woman."

"You don't know that."

Caitlin groaned. "Ugh, why did I get so caught up in him?"

"C'mon, Caitlin," said Lindsay.

"What?" asked Caitlin.

"He likes you. Plus he's got a great smile, warm eyes, and an amazing voice," said Lindsay.

"And gorgeous dark hair. And he's an amazing kisser," said Caitlin with a grin.

"See?"

"And then this random woman shows up—for all I know, she's his wife—"

"She's not his wife," said Lindsay.

"How do you know?" asked Caitlin.

"He wouldn't ... I just don't think—" began Lindsay.

"I never should've gotten involved," said Caitlin.

Lindsay tried to motion for Caitlin to quit talking, but Caitlin was on a rampage. She didn't see Angus heading toward their table with a filled plate. The grin on his face faded as he heard Caitlin say, "He's just some superficial grifter musician. Who still tries to be a musician at his age, anyway?"

Caitlin finally caught sight of Angus just as he quickly changed course and went into the storage room.

"He's alone now," said Lindsay.

"Do you think he heard?" asked Caitlin.

Lindsay nodded.

"Fine. I mean, really?" said Caitlin, fuming now. "He just took off last night and now expects to sit here for breakfast like I'm some groupie waiting for him?"

Caitlin stood.

"Where are you going?" Lindsay asked.

"I'm going to move some big-ass trees so we can get out of here."

Caitlin put on her hat, snow pants, and coat and blew through the front doors of the inn.

LINDSAY WATCHED Caitlin hurry toward the frenzy of activity as guests and locals joined the brigade of snowmobiles zooming across the sparkling snow on the clear, sunny morning. She couldn't help but feel pride in her fellow Scotsmen. All you needed to do was say that help was needed, and they rose to the challenge. Especially if that challenge was a competition involving wearing kilts, lifting heavy things, and winning single malts.

CAITLIN RODE on the back of a stranger's snowmobile. Her helmet was ill-fitting, and the stranger drove a tad recklessly, in her opinion, as they roared over the snowy roads. When they reached their location—the downed tree that first brought her to the inn—there were already seven or eight men and women assembled to lift it. Caitlin bent down to lift and was greeted with sideways glances right away.

"Have you done this before?" asked an athletic woman with long dark hair and a bright smile.

"Um, no, but I wanted to help," answered Caitlin.

"You'll put your back out doing it like that. We've been training for the Highland Games all year. But if you really want to help, crouch low, lift with your legs, and—did you ever play 'Light as a Feather' as a lass?"

"Yeah," answered Caitlin.

"We're gonna do it like that. I'm Sydney, by the way. Nice to meet you."

"Caitlin."

Sydney smiled.

Caitlin crouched low and lifted with her legs. Her hands were light on the tree trunk. She suspected the more experienced Highland Games participants were doing the real heavy lifting because it did feel "light as a feather," but it worked! Soon the tree was up and over. They heaved it to the side of the road and cheered.

Sydney wiped the bark from her gloves and grinned. "We're cracking now. Just 157 more to go, and then we bring in the plows!"

"Someone counted?"

"I exaggerate. Have you seen my brother around?" Sydney asked as though Caitlin knew him.

Caitlin just shrugged.

"I saw you two playing together last night. I haven't heard him play like that since Sophie ..." began Sydney.

"Angus is your brother? Wait, who's Sophie?" Confusion washed over Caitlin as she tried to process this new information.

"Oh, gosh, I'm sorry. I thought you knew him fairly well. I mean, I haven't seen him like that in so long."

Sydney seemed to be waiting for an answer, so Caitlin finally replied, "We just met."

"Well, he's smitten, that's for sure."

"I don't think so," said Caitlin.

"No. Believe me. I haven't heard him play like that or look at anyone like that in years. You're definitely what the doctor ordered," said Sydney.

"It sounds like Sophie may be what the doctor ordered. There was a woman with long, blonde hair who came up to him after our second set and asked to 'steal him away' so they could talk about how to 'get back together,'" said Caitlin.

Sydney stood thinking. "Well, it wasn't Sophie. Sophie died several years ago."

"Oh. I'm sorry."

But Sydney couldn't hold back the slight grin spreading across her face. Finally, she dug into her pocket and pulled out her phone. She began flipping through pictures.

"Is this the woman?" asked Sydney.

Caitlin nodded. "The very one."

"And she said she wants to 'get back together'?"

"Yes. That's what she said," replied Caitlin.

Sydney burst into an elaborate happy dance, and Caitlin felt her stomach twist into knots. Before she could ask why Sydney was so happy about the woman when she'd seemed in favor of Caitlin's relationship with Angus, Lindsay pulled up in her car.

"It took me forever to dig out, but they've got the road to Inverness open! I told Melissa we'd be there in an hour!"

"Oh. That's … I mean, that's great. If you can just take me back to the inn, then I can—"

"I already packed your things. We're all set! Isn't this great? Just what we wanted!"

Lindsay opened the car door, and Caitlin stood there for a minute, trying to process what had just happened. It was all a little too much, so she surrendered and plopped into the car, still a little dazed. "Nice to meet you, Sydney."

"Hey, yeah. Really nice to meet you, Caitlin. I'll give your regards to my brother."

"Uh, yeah."

. . .

"WHAT WAS THAT ABOUT?" Lindsay asked once the door was closed.

"Um. I'm not sure. That was Angus's sister. She was really nice. She was pretty sure we were together. She said she hasn't seen Angus look like that since he was with someone named Sophie. But she was also ridiculously, utterly shamelessly excited that the blonde woman from last night wants to get back together. So I have no idea. Let's get out of here and have a proper New Years with our friends."

"Absolutely."

As they drove away, Caitlin tried to sort out her thoughts, but she couldn't make sense of it all.

CHAPTER 14

Melissa burst through the front door to welcome her friends as they drove up the freshly-plowed driveway. Jingles followed at her side, eager to see who'd arrived. Colin stood in the doorway on his crutches, but Melissa waddled out to the driveway in her leg brace to help with their bags.

"Caitlin! I am so sorry! You came all the way here to visit, and it's been days ..."

"No worries, Melissa. Lindsay and I got to know each other better, and we had fun at the Inn." *Until we didn't,* Caitlin thought. But she didn't include that part.

"Yeah, it was a good time. Great room, beautiful inn. We'll tell you all about it later. But first, let's get you inside so you don't slip again!" said Lindsay.

"We salted the sidewalks like crazy, so we should be good," replied Melissa.

They carried their bags up the stone walkway, and once again, Caitlin marveled at what a beautiful house Melissa had inherited. The wreaths on the door and the greenery were so welcoming and cheerful, and the snowy walkway just added to the magic.

INSIDE, Melissa had taken down the more overt Christmas decorations but had kept up the greenery and white lights. The scent of fresh pine and smokey peat filled the air, and fires crackled merrily in the numerous fireplaces throughout the house.

Jingles followed them around as they carried their bags into the hall, then curled up in his bed, his little head on his paws as he watched the newcomers.

"SO WHAT'S THE PLAN?" asked Caitlin.

"As you probably noticed, Inverness is still clearing the roads, but we're thinking it'll be great by tonight. No snow predicted for tonight or tomorrow. If it snows, we have a lot of space, so people can just stay here. Colin's inviting his crew. Lindsay, you invited yours, right? And the people I know are mostly through Colin and Lindsay. We made a great playlist. We've got champagne, and we're going to make some amazing appetizers."

It all sounded fun, but at the mention of a playlist, Caitlin couldn't help but think how much fun it would be to have a band. Specifically Angus, strumming his guitar. Lindsay noticed Caitlin's smile beginning to waiver, and she quickly changed the subject.

"I'll get started on whatever you need me to do for the food. Caitlin can help," Lindsay offered.

CAITLIN AND MELISSA were soon chopping vegetables, making dips, and slicing cheese for cheese plates. Meanwhile, Lindsay prepped a roast, and Colin stocked the bar. Melissa's new playlist kept them in the New Year's spirit.

"So, Lindsay, please let us know what we're getting into here with this. How is Hogmanay different from a traditional New Year's Eve like we'd celebrate in the States?" asked Caitlin.

"Well, I've never celebrated in the States. But from what I understand, it's a one night thing, right?"

"Yeah. It's pretty much a night where you try to find a date, put on your glitziest outfit, go to parties or bars, and then do a countdown at midnight," said Melissa.

"And ideally kiss a special someone as the clock strikes twelve," said Caitlin.

"And then it's kind of all over, right?" asked Lindsay.

"I mean, once the ball drops on TV, people generally leave within an hour or so," said Caitlin.

"Then what do you do the next day?"

"We sleep in, and then there's football." Melissa saw Colin raise an eyebrow. "American football, that is," she added.

"We watch football, have snacks—like a seven-layer dip, chips and salsa, or Buffalo wings—and sometimes people organize a pool to win money each quarter depending on how the score comes out," said Melissa.

"Then we go back to work tired and bleary eyed, with nothing to look forward to except dieting and ruining said diet with more Buffalo wings for the Super Bowl," said Caitlin with a wry grin.

"That's definitely not how we do it here. At midnight, we countdown and have fireworks, but the big event is First Footing. We have a lot of ancient traditions around here, and most of them come with superstitions and rituals about bringing good luck, health, and prosperity for the new year. It's all about starting out on the right foot. So First Footing means that the very first person to step through your door after midnight can make or break your whole year. Back in the day, people were scared of the Vikings—they often had blond or red hair—so it was good luck for a dark-haired man to be the first person through the door."

"Then what?" asked Caitlin.

"The dark-haired man should bring gifts," said Lindsay.

"I like that idea," said Caitlin with a grin, though her mind went straight to Angus. "What do they bring?"

"Well, a black bun so no one goes hungry. Sometimes it's shortbread and single malt. Some people bring salt. And coal or peat so the house remains warm. But it's all to bring good luck to the household," Lindsay explained.

"Well, I wouldn't turn that away," said Melissa.

"So anyway, Caitlin, you and I with our light hair have to be extremely careful to not enter a home until someone says it's okay. Even though it's an old tradition, it's not something you want to mess with," said Lindsay.

"What then? So someone comes in ..." said Caitlin.

"Yeah. The First Footer comes in, and then the party gets started!" said Melissa.

"So it's a late-night thing," said Caitlin.

"Honey, it's an all-night, into-the-next-morning, and maybe-the-day-after kind of thing. This is a serious party!" said Lindsay.

"So you can really see how the snow has put a damper on the daft days," said Colin.

"The daft days?" asked Caitlin.

"Yeah, it's all called 'daft days' between Christmas and Hogmanay. Lots of parties, gatherings, festivities, music ... I'm so sorry you were trapped and didn't get to experience all of it," said Colin.

"We did okay for ourselves," Lindsay said, grinning mysteriously.

Melissa's jaw dropped. "Come on. Spill the tea!"

Lindsay continued to chop vegetables as she told Melissa about Drew and Angus.

"So have you invited them?" asked Melissa.

"To your party?" asked Lindsay.

"Of course!"

"Um. No. Maybe I should?" Lindsay looked at Caitlin.

Caitlin felt a pit in her stomach. "You can invite Drew if you want," said Caitlin. "I think Angus is ... not ..."

"What?" Melissa asked.

"I think he's got other plans."

"Invite him anyway. Everybody has plans, but if the roads are clear people really do go from party to party," said Colin.

Caitlin kept chopping, and Lindsay and Melissa looked at each other and shrugged.

CHAPTER 15

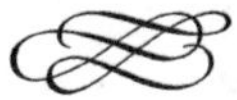

White string lights hung over a bonfire on the patio. Music streamed from bluetooth speakers. And a table with single malts, bottles of wine, and a pitcher of a seasonal cranberry and vodka punch stood waiting.

The snow fell lightly, but it felt warm near the crackling fire. The patio had been cleared of chairs so it could be a make-shift dance floor. Soon guests began arriving, and Melissa was back in her favorite role, hostess.

The party in full swing, Colin's playlist blasted through the house as revelers dressed to the nines in their New Year's finest danced, mingled, and munched on appetizers. As Lindsay and Colin mixed drinks and bantered with guests, Melissa carried around trays of appetizers. Caitlin filled more trays as fast as Melissa could empty them. It was about half ten when the thunder grew louder than the music. A few minutes later, guests crowded around the windows to watch the "thundersnow."

Thunder crashed, lightning flashed, and wet, sleety snow poured out of the sky in sheets. Caitlin noticed a car coming up the driveway. A man in a dashing wool coat emerged carrying two guitars. Behind him was a big guy with long, dark, wavy hair escaping from underneath his hat.

"They're here," Caitlin said to Lindsay. "Drew and Angus."

She rushed to open the door just in time to see Angus help someone out of the back of the car. The first had long, dark hair, and Caitlin recognized her as Sydney, Angus's sister. The next to emerge was the blonde who had stolen Angus away at the inn. Caitlin's heart sank, but she put on a big smile and waved as the four carried bags of goodies for the party.

"Lindsay and Caitlin, I'd like you to meet Sydney and Elspeth."

"Nice to meet you," said Lindsay.

"Thanks for coming," said Caitlin, hoping it sounded like her heart was in it. "Elspeth? I thought your name was—"

"Elspeth," said Sydney quickly, as Angus looked from Caitlin to Sydney.

"Thanks so much for helping us patch things up, Angus"

"What?" Caitlin asked, confused.

"Elspeth and I had broken up, but she came back. And now …"

"Oh!" said Caitlin, the pieces finally falling into place. "Oh. Congratulations!"

"A fresh start for a new year!" Sydney smiled.

"Come on inside before that sleet ruins your hair!" said Lindsay with a laugh. She ushered the women and Drew inside, while Angus stayed on the front steps with Caitlin.

"You thought Elsepth was … a girlfriend?"

"I didn't know who she was. I just knew that she took off with you and …"

Angus grinned. "You were jealous."

"Hell yeah, I was jealous. You took off with this beautiful woman and …"

Angus took her hand. "She's my little sister's girlfriend."

"I see that now."

"And you just left without even saying goodbye."

"Well, what was I supposed to think when you took off with this gorgeous woman and were gone all night."

"We were up all night coming up with a plan to get the two of them back together," said Angus.

"What was the solution?" asked Caitlin.

"Showing up. Talking. Which is what I'm trying to do right now."

Caitlin looked up at his sincere brown eyes and brushed his long, dark hair aside.

"I'm glad you showed up."

"I'm glad I knew where to find you."

He looked to the front door. "Better get you inside before midnight. We can't have a blonde be the first one inside. And actually, we should leave one of those bags outside. It's got everything for First Footing—a peat log, a bottle of single malt, shortbread, a black bun ..."

"Which bag is it?"

"That one there. The rest you can bring in. It's just more of the same, but someone with dark hair will need to carry it in."

"You have dark hair," Caitlin pointed out.

"Aye. And the dark-haired man who brings it in should have someone to kiss at the stroke of midnight."

"I might be willing to oblige," said Caitlin.

"Oh, you would?"

Angus's eyes crinkled as he looked down at her. The sleet was turning into heavy snow and now covered his jacket and hat. "Maybe we should practice."

Drawing closer, their breath visible in the chilly air, Caitlin brushed her lips against his. Gently dropping the bag to the ground, Angus wrapped his strong arms around her. The kiss was soft and tender, but the electricity between them was intense.

"Come inside and get warm," said Caitlin in a whisper.

Angus brushed his lips against hers again, kissing her hungrily now as the snow fell down on them.

"I'm not losing you again if I can help it," he said.

"Keep doing that, and I'll hang around as long as you want," said Caitlin, trying to catch her breath.

"Good."

He took her hand, and together they crossed the threshold into what promised to be an exciting new year.

CHAPTER 16

It was 11:30 when Melissa began filling champagne flutes. Lindsay and Drew passed out noise makers and little hats and glasses with the new year written on them.

The playlist was cranking out the best hits, the most New Year's-worthy songs. Then, with a clap of thunder and a flash of lightning, the house went dark and the music stopped.

Melissa hurried to the basement with Colin right behind her. They returned with lanterns and battery-operated, flameless candles.

"What are we going to do? We can't ring in the new year without music!" lamented Melissa.

"I brought two guitars," said Angus quickly. "Caitlin, will you do me the honor of playing with me?"

"We did rehearse a setlist," replied Caitlin.

"We did at that."

"I always say I don't believe in coincidences."

Angus scanned the living room for a place to play. "What do you think?" he asked Caitlin.

Caitlin looked at Melissa. "We could play in front of the fireplace, but it might be a little hot for the guitars. And we don't want to block the heat and the light. We could play outside on the porch? But we don't want to leave the sliding door open and lose all the heat."

Colin found two chairs and set them up in front of the long line of windows in the living room. "This way people can still get the light and heat from the fire, but you can still be near it as well."

"Perfect!" said Caitlin. "Oh! Colin, this is Angus. Angus, this is Colin."

"Nice to meet you," said Angus, extending his hand to Colin.

"Thanks for playing on short notice."

"No worries. We actually had a gig planned for tonight, but my bandmate skipped town. I had to chase after her," said Angus, grinning.

"If she's anything like the friend she chased here, she's worth it."

Lindsay waved toward the chairs. "It's half eleven! Time to get this party started!"

Angus tuned his guitar while Caitlin quickly jotted down what she remembered of their setlist. He then tuned hers as he looked the songs over. Angus looked at Caitlin. "Ready?"

She nodded.

They launched into a song by the Proclaimers, and everyone started dancing. Melissa breathed a sigh of relief as she saw that not only was Angus as good a guitar player as her friend, but they sounded great together ... and there was an obvious spark between them.

They launched immediately into the next song, then the next, and soon it was almost midnight.

Melissa and Colin circulated trays of champagne flutes and made sure everyone had little hats and noisemakers.

Suddenly, it dawned on Angus. "We gotta do 'Auld Lang Syne,'" he whispered. "Do you know it?"

Caitlin shook her head. "Not at all. Just the chorus. You're gonna have to go solo."

It was 11:55. Angus quickly called up the lyrics on his phone. "Scots or English?" he asked.

Caitlin shrugged. "The way you most fondly remember it?"

Angus nodded and scanned the lyrics. "Sing with me?"

"Of course."

As they played one last, short song, both with a keen eye on Melissa's antique walnut clock still ticking its analogue sounds, the crowd began their countdown. As they reached one, Angus kissed Caitlin deeply, then launched into a beautifully soulful version of "Auld Lang Syne." Everyone joined hands and crossed arms during the chorus as they sang together. Caitlin glanced around the candlelit room, the warm fires crackling, the people singing together. Lindsay and Drew were hand in hand, swaying to the music. In the hallway, she spotted Angus's sister, Sydney, hand in hand with Elspeth, both of them radiant. Tears filled Caitlin's eyes as she read the lyrics along with everyone else. It didn't matter that she didn't know the song. Everyone else did, and their voices together more than made up for her. As Angus strummed the last note, everyone cheered and wished each other Happy New Year.

Angus rummaged in his bag and found a small-but-mighty battery-powered speaker and set it up with his own playlist of New Year's songs. "We're gonna take a wee break to do some First Footing. See you soon!"

"That was beautiful," said Caitlin.

Angus put his muscular arms around her and kissed her gently on the head until she turned and they could have a proper kiss. His lips were warm, and she felt like she was melting into him.

When they came up for air, Angus had a sparkle in his eye. "I've got to get outside and then come back in to ring in the New Year's good luck."

. . .

ANGUS PULLED ON HIS COAT, grabbed his hat, and went outside. Jingles raced out into the snow right behind him.

"Jingles!" Caitlin rushed through the door and did her best to herd the border collie. "Back inside!" She reached for the doorknob to go back inside, but she'd only taken a single step when Angus lunged for her.

"What?" Caitlin gasped.

"Don't move!"

"What?!" Caitlin looked around wildly. Was there an animal or something?

"You've got blonde hair. You can't be the first one to enter the house, or your friend will have bad luck all year!"

"Shit!"

Angus moved forward to knock on the door, but it was already open. Lindsay stood in the doorway, drawn by the activity outside.

Lindsay shook her head and sighed. "Angus, First Footer can't have been in the house when the clock struck midnight."

"That's right! I wasn't supposed to be there, but with the power out, I had to play 'Auld Lang Syne.'"

"So can we come back in?" Caitlin asked, starting to shiver.

"No!" Lindsay shouted. She was so emphatic that Caitlin couldn't help but giggle.

"Can you at least throw me my coat, then?"

"I'm sorry, but I don't want to be half in and half out. I think it's totally sexist, but the tradition holds that the First Footer really should be a dark-haired *man*. I just think Melissa's been through enough lately, and we really need to give her the best luck we can."

Colin emerged from the back yard with a twinkle in his eye. "And that's why I popped outside just before midnight to get more firewood."

Melissa now stood next to Lindsay near the door. "I couldn't believe you weren't there for the midnight kiss!"

"I'm here to bring you a whole year's worth of luck, Melissa," said Colin.

Carrying a log for the fire, Angus's single malt, a black bun, shortbread, salt, and a lump of coal, Colin struggled to balance as Angus poured him a dram.

Angus laughed. "Maybe the dram should go through the threshold via your stomach instead of the dram glass?"

"I've got a lass to share this with," Colin said, as he carefully balanced the dram glass on top of the firewood.

Colin walked through the door, presented Melissa with the gifts. "*Lang may yer lum reek,* Melissa!"

"Uhm ... what?"

"It's a Hogmanay wish that means 'may you never be without fuel for your fire.'"

"Oh ..."

"Now take these gifts and set them down so I can kiss you already!"

Laughing, Melissa accepted the gifts and handed them to Lindsay.

Colin kissed Melissa deeply, and then with a hearty *slàinte,* they shared the dram. "Happy New Year, Melissa."

"Happy New Year, Colin. *Long may your rum leek.*"

"That's '*lum reek,*'" whispered Colin as he kissed her again.

CHAPTER 17

Angus and Caitlin played acoustic tunes into the wee hours. Some revelers nodded off, while others moved the party into the kitchen for a second supper, or an early breakfast, around the fireplace.

At dawn, the lights flickered on and music roared from the speakers, waking everyone in the house. Drew and Lindsay dragged their weary selves off the couch, and soon they were cheerfully cracking eggs and sizzling sausage.

"You two seem to be pros at this!" said Melissa.

"We've had some experience this week," said Lindsay.

"I can't believe you're not cooking professionally," said Drew.

Lindsay blushed. "Maybe someday."

"How soon is now?" asked Drew.

"You're a Morrisey fan?"

"No. Why wait until someday? You already know your way around the kitchen at my inn, and you've met the staff."

"But you have a chef, and you have line cooks. They just couldn't get there because of the snow."

"Right. So how will they be able to get to my new inn in

Inverness—say that three times real fast—if they can't even get to the one in the town where they live."

"You have a new inn? In Inverness?"

"Aye. A new inn in Inverness," Drew said with a grin. "Opens this spring. What do you think? Executive chef?"

"Oh Drew. That would be amazing!" Impulsively, Lindsay kissed him. As she realized what she'd done, she quickly stepped back.

"What's wrong?" Drew asked.

"You'd be my boss."

Drew shook his head. "Nope. I just sold some shares in it, so I'd no longer be your immediate boss. That would be Angus's sister, Sydney. She'll be serving as general manager."

"That's awesome!"

Sydney and Elspeth padded over in their PJs, carrying cups of tea. "We can't wait to move here! We're going to stay in the apartment above the inn. We just need an interior designer to help with renovations."

"I can do that!" said Melissa, handing them a plate of crumpets. "I've done work on homes, restaurants, and businesses. An inn would be a wonderful project!"

"She did all the design on this house," said Lindsay.

"It's incredible," said Sydney.

"There's a lot more to do. I've really just scratched the surface, but—"

"Don't discount it. This place is beautiful. It looks like you've lived here for years," said Sydney.

"Sure does," said Melissa with a laugh, gesturing to the mess. "I'll get started on the clean up efforts soon."

"No worries. It's a party, Mel," said Caitlin.

"Can you stop by one day this week to do an assessment and write an estimate?" asked Sydney.

"I'd love to! Thank you so much, Sydney. You have no idea what this means."

"It means Melissa has her first step toward being able to stay here!" said Lindsay.

"And you all joining the team means Sydney and I can finally work together. We broke up when I moved to London, but now that we have the inn ..." said Elspeth.

"It looks like we'll all be able to stay in Inverness," said Melissa with a grin.

"I'll come visit," said Caitlin.

"Aye, and you can come visit me in Boston," said Angus, clasping Caitlin's hand and pulling her closer to him.

"And when you book your ticket home, you'll have to come see me," said Colin quietly.

"Of course," said Melissa. Then it sank in. He meant the United States. "That's right. Home. You have to go home."

Sydney, Elspeth, Lindsay, Drew, Caitlin, and Angus all casually excused themselves into the other room so Colin and Melissa could have some privacy.

"I'll be back, of course," said Colin.

"Of course."

"And I'll help Sydney draw up the materials you'll need to show you have a job. That will help with the immigration documents. And when you book your ticket to the US, that will be another positive. And—"

"How often do you come back?" Melissa asked him gently.

"I mean. It's ... I come as often as I can. Lately, that's just been for Christmas."

Melissa nodded. "I never even asked. When's your return flight?"

"Sunday. I go back to work on Monday," replied Colin.

Melissa blinked away pesky tears.

Colin put his arms around her and held her close. "Melissa, hey ..."

"It's just ... I mean, I'm ridiculous. We just met. I had a wonderful time. This place means so much to me, and I'm sure I got confused between the place and your family and thinking that this was—"

"But it is—"

"It can't be. I had a long distance relationship in college. It was with Dave. That's when he first met Samantha," explained Melissa.

"I had a long distance relationship with Fiona. She tried to make it work, but the spark was gone."

"See?"

"But *we* have a spark! We have more than a spark. We have—"

"We have a good, solid friendship, and I love your family and the town where you live and the dog your father raised. I just got a divorce. It's too soon."

"What are you saying?"

Melissa took Colin's hand. "You have to follow your heart. And everything in you has told you for years that you belong in the United States."

"And everything over this past week has told me I belong here. With you."

"It's just ... It's not us. It's the connection with your father. It's realizing that these dogs are awesome, that you live in a wonderful community—all of it."

"You've made me realize all that, Melissa. How much I love it here. How much I love the landscape, the lochs, the food, the *craic*. But most of all, Melissa ... it was Fiona that made the long distance relationship not work out. Well, and myself as well. We didn't have that magic. But I have it with you. And I want to try. I want this to work. I have to go back. I'm just on holiday. But once I get things in order ... people live and work on different continents every day. We've got video conferencing, texts, emails, carrier pigeons."

"Maybe I'm just the first person that—"

"You're not. No offense, Melissa, but this isn't my first rodeo.

My dad may have painted a picture of me as some lonely guy mooning over a lost love from years ago. But as you can see from Fiona, I've dated plenty, and I never sparked with any of them the way I have with you. Give this a chance. I won't stay away long, and you have to come back anyway. Please?"

"Rodeo?" asked Melissa, trying to ease the tension.

Colin reached into his pocket and pulled out a small box.

"Colin, you're not—"

"No worries. I'm not."

Melissa opened the box. It was a new mobile.

"No more finger cuts or plastic tape. And I've already programmed all my contact info into it. That is, if you'll have me."

"Absolutely!"

CAITLIN SMILED as she saw Melissa embrace Colin.

"I guess my work here is done," she said to Lindsay.

"Actually, I think it's just beginning. We're gonna have to scheme to keep these two together and get Colin back sooner than he plans."

Caitlin raised an eyebrow. "Great minds think alike."

Lindsay grinned.

CHAPTER 18

Sunday night, the Inverness airport was bustling—cars dropped off travelers, people were hugging on the sidewalk, others were rushing into the terminal. Melissa slid into a parking spot by the curb. As they walked to the trunk, Melissa said, “Thanks so much for coming!”

Caitlin replied, “I had a wonderful time. I can see why you love it here.”

“Please come back soon. I’m sure spring and summer are amazing.”

“I bet we can make it to the Isle of Skye if we go in the summer!” said Caitlin.

“And I’ll be back in Boston in late spring.”

Caitlin hugged Melissa and reached for her bags, then paused. “What about Dave and Colin and all of—”

“I don’t care about Dave. We’ve got everything settled.”

“What does that mean?” asked Caitlin.

“He’s keeping the house. It’s his. That’s fine. We split our joint accounts. I’ll sell him the furniture. And it’s just done.”

“He’ll agree to that?”

Melissa replied, "He already has. So it'll be official as soon as we get the paperwork signed."

"Well, that's great. Right?"

"Yeah."

"And the house is all set?"

"Yep. And once I submit my paperwork showing I have a return ticket home and a means to support myself, I should be able to stay on a visa."

"That's a relief! Thank goodness." Caitlin gave Melissa another hug. "You take care, have fun, and I'll come visit soon. I definitely understand why you love it here."

CAITLIN CHECKED her bag and made her way to security. She found herself in line behind a burly guy with long, dark hair and a guitar strapped across his shoulder. As he set the guitar on the conveyor belt and began stripping off his belt, jacket, and shoes, he turned, and Caitlin found herself staring into the deep brown eyes of Angus.

Caitlin smiled. "Hey!"

"Hey yourself!"

Caitlin slipped off her coat and shoes and put them in a box while Angus walked through the metal detector, setting off an alarm.

Security patted him down to discover a guitar string in his back pocket.

Caitlin walked through the metal detector. As she waited on the other side for her bags, she noticed the security agent pull Angus aside.

"Is this your bag, sir?" asked the guard.

"Yeah," replied Angus.

The agent rummaged through it and pulled out a set of darts.

"You can't fly with these."

"I'm so sorry. I had no idea I'd packed them."

The agent glared at him and took the darts and guitar string.

"You got anything else I should know about? Liquids? Fireworks? Knives?" He was now eyeing Angus's long hair and tattooed arms.

"No, I'm so sorry. I was just in a rush to clear the hotel room and threw everything in my bag."

Things were just beginning to look dicey when Caitlin came up and put her arm around Angus. "Did you grab the wrong bag, babe? I thought I'd made sure you had taken those out."

The agent looked from Caitlin to Angus, then finally let Angus pass. Angus slipped on his shoes and belt and looked at Caitlin sheepishly.

"Gate 32?" asked Angus.

"Yep."

They wheeled their suitcases toward the gate and plunked themselves down in chairs.

"I'll go grab us some coffee if you'll watch the suitcases," said Caitlin.

"Sure."

She paused. "I don't even know how you like your coffee."

Angus replied, "Generally, black tea and a splash of milk is how I like it when I'm here. At home, coffee black."

Caitlin grinned. "Home?"

"Boston is home now. I love going back, but Boston is where I belong."

Caitlin nodded and left him to guard the bags.

Standing in the long line at the coffee shop, Caitlin looked at various muffins and scones, trying to decide what to get for Angus to go with his tea. A Scotsman in front of her wearing a tweed jacket and talking quietly on his cell phone got her attention.

"That's absurd ... Of course not ... You can't—" The person on the other end must've hung up.

Caitlin stared as the man put his phone in his pocket and turned. It was Colin.

Panic washed over Caitlin—something was definitely wrong.

"Everything under control?" she asked, trying out the British phrase she'd learned.

Colin sighed. "Melissa's ex heard about the house."

"Well, he can't have it."

"There's no pre-nup and the divorce isn't finalized yet. He thinks he hit the jackpot," said Colin.

The airline announcer announced a flight to New York was boarding.

"That's me. Blast," said Colin.

"Want me to bring your coffee to the gate?" asked Caitlin.

"Nevermind."

"No, I'll catch you. I'm next in line. Which gate are you?"

Colin replied, "35."

"Just down the aisle. What are you drinking?"

"Black tea with a splash of milk."

"I'll be right there. And don't worry. I'm sure this will all work out."

Caitlin approached the counter and ordered. Quickly grabbing the two teas and her coffee, she carried a bag of muffins in her teeth and hurried to Colin's gate.

When she got there, a woman with beautiful, long, red hair was standing next to him.

Colin looked even more miserable.

The flight attendants had already started boarding, and Colin was queued up with the rest of his zone. "Here's your tea."

She looked from Colin to the woman and back.

"Thanks, Caitlin. Caitlin, this is my old friend, Fiona. Fiona, this is Melissa's best friend from home."

"You're not taking Melissa back with you?" asked Fiona.

"No, she's staying," replied Caitlin.

"And without Colin? That's too bad. What a lonely winter that will be."

Caitlin's eyes widened with fury, but she said nothing.

They stood awkwardly for a few moments, then Caitlin heard her own flight announced over the loudspeaker.

"That's me. I've gotta run. Colin, good luck with the … thing. And Fiona … nice to meet you."

Caitlin hurried back to the gate. Her fury melted away as she saw Angus—his long, dark, wavy hair and the rock star tattoos canceled out by his reading glasses and the bits of gray dotting his beard. He smiled as he put down his book to take his tea. He had such a warm smile. It made Caitlin feel like she was the only one in the room.

"Glad you made it. They just called for people who needed extra time to board."

Caitlin nodded. "I got you a muffin."

"Thanks. You okay? You looked so happy when you left and now …"

Caitlin sat down beside him. "I ran into Colin. He's run into some trouble with Melissa's divorce trial."

"Oh no!"

"And his ex-girlfriend is on the flight with him."

"He can deflect that," said Angus.

"I don't know. She's really beautiful."

"Beautiful isn't everything. I've seen the way he looks at Melissa."

Caitlin felt the tears brimming up. "She was so happy, and everything was settled."

"It'll work out. John Lennon once said 'Everything will be okay in the end. If it's not okay, it's not the end.'"

He took her hand in his, and they walked toward the gate to board.

As they scanned their tickets and boarded, Angus turned back to Caitlin. "Where are you sitting?"

"38 A," replied Caitlin.

"I'm 38 B."

"Really?"

"Truly."

"I don't believe in coincidences."

"That's good, because it would be hard to explain getting into the same cab as you back in Boston," said Angus.

Caitlin laughed. "Rather presumptuous of you."

"More presumptuous is that I'm taking you to dinner. That is, if you'll have me."

Caitlin flashed him a grin, and they settled into their seats.

"I think we're good together," Angus said tentatively.

Caitlin slipped her hand into his and nodded. "Me too."

The flight attendants called for cross checks, and then they took off, flying above the green hilly highlands toward Boston, the New Year awaiting.

HIGHLANDS HOMECOMING

BOOK 3

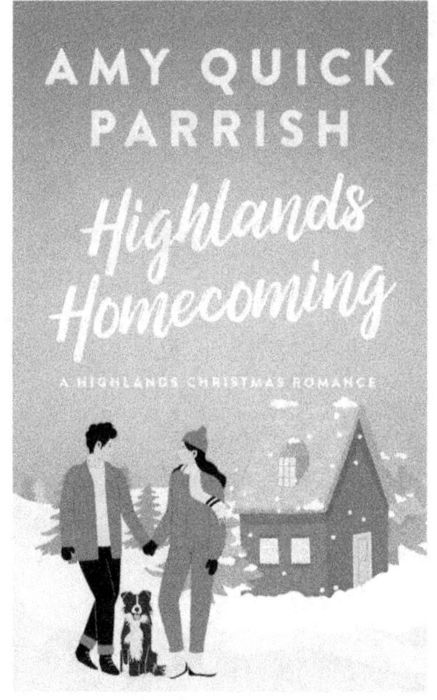

Nessie believes in you.

CHAPTER 1

Bursting with excitement, Melissa MacKenzie wheeled her small suitcase through the bustling Boston Logan airport. Her heart pounded in anticipation as she drew nearer to the passenger pickup. There was her best friend, Caitlin, waving enthusiastically as she hopped out of her car and rushed to help Melissa hoist her luggage into the back seat.

"Welcome home!" exclaimed Caitlin, her cheeks flushed from the cold and her blonde curls tucked snugly into a cute blue knit hat.

Melissa threw her arms around her in a tight hug and exclaimed, "Oh my goodness, it's so good to see you!"

Melissa walked to the left side of the car, excited to start the drive back toward her hometown. When she saw the steering wheel, she laughed. "Oops. Looks like I finally got the hang of it, just to be all mixed up again back in the States!"

"I'll have to reintroduce you to our culture," Caitlin teased with a playful wink. "We drive on the other side of the road over here, we spell *whisky* with an *e*, and ... what else?"

"Do you drive with your middle finger in the air?" Melissa joked back, feeling at ease in her longtime friend's company.

"Guilty as charged," giggled Caitlin as she deftly navigated through traffic toward the Mass Pike.

"So what's on the agenda for this trip?" asked Caitlin.

"I need to ship my belongings back to Inverness, spend time with my family, finalize the divorce paperwork, and get everything sorted before officially making Scotland my new residence."

"Sounds like a busy but exciting trip," Caitlin remarked.

"And I definitely want to make a stop at Angus's bar," added Melissa.

"Absolutely," agreed Caitlin.

"And maybe surprise Colin while I'm at it," Melissa said, causing Caitlin to do a double take.

"You didn't tell him you were coming?!"

"No, I thought it would be fun to surprise him," said Melissa with a mischievous glint in her eye.

"He doesn't strike me as the type who enjoys surprises," mused Caitlin, brushing a loose strand of her blonde curls behind her ear.

Melissa considered this for a moment. "You're right. But I'm always full of surprises, so I guess this can be an early test of our relationship."

As they emerged from the Ted Williams Tunnel into the bright sunlight, Caitlin asked, "So where should we go first?" Her bright blue eyes scanned the bustling streets of Boston, eager to explore. "We could grab some lunch if you're hungry. Maybe shop on Newbury Street or visit Harvard Square. Or maybe we should freshen up at my place before heading out?"

"That actually sounds perfect," agreed Melissa as they made their way through the busy streets. "It was a short flight, but I still feel like I have a layer of 'airplane' on me."

"My house it is, then," declared Caitlin.

* * *

CAITLIN'S cozy two-story condo boasted a stunning view of the January ice shimmering on Jamaica Pond. As they walked up the salt-covered wooden steps and entered the spacious living room, Melissa felt nostalgia for all the good times they'd had there.

"I've always loved your place," Melissa said as she took in her surroundings. "And what a gorgeous view of the pond!"

Caitlin led the way up the oak banister staircase to the bedrooms and bathroom on the second floor. "It's small, but it suits me for now," she said with a shrug. "Hey, we could grab lunch at Angus's place if you want," offered Caitlin.

Melissa raised an eyebrow playfully. "How are those two thoughts connected? Thinking of moving in together?"

Caitlin's cheeks flushed as she stumbled over her words. "My lease is up in September and, well, we *have* discussed it."

"So things are going well," observed Melissa. "You move fast!"

"Once you've been snowed in together, things tend to ... accelerate?"

"Good. You deserve it. And you're adorable together."

* * *

MELISSA EMERGED from the shower with a radiant glow, her damp hair falling in soft waves around her shoulders. She wore a bright blue sweater that brought out the color of her eyes, and her jeans hugged her curves in all the right places.

"Feeling better?" asked Caitlin.

"I feel like it's morning ... again."

Caitlin laughed. "Are we forwards or backwards?"

"I don't even know anymore. What time is it here?"

"Time for something to eat. Let's go see what's on special at the Iron Brew," answered Caitlin.

"Angus picked a great name for a Scottish pub."

"Definitely. No trademark issues, and the Americans can pronounce it."

* * *

The Iron Brew was a cozy corner pub on a bustling street in a funky up-and-coming Boston neighborhood. The outside was clearly a Scottish pub—a blue and white Saltar flag waved in the breeze, and the windows sparkled with thistle decorations painted in a lovely ornate gold.

Stepping inside, Melissa felt transported back to Scotland. The whole place was a whirl of exposed brick and old wooden beams, with tartan pillows, a framed photo of Robert Burns, and a large wooden bar made from what appeared to be antique, up-cycled wood. They even had a little wooden sheep sitting on the bar.

And the music—a rich rumble of guitar with soft crooning felt like the Scottish indie rock that Melissa hadn't quite grown up with, but had always loved. In short, the place felt as much like home as Greenhill House did the moment she first stepped inside.

"This is incredible!" gushed Melissa.

"I know, right?" said Caitlin.

"Do you want a table, or do you want to sit at the bar? Or they have tables in the bar." Caitlin gestured to a table next to a window in the bar room.

Melissa nodded. "Definitely let's take that one. We can watch the snow and enjoy the atmosphere at the same time."

They settled in, and soon a young man in a plaid flannel and jeans came over to them. "Welcome to the Iron Brew. We're known for our hearty Scottish pub grub, our extensive list of Scotch, and our good banter."

"We're glad to be here," said Melissa.

He handed them menus.

"So many Scottish beers," noted Melissa.

"They also have a lot of mocktails, teas, and coffees for daytime. And they run the brunch menu well into the afternoon, so if you want porridge or their sticky toffee French toast you're in luck," said Caitlin.

"Sticky toffee French toast? You've gotta be kidding me," Melissa hadn't realized how long it had been since she'd eaten an actual meal.

"Dead serious," said Caitlin.

"Bring it!" said Melissa. They sat back and listened to the music pour from the speakers overhead. Melissa hadn't felt this relaxed in ages, and it was doing her a world of good.

The waiter came back.

"I'd like a cappuccino and the sticky toffee French toast," said Melissa.

"And I'll have the full Scottish breakfast," said Caitlin.

"Anything to drink?"

"Just tea. Earl Gray," said Caitlin.

"You've gone full-on Scottish," commented Melissa.

"It was a life-changing trip, and I have you to thank for it," said Caitlin.

"And I also like to take some credit," said a tall man in a blue flannel shirt and jeans. A cascade of long, wavy dark hair fell over his face as he greeted them. "Welcome, Melissa! Thanks for coming!"

Melissa stood and gave him a hug.

"Angus! I love your place. It's fantastic. I love the decor. I love the atmosphere. And the music is absolutely you."

"Thanks. I try to make it feel like a little bit of Scotland here in Boston. The parts I miss the most," said Angus as he pulled up a chair. "You're not back here permanently, are you? Not that we wouldn't love to have you."

"No, I'm just here to get my ducks in a row before I finalize all the paperwork to stay in Scotland," said Melissa.

"Grand. It really suits you. And your home is wonderful," said Angus.

"Right on Loch Ness. My eleven-year-old Scooby-Doo-watching self is thrilled. Heck, my present-day self is thrilled!" said Melissa.

Her gaze lifted to the wall behind the bar where the infamous grainy black and white photo of Nessie hung. She was aware that this particular photo had been debunked as a hoax, but she appreciated that Angus was a believer. After all, what's life without a little mystery and wonder?

The waiter brought their drinks. "Anything for you, Angus?"

"I'm good, thanks." Angus got up. "Back to the salt mines."

Caitlin gave him a quick kiss. "Stop back later?"

"Of course."

They sipped their warm drinks and looked out the window. The city bustled with pedestrians—families with strollers, dog walkers, and some ambitious joggers bundled for the cold.

Melissa scanned the rest of the Iron Brew, taking in every detail of the bar area. The walls were adorned with exposed wood and bricks, each one decorated with paintings of breathtaking Scottish landscapes. Highland cows and sheep grazed peacefully in the scenes, while maps of Scotland and photos of notable Scots added a touch of history to the room. A cozy stone fireplace crackled in the corner, casting a warm glow over the fifteen wooden tables scattered throughout the main restaurant area. The air was filled with the comforting smell of hearty food and chatter from other patrons, creating a welcoming atmosphere. "This place is just perfect. If I had come here before finding out about Greenhill House, I might have never left!"

"Not true. I truly believe that house and that land are your destiny," said Caitlin.

Melissa threw back her head and laughed. "Who are you, and what have you done with my practical, no-nonsense friend Caitlin?"

The waiter returned with their orders. Melissa's plate had thick slices of brioche drizzled with sticky toffee sauce, topped with a whipped toffee butter, with blueberries sprinkled over the top.

Caitlin's full Scottish breakfast included eggs, potatoes, white pudding, black pudding, and a tomato.

As they finished their breakfast, the snow started falling harder. "It's beautiful out there," said Melissa, watching the giant flakes cascade to the ground. They were beginning to stick. "The last few winters, we've hardly had any snow."

"I know, right? We might actually live up to our reputation for snowy New England winters again."

Melissa dug around in her purse for her credit card, but Caitlin shook her head. "Angus won't allow it."

"That's ridiculous."

Caitlin shrugged. "He's a proud man."

"Well, I'll have to leave a hefty tip."

"That's the way."

"Except I don't have any US dollars," Melissa said, flushing.

"I've got it."

"How ridiculous. You're driving me around. You're hosting me … I'll get dinner."

"No worries, Melissa."

They left a hefty tip for the server and thanked Angus before walking back to the car. Melissa pulled her relatively thin coat around her. "I bet I've got a better coat and snow boots in storage."

"Do you wanna go there now?" asked Caitlin.

"Ugh. No, I'll suffer through today. I don't want to tackle that mess until the jet lag wears off."

* * *

As they drove across town to the building where Colin worked, Melissa couldn't contain her excitement. It had only been a few weeks, but she already missed him and couldn't wait to see him.

"Want me to just drop you off, or should I go in with you?" asked Caitlin.

"Whatever is easier," said Melissa. "Actually, you probably need a break from me to do your own thing, right? Go ahead and run your errands or go home and do what you need to do."

"I'll come back in an hour? Two?" asked Caitlin.

"Seriously, whatever works for you. He'll certainly be working, but maybe I'll grab coffee with him."

"Text me."

CHAPTER 2

Colin sat at his desk looking out at the cold, bleak Charles River. Years ago, when he'd first moved to Boston from Scotland, the snow piled up everywhere each winter. However, the last few years, it had been just cold enough to chill someone to the bone as the rain washed away what little snow had fallen. He was happy to see it was snowing steadily for once.

Colin had always loved Boston winters. When he wasn't cross-country skiing in the Boston suburbs, he drove a few hours north to Vermont and New Hampshire for downhill slopes. He dined out, saw Broadway-in-Boston shows, and could often catch a show in previews before it made its debut in New York. He'd moved to the US eager to carve out a life for himself, and he'd done it. He'd cultivated a great circle of friends, co-workers, and clients, and he'd made himself a real home in Boston—he'd thought. But after spending the past few weeks in his hometown of Inverness, Scotland, his old life in America that once had felt so full of promise now felt hollow.

He glanced through the stack of briefs that he needed to get back up to speed on after the holidays and this past MLK weekend. It was going to take a lot of coffee to keep him alert enough to get through those. His ex-girlfriend, Fiona, had talked almost the whole flight back from Scotland. She was also a lawyer, and one who never lost, which meant that she couldn't take no for an answer. Somehow—even though she knew he'd met someone recently and there'd been significant sparks—Fiona had strong-armed her way into having dinner with Colin. She had implied it was just as friends, but he doubted that was her full intent. She couldn't lose. Even if she didn't want to win, she would try to do anything she could to avoid the loss.

He'd been so caught up in getting away and starting anew that he hadn't realized what he was leaving behind. Melissa was so full of wide-eyed innocence and joy. She loved exploring Scotland, and Colin had loved every minute of their time together. Why had he left so suddenly? Just because he'd bought a ticket didn't mean he'd had to use it. Colin had never felt so depressed. This wasn't the post-Christmas blues, either. This was something new. What he needed was a pint with some friends, not dinner with Fiona.

* * *

COLIN WAS FINALLY ABSORBED in his work. But soon the door burst open, an angry Dave charged in with Colin's apologetic assistant, Meghana, shaking her head as she followed him into the office.

Dave was Colin's client and Melissa's ex. Colin didn't even want to think about what this situation could do to his law career. He never should've gotten to know Melissa, but fate had other plans. They'd first met at the airport, then rode the same plane to Edinburgh, then the same train to Inverness. When the man at the hardware store had sent Melissa to Colin's father for firewood, that had sealed their fate—at least the getting acquainted part. The rest had just unfolded, and now he could very well lose his job … or get disbarred.

"Hello, David," said Colin calmly. "I don't believe we had an appointment today. I'm deep in a case right now. I'm afraid we'll need to schedule something for tomorrow morning."

"I had an idea," said Dave.

Colin set down his cup of coffee and looked at his phone. "All right. Have a seat. Would you like some coffee?"

Dave leered at Meghana. "I'll take two sugars, honey."

Meghana blinked at him and pointed to the Keurig machine in the corner of the office. "Coffee machine's over there." She rolled her eyes and walked out. Colin hid his amusement.

"What can I do for you?" asked Colin.

"I want to speed things up," said Dave.

"Okay. Your ex-wife has agreed to let you have the house and half of the money. I believe that's more than generous."

"And as you know, I want half of her inheritance. That house in Scotland I've been hearing about," said Dave.

Colin took a deep breath. "Then you'd be collecting more than half of what—"

Dave interrupted, "No, half means half. Cut down the middle. 50% for me, 50% for her."

Colin nodded. "Well, that's a good idea, but unfortunately the divorce has already been finalized."

"Then why don't I have the notarized final copies of the divorce in my hands?"

"They're on their way. We were closed yesterday for Martin Luther King Day and I just need to—"

"No, you don't need to. You're my lawyer, and I'm telling you to stop the divorce until I can sort this house thing out."

Colin froze. "I can't do that."

"You can, and you will. I wanna put that Scotland house on the market. Me and my girlfriend wanna sell the place and get a condo in Vegas," said Dave.

"I understand," said Colin through gritted teeth. "Well, these things can take time. And we'd need a buyer. Not a lot of people want a broken-down old place in the middle of nowhere."

"Her friends made it sound like a palace," said Dave.

"I can assure you, the closest thing to a palace is Inverness Castle, and it's nothing like that," said Colin.

Dave blinked. "You've seen it?"

Damn. "I'm from the area," Colin said.

"Well, maybe you can buy it, then. Fix it up," said Dave. "In the meantime, I'm gonna go check out some condos online."

CHAPTER 3

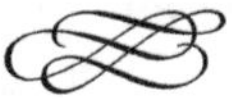

Melissa loved walking past the line of old brick two- and three-story brownstones in the Back Bay, and as luck would have it, Colin's office turned out to be in a particularly quaint brownstone right across from the Charles. She wondered when and how her ex, Dave, had found Colin. This part of Boston wasn't Dave's cup of tea, but Colin's law firm probably was well known and well-advertised.

She climbed up the snowy steps and opened the heavy wooden door. What must have been an entryway for the original home was now a small lobby with signs for the various offices and where to find them. She read *Colin MacGregor - Attorney at Law, Suite 303.* She eyed the tiny elevator warily and decided to take the stairs instead.

Melissa hefted herself up the two flights of stairs and finally reached the office. She decided to do the "old school" trick—calling him from a few feet away and then popping in while they were chatting. In fact, it was kind of how they first met.

She dug into her purse, found her phone, and dialed.

As the phone rang, her heart pounded in anticipation. Finally, he answered.

"Uh, hi ..."

"Hi, Colin! How are you doing? I've been really missing you. Don't you just wish we could get together for coffee or something in person? Long distance relationships are so hard."

"Uh, yeah ... that sounds good. Listen, I have a client here."

"I sure would love to see your office. I bet you have a great view of the Charles," Melissa said.

Melissa was still standing outside Colin's office when she heard a commotion from within. Her stomach twisted into knots as she recognized her ex-husband's voice.

"Enough with the personal phone calls. I'm a paying customer," said Dave in his flat, always-annoyed voice.

"Thank you for that, but I'm with a client now. I'll, uh, talk soon," said Colin.

"Oh my God. I'm here, too," whispered Melissa. Her face flushed as she turned and raced toward the stairs, her heart pounding.

"Fine. You're on the phone? I'm leaving!" snapped Dave.

Dave brushed past Meghana and opened the door to find Melissa standing at the top of the stairs.

"What are you doing here?" he asked.

"I, um ..." Melissa's thoughts raced as she tried to come up with a plausible explanation. *How could this possibly be happening?*

"Are you spying on me or something?"

Melissa glanced around the signs and spotted a dentist opposite Colin's office.

"Why would I spy on you? I was just, um ... looking for my dentist," she said lamely, walking toward the door.

Dave blocked her path.

Meghana stepped into the hall. "My mistake," said Meghana. "This woman came in looking to use the restroom, and I wasn't very clear with my instructions. She must have taken a wrong turn while I was on the phone. Ma'am, the restroom is just down the main hall. We don't have public restrooms in the offices."

Relief washed over Melissa, and she nodded a silent thank you to Meghana. Dave looked from Melissa to Meghana, knowing something was up, but still trying to put two and two together.

"What were you even doing here?" Dave asked.

"I was just out and about, taking a walk and ... Well, you know me. I had to go. This seemed like a place that would have a restroom, so ... " Melissa winced, realizing her story had changed.

"I thought you'd moved to Scotland." Dave's eyes narrowed in suspicion.

Melissa nodded. "I'm just back to collect some things from storage, see friends and family. So I'll just be on my way."

"Where are you staying?"

"That's none of your business," said Melissa, crossing her arms in front of her.

"So was it the dentist or the restroom? Why would you come back here to the dentist?"

"I lost an aligner and needed a new one," said Melissa. "Remember? You were mad they cost so much. Silly me."

"They can't mail them?"

"Uh, they needed to check the fit. Remember, they did a scan of my mouth. They needed me to come in and check that it was the same. It's like when you need to see the doctor before they can refill a prescription ... you know?" She knew she was a terrible liar, and this was getting her nowhere, but for whatever reason she couldn't stop.

He was still blocking her way. When they were married, he'd been gruff, but he'd never been like this. Melissa had never been scared of him before, but now she was.

"I need to get by, Dave," said Melissa in a voice that she knew sounded weak and meek. But she was a different woman now. She was independent. She could face this oaf.

Gathering her resolve, Melissa pushed past him like he was a high school bully blocking her path to the locker. Astounded, he turned and watched as she hurried down the stairs.

Dave called after her, "Don't you need to see the dentist?"

"I already did," she called back.

She walked with purpose down the street in case Dave could see her. Then, shaking, she pulled out her phone and texted Caitlin.

M - Can you pick me up or should I call a ride?

C - I'm in Kenmore Square. BRB.

M - I'll wait on the corner.

Caitlin was already waiting in her car at the corner when Melissa arrived, shaken but proud that she'd made it through her first face-to-face confrontation with Dave. Baby steps. But she had taken them.

"That was fast," said Caitlin as Melissa hopped into the car.

"Yeah. It didn't exactly go as planned."

As Melissa explained what happened, Caitlin tried to comfort her.

"I mean, I'm just too impulsive. I should have let Colin know I was in town."

Caitlin shook her head. "There's no way you could have known Dave would be there."

"Yeah. He's just getting worse. Now that I'm away, I can't believe I was ever married to him."

"You were kind of ... sheltered. I'm not sure what the word is, but you didn't know any better."

Melissa groaned. She knew Caitlin was right, but the gut punch of being called out was a wake-up call.

"But now you do. So we're going to celebrate you all weekend. First stop? Shopping on Newbury Street. We can get together with Colin once he's off the clock."

Caitlin parked in the structure underneath the Boston Common, and they emerged to the grand park blanketed in soft, giant snowflakes. Melissa tucked her hair into a lavender knit cap and wrapped a matching scarf around her neck.

Melissa's phone rang. It was Colin.

"Hey, Melissa ..." Melissa drew in her breath at the sound of his lovely Highland accent, as she always did. "So, you're coming to Boston?" he said with amusement.

She flushed with embarrassment but was grateful that he was always so laid back and understanding. The complete opposite of Dave.

"I don't know what I was thinking trying to surprise you at work like that. I'm so sorry," said Melissa.

"It was a wonderful idea, just bad timing. And, well, you know how Dave can be."

"No kidding."

"I get off at six tonight. Shall I meet you and Caitlin for dinner?" asked Colin.

"That would be wonderful. I'm so sorry," said Melissa.

"It's okay. I just hope you're all right. Meghana said he really had you rattled," said Colin.

"Yeah. I'm good," said Melissa.

"See you soon."

Melissa hung up and took a deep breath.

"Does dinner at the North End sound good?"

"You know, thinking of you and Colin and all that amazing Italian food, I'd rather let you have your Lady and the Tramp spaghetti moment. I can sit at the bar at the Iron Brew," Caitlin said with a playful twinkle in her eye.

"You sure?"

"Absolutely!"

As they walked down Newberry Street, Melissa and Caitlin passed by rows of colorful storefronts, each adorned with unique window displays. The boutiques and high-end stores they visited were filled with racks of clothing in all different styles, and the cozy corner cafe had a homey atmosphere with wooden tables and chairs and a cheerful view of the snow-covered park.

They each ordered a coffee and sat at a table by the window.

"Shopping therapy works every time," said Caitlin.

Melissa looked at their collection of little bags and packages. "You'd think it was Christmas," she said, sipping her coffee.

"Nothing like January sales. You'll probably be needing winter hats and gloves well into March in the Highlands," said Caitlin. "So what have you missed most?"

Melissa thought for a moment. "I mean, mostly friends and family. You always hear about Americans living abroad and sending away for American foods like peanut butter or something. But really, anything I want is available, and if it's not, I can order it. That said, it's good to walk down a familiar street and know what the shops are."

"What do you want to do next?" asked Caitlin, biting into a biscotti.

Melissa thought about it. She'd lived in the Boston area for a while. "Well, I think I've done all the touristy things: Paul Revere's home, the Old North Church, Faneuil Hall and Quincy Market, the Freedom Trail ..."

Caitlin nodded. "What's something you can only do in Boston that we haven't done?"

She thought for a moment. "Duck boat tours?"

"Not in this cold!"

"Museum of Fine Arts? Isabella Stewart Gardner museum?" Caitlin asked.

Just then, Melissa's phone buzzed. Dreading the idea that it could be Dave, she didn't even want to look at it. It buzzed again. Then it rang. Melissa reached for her phone, then breathed a sigh of relief. It was her sister, Emma.

"You've been in town nearly a whole day, and we haven't made plans. Why don't we meet up at the golf course and do a little cross-country skiing, and then you can have dinner at my house?" Emma had a way of jumping past pleasantries and getting to the point.

"Great idea, Emma! And I was going to call you. I just haven't had a chance yet."

"A likely story ..." said Emma, her tone teasing and warm. "I've got a pot of clam chowder that Thomas will keep an eye on. I can be at the golf course in fifteen minutes."

"Perfect!" said Melissa. "But can I ask a favor?"

"Of course."

"Can Colin join us for dinner? We can bring more—"

"Absolutely! And don't bring a thing. I definitely want to meet this guy!"

CHAPTER 4

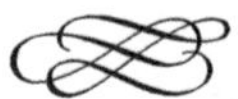

Melissa called Colin and let him know about the change of plans, then Caitlin drove them to a golf course in Auburndale where they met up with Emma, who was already in line to rent skis.

"So good to see you!" said Melissa as she hugged her older sister. Emma's bright blue eyes complimented the riot of auburn curls that poked out of her green ski hat.

"I've missed you so much. Thomas and I are hoping to visit in the summer when we have more vacation time," said Emma.

"That would be fantastic! I'd love to show you all around," said Melissa.

They reached the front of the line. As they filled out the paperwork, they shared updates on Emma's life and Melissa's new home, while carefully avoiding the subject of Dave.

Melissa donned her skis. Initially, she felt like a klutz following her sleek, athletic sister and Caitlin, who seemed to be naturally good at everything. First she veered too close to the snow machine, then had trouble following the tracks someone had cut into the snow. Emma pointed toward the woods, and they followed her down a small hill where Melissa finally lost her balance. Emma held out her hand as Melissa looked up at her from the snowy ground. "I've got you, sis."

She hoisted Melissa up, and soon they were back on course with Emma in the lead, Caitlin following, and Melissa marching to the tune of her own drum behind them.

As she zipped and glided through the snow, the exercise did wonders for Melissa's mental state. She reflected on her encounter with Dave. That was the first time she'd ever stood up to him, and she felt so much better for it. With each *zip* and *zas* through the snow, she felt stronger. The bright Boston sun on her face, the clear blue sky, and the shimmer of snow made her feel that anything was possible. And for the first time in her life, she began to realize that anything really was possible. She was strong. Each dig of her ski pole into the ground propelled her further ahead. She reached a bend in the pre-formed track and nearly slid over, but somehow she leaned at the perfect moment and regained her balance. Soon she was gliding onward. It was exhilarating, and exactly what she needed.

When they circled back toward the parking lot, Melissa was confident, rosy cheeked, and relaxed for the first time all afternoon.

"I have to remember that just because it's winter doesn't mean I can't get outside," said Melissa.

"It must be dark there in the winters," said Emma.

"Incredibly. I thought it was bad here in Boston when it gets dark at 4:30, but over there …" Her voice trailed off.

"But you like it?" asked Emma.

"I love it. The people there are all so friendly. The homes are cozy. They have a whole thing, *coorie*—you know that *hygge* movement you saw on the Internet a while back? That cozy, warm feeling you have when …" Melissa paused, not quite sure how to explain the Danish lifestyle trend of warm blankets, cozy sweaters, tea by the fire, and good company.

"When you've just finished skiing and now you're going to cozy up by the fire?" ventured Emma.

"Exactly. That's a whole movement in Scotland, and with the weather and darkness, it makes a lot of sense."

Emma nodded. "It's on! C'mon, let's get to my house!"

They peeled off their ski gear, made their returns, and got back into their respective cars. "I'm just about five minutes away, Caitlin. Follow me," said Emma.

As they drove in Caitlin's car, Melissa breathed a deep sigh of relief.

"Feeling better?" asked Caitlin.

"So much. There's nothing quite like a little time in nature to set me straight. I think it's exactly what I needed."

"This afternoon must have been worse than you let on."

Melissa nodded. "I don't want to talk about it."

* * *

EMMA'S HOUSE was a cozy two-story Cape Cod nestled in the woods, surrounded by pine and maple trees, with an old-school New England stone fence along the driveway.

"What a great place!" said Caitlin, getting out of the car and walking toward the front steps where Emma waited.

"It's perfect. A fifteen minute drive into Boston, easy access to outstanding museums and restaurants, and yet we're in the woods," said Emma.

"Amazing."

As they strolled up the sidewalk, Colin pulled into the driveway. Melissa ran back to meet him. He was still sitting in the driver's seat when Melissa opened the car door and planted a warm kiss on his cheek. He laughed and quickly got out of the car to give her a proper kiss.

Hand in hand, they strolled up the driveway to join Caitlin at Emma's front door.

As Emma opened the door, Melissa felt butterflies in her stomach as she looked between two of the most important people in her life.

"Emma, I'd like to introduce Colin MacGregor. Colin, meet my sister, Emma."

Colin stuck out his hand for a handshake while Emma leaned in for a hug. They both laughed at the confusion before finally settling on a quick embrace and an awkward handshake.

"We're a huggy family," said Melissa with a laugh as she put her arm around Colin.

Thomas, Emma's husband, arrived at the door and greeted Melissa with a hug, then shook Colin's hand. "Come on in, Colin, and welcome! Caitlin, good to see you," Thomas said with a quick embrace.

Inside Emma's house was just as cozy as the outside. A fire crackled in the fireplace, an inviting sectional couch was covered with handmade throws and pillows, and a gray-and-white kitten snoozed on a braided rug next to the fireplace.

"And who is this?" asked Melissa, getting down on the floor next to the kitten.

"Big Papi," replied Thomas.

Melissa laughed. "Of course it is. Only the biggest Red Sox fans would name their tiny kitten—"

"We're optimistic about this season," said Thomas.

"And Thomas is a lifelong fan," said Emma.

"What a lovely home," said Colin as he looked at the childhood photos of Emma and Melissa by the fireplace.

"Thank you," said Emma. "It's a work in progress. I wish I had someone with Melissa's eye for interior design for the new paint job we need."

"You know I'll help with whatever you need, Em," said Melissa.

"Soup's on," said Thomas.

They sat around the dining room table with blue pottery

bowls full of steaming, thick clam chowder. Melissa shook a hefty portion of pepper onto hers and dipped a piece of crunchy bread into the creamy soup.

"This is amazing, Thomas. I must have the recipe," said Melissa.

"It's easy," said Thomas with a twinkle in his eye. "My mother's family secret. Go to the store. Find the frozen section. Get the local bestselling, award-winning chowder. Heat. Impress your friends and family."

"Well, you did a great job," Melissa said with a laugh.

"All right, I think we've had enough of the pleasantries," said Emma. "Spill the tea. Tell me what's going on with you!"

"So much I can't even decide how to begin," said Melissa.

"Come on …" Emma said, all but pleading.

"Well, you know Dave surprised me with his request for a divorce right after Thanksgiving. Then there was that letter I received about inheriting a home in Scotland."

"So you jumped ship immediately?" asked Thomas.

"I'm sure Emma has told you I'm pretty impulsive. But what else was I going to do? Dave was getting the house, and I just … didn't want to be here. No offense."

"We totally understand," said Emma.

"Then I met Colin in line for coffee at the airport." As Melissa gestured toward Colin, their hands brushed, and she felt gooey inside again. "He had this fantastic accent, and he defended me when the barista messed up my order. So that was nice. But then I kept running into him—at the train station and in Inverness," Melissa continued.

"When she finally showed up at my dad's croft for firewood, I started feeling like this wasn't a coincidence," said Colin.

"You knew she was stalking you, eh?" said Emma.

"I was not!" said Melissa in mock offense.

"I think it was meant to be," said Colin, planting a kiss on her cheek. Melissa's face suddenly felt very warm.

"And then Caitlin set off to 'rescue me.' We got separated, and somehow, she found herself snowed in with a handsome musician!" laughed Melissa.

"Do tell," said Emma.

"His name is Angus. I ended up going off with Melissa's friend, Lindsay, after Melissa decided to run off with her new boyfriend."

"I didn't decide anything! But you might say I fell for him," said Melissa, taking Colin's hand.

"We fell for each other," said Colin, laughing.

"And it landed us in urgent care!" said Melissa.

"So how did you end up with the musician?"

"Long story, but we thought we'd meet up with Melissa and Colin later, so we went sightseeing on Loch Ness."

"As one does," joked Emma.

"Well, I do ..." said Melissa.

"Of course you do," teased Emma.

"And we met Angus and Drew, who warned us about the impending storm, and we ended up staying at Drew's Inn," finished Caitlin.

"And that's when she fell for Angus," said Melissa.

They stayed late into the night, chatting by the fire, catching up. At first, Melissa felt guilty about leaving home for Inverness, but as the evening went on, it became clear that she was only a plane ride or a phone call away. They really had started up right where they'd left off. And with Colin living in Boston, there would be multiple reasons to come back. *But ... then why live in Scotland?* The guilt came flooding back, and she felt the little pit in her stomach again. *Or maybe she was just tired?*

Caitlin noticed her friend was losing steam. "You must be so jetlagged."

"I didn't even think of the time difference," said Emma.

"It's all good. But I do think the travel, shopping, and then skiing is beginning to catch up with me. We probably should get going," Melissa said as she hoisted her sore body from the comfortable chair. "Thanks so much for everything, Em," said Melissa.

"Thanks to you for coming over, M," Emma said, getting up to see them all out.

Melissa turned to Colin. "We were *M&M* in middle school."

"*Eminem* in high school," laughed Emma.

Melissa gave her sister a long, warm hug. "So good to see you," said Melissa. "I really hope you can come in the summer. There's so much I want to show you."

"I'll be there with bells on," said Emma.

"So wonderful to meet you both," said Colin, shaking hands with Emma and Thomas.

Suddenly, the reality of not seeing her sister other than a few quick visits a year overwhelmed Melissa. "Please don't forget to call or FaceTime."

"You know I will," said Emma.

"You'll forget?!" asked Melissa.

"I'll remember, you goof!" said Emma, swatting her sister.

Melissa began to blink back tears, and Emma hugged her again. "Hey, I'm just a phone call away. And I'm not busy. Let's get together tomorrow, too."

"Good idea. Somehow this goodbye felt so final." Melissa fanned her face, hoping the tears gathering in the corners of her eyes wouldn't fall.

"Mel, I'm right here. Only a phone call away. Just like Caitlin," Emma said, reassuring Melissa, just like she had been doing since they were young.

Melissa took a deep breath. "You're right."

Still a little emotional, Melissa followed Caitlin and Colin down the snowy sidewalk to their cars.

"Maybe we can grab dinner in the North End tomorrow night after work?" asked Colin.

"I'd love to."

He gently brushed her neck with a kiss, leaving Melissa wishing she could never leave him.

"Why did I get so excited about living in Scotland when everyone I love lives here?" Melissa wondered aloud.

"Everything's going to be alright," said Colin. "See you tomorrow?"

She nodded and pulled herself away from him and got into Caitlin's car.

Melissa could barely speak as Caitlin backed up the car.

It's one thing to impulsively go after your dreams, Melissa thought to herself as Caitlin drove. *But it's another thing to take time and consider the consequences.*

CHAPTER 5

The next day, Colin had trouble focusing at work. Meghana noticed him getting up for his fourth cup of tea and finally laughed. "Mr. MacGregor, you never take vacation time. It's Friday. You have no meetings, no appointments, and as far as I can see, you're completely caught up since your trip. That nice woman is in town, and, if I may be so bold, I think you should go spend time with her."

Colin set down his Earl Gray. "You're right."

"I know I'm right," said Meghana. "Go on. Get out of here."

"I expect you to take a day full of … whimsy. Or whatever it is you enjoy," said Colin awkwardly.

She laughed, but he looked at her seriously. "I appreciate this. You're right. All I do is work."

"Work isn't everything … Although you're my boss, so I should be careful saying that."

Colin laughed.

"Come on, Colin. Live a little," Meghana insisted, her words hanging in the air as he shut down his computer and packed up his briefcase.

She arched an eyebrow, and he looked down at his briefcase. "You're right. I don't need this," said Colin.

"Exactly. Leave it behind. I'll take care of any emails that come through," said Meghana.

"Nope, you should take some time off too. Have you ever had tea at the Boston Public Library? Or lunch at the Isabella Stewart Gardner Museum? Use the company card. Seriously. My treat."

"Oh, I couldn't possibly," she protested.

"You went through a lot with my client yesterday, and you helped Melissa. You deserve a treat."

Colin put on his tweed cap and coat and walked out of the building without a briefcase for the first time in his memory. It felt good. He felt lighter. The snow was falling, the sky was somehow still a brilliant blue, and the air was crisp and cold. Colin couldn't believe he hadn't considered taking the day off to see Melissa. *What was wrong with him? So focused on all the wrong things.*

* * *

DESPITE THE CHILLY DAY, Boston Common bustled with people. Parents walked with strollers and dogs, the scent of grilled onions and sausage filled the air, and street performers entertained the crowds. As they walked, they passed by vendors selling hot cocoa. The skating pond was frozen over, with people twirling and gliding on the ice, their laughter and shouts filling the air.

"The skating pond!" said Melissa, her rosy cheeks painted with excitement. "Emma and I used to love to come here as kids. Did you skate when you were younger?"

Colin shook his head *no*. "We mostly went sledding and worked on the croft. I played hockey as a lad, though."

"So you did ice skate."

"More like, I went into battle with blades on my feet and a stick in my hand, but sure … you can call it ice skating," said Colin.

Melissa laughed, but Colin was reflecting. *Had he always been this way? Wound up so tightly? He'd never even skated for pleasure.*

They stood in line, rented skates, and put them on.

Colin helped steady Melissa as she wobbled on the ice. She loved the feeling of his arm wrapped around her waist as they slowly made their way onto the pond. The ice was smooth and glistened in the afternoon sunlight. Traces of snow dusted its surface. As they grew more confident in their skating abilities, their movements became fluid and graceful. Their laughter echoed across the pond. Colin realized he hadn't had this much fun since … he was home in Scotland. And before that? He couldn't remember. *When had he started taking life so seriously?* He listened to Melissa's contagious, joyful laughter and was glad to have her in his life.

As they returned their skates, Colin looked at his watch. "Tea time back home. Fancy a hot chocolate?"

"Always."

The hot chocolate was steaming in their mugs, topped with a generous serving of tiny white marshmallows that bobbed on its surface. Melissa took a sip, coating her lips and nose with a fluffy layer of melted marshmallow. Colin couldn't help but laugh and tease her playfully for the sweet mustache she now sported.

"It suits you, Mel."

"I'm sure it does …" said Melissa.

The once bright blue sky was now painted with hues of pink, orange, and purple as the sun began to dip below the horizon. The cityscape was illuminated by the warm, golden light as buildings and landmarks stood silhouetted against the colorful backdrop.

"Shall we have an early dinner?" asked Colin.

"Sounds good," said Melissa.

They walked hand in hand, their breath visible in the cold air as they chatted and laughed. The snow-covered ground of the Boston Common made a crunching sound under their feet, and the trees were adorned with twinkling lights. As they made their way toward the North End, their faces were flushed with rosy cheeks, and their eyes sparkled with excitement. Colin felt relaxed and carefree—more alive than he had felt in years.

The streets were bustling with people hurrying home, bundled up in winter coats to shield themselves from the chilly air.

The North End—a Boston neighborhood known as Little Italy that dates back to colonial times—sparkled with white lights and old-world splendor. They passed tiny Italian bodegas, gelaterías, cafés and pastry shops, as well as the myriad of elegant Italian restaurants the neighborhood was known for. As they walked the cobblestone streets, they passed the quaint, white Old North Church—made famous by Paul Revere and Longfellow—and made their way down Hanover Street, where there was already a huge line around the corner of Mike's Pastry, home of the best cannoli Melissa had ever had.

Colin held the door for Melissa as they reached a tiny, elegant, but comfortable restaurant called *Fatto a Mano*. The place was a long, narrow space with only about a dozen small tables for two alongside an exposed brick wall. Each table had a white table cloth, a candle, and wine glasses. "It smells amazing in here!" said Melissa. "You won't believe it, but this might be the thing I missed most about Boston—the smell of fresh tomato sauce and garlic bread!"

"I know. We have it in Scotland, but not like this. And since we can't have dinner in Venice tonight, I thought this would be the next best thing," said Colin.

"Have you been here before?" asked Melissa.

"No, it's new. A friend recommended it. Everything's—"

"Made by hand," finished Melissa.

"Do you speak Italian?" he asked.

"No, just important things: *formaggio, vino, gelato di nocciola,*" she said.

"Ah. I still have much to learn about you, m'lady."

The waiter handed them wine lists and a menu and poured still water from a cobalt blue bottle. With the soft glow of the candlelight and the nostalgic Italian music, Melissa finally began to relax.

"You know, is this our first actual date?" said Melissa.

"I think so," said Colin.

"I mean, we've been to lots of places in groups. And we've been to urgent care together," said Melissa.

"I cherish those memories of us hobbling around on ice," said Colin. "But this ..."

"This is nice," said Melissa.

They ordered chianti and fried calamari to start.

The waiter poured the wine at their table and soon returned with a basket of amazing crusty bread accompanied by dark green olive oil and a tapenade. As their hands brushed while reaching for the bread Melissa felt a tingling surge of electricity race through her and she couldn't help but admire how handsome he looked, his cheeks still rosy from the cold and his blue eyes twinkling as he raised his glass of wine.

"Cheers!" said Colin.

"Sláinte!" said Melissa. "Wow, this looks amazing. Homemade Italian bread, straight out of the oven."

As the waiter brought various courses—salad, pasta, cheese, and finally espresso—they laughed and talked and almost forgot that they lived on opposite sides of the ocean.

"We should do this more often," said Colin, before realization sank in. They lived thousands of miles apart now.

"We should," said Melissa. Colin noticed that her face was filled with doubt.

"We will, then," said Colin. "We'll make it all work out."

As he helped her on with her coat, and they stepped out into the magical snowy sidewalks of the old North End, optimism swept over Melissa again. "They have frequent-flyer credit cards. Business trips. Family visits and holidays. Facetime. We've got this."

As they strolled down Hanover Street, Colin and Melissa noticed the line at Mike's Pastry was unusually short.

"Do we dare?" Colin asked with a playful glint in his eye.

"Absolutely," Melissa replied without hesitation.

The bright fluorescent lights inside were a stark contrast to the street, but Melissa's discomfort quickly faded as she admired the array of pastries in the display case.

They had everything from birthday cakes, black-and-white cookies, brownies, lemon bars, eclairs, Boston Cream Pies, lobster tails—puffed pastry filled with cream. But the star of the menu was their cannoli. Colin and Melissa studied the menu: limoncello, pistachio, chocolate, hazelnut, chocolate chip, plain, strawberry, peanut butter, chocolate covered, Florentine, chocolate cream, amaretto … The list was endless.

"I have no idea," said Colin. "You decide."

Melissa stepped up to the counter. "We'd like a dozen cannoli. Cannolis?"

The clerk nodded.

"Two Florentines, two chocolate covered, one chocolate cream, two plain, one hazelnut … How many is that, Colin?"

"Eight," said Colin.

"What else?" asked Melissa.

"And two limoncello, a chocolate mint, um … peanut butter? Actually, another hazelnut."

The clerk gathered them all. "Powdered sugar?"

Colin looked to Melissa, who nodded *yes*.

"Yes."

The clerk dusted the cannoli with a light sprinkle of white

powdered sugar, then tied the box securely with string. Colin handed over a wad of cash, and they turned toward the exit, carrying the giant box with a mix of smug satisfaction and lingering guilt after their heavy meal.

"We'll enjoy these in the morning," Melissa said, perhaps louder than she meant to. Just as if she had summoned him with her words, her ex, Dave, walked through the door with his girlfriend, Samantha.

CHAPTER 6

In the crowded shop, there was no escape. No place to hide.

Melissa locked eyes with Dave, catching his astonished double-take as he shifted his gaze from her to Colin and the conspicuous box of pastries.

"Melissa. You're certainly getting around now that you're back in the States," said Dave.

"Have you lost weight?" asked Samantha in a syrupy, condescending voice as she glanced from Melissa to the pastry box.

Melissa was so flustered she stood frozen. So Dave kept pecking away at her.

"Lemme guess. You couldn't decide, so you got a dozen. Two of each of your favorites?" said Dave.

"Gonna eat those all by your lonesome, tonight?" asked Samantha.

Dave locked eyes with Colin. "No. It seems she's going to share them with my divorce lawyer. Samantha, meet Colin MacGregor, attorney at law. It would appear he likes to get up close and personal with his work."

“Good evening,” said Colin as he tried to brush past. Dave blocked him just as he had Melissa.

Dave was short and heavy, while Colin was lean and strong.

“Why don’t you just sod off!” said Melissa, grasping for words and realizing too late that she couldn’t pull off the Scottish colloquialism.

“Sod off? Really?” said Dave, a twisted smirk on his face. “By George, that chap’s already got you turning British, *innit*?” His horrible mockery of the accent made Melissa’s sound like that of a proper Scottish lass.

“You’ve got your divorce. I’ve signed all the paperwork. The house is yours. What more can you want?” she said, trying to mask her trembling voice with as much force as she could.

Dave's eyes darted back and forth between Colin, who clenched his fists, and Melissa, who avoided eye contact. His face contorted into an angry scowl.

"What else do I want?" he pondered aloud. "In negotiations, they say if the other side hasn't said no, you haven't asked for enough."

Melissa’s stomach twisted into a giant knot. *Was she going to be sick, right here, on Dave?*

“I think I know what I want. That is, if my lawyer’s still working for me and not the enemy,” said Dave.

“Oh, is this billable time?” said Colin. “I thought it was the weekend, but if you want me on the clock, I’ll be sure to—”

“Not so fast, MacGregor,” Dave said, inching closer to Colin and appraising the situation. “I smell wine on your breath. I see you sharing a box of pastries with my ex, at nine o’clock in what is arguably the most romantic neighborhood of Boston. And you call yourself a licensed lawyer?”

“It’s the weekend,” repeated Colin.

“How long have you been dating Melissa?” asked Dave. “Can’t find yourself a normal girlfriend? Gotta go look in the recycling bin?”

"Did ye, aye?" said Colin, and Melissa was shocked to see Colin puffing up like a bloke about to brawl in a pub over a football match. "Like Melissa said, sod off. I'll be happy to discuss this on Monday."

"I'll be looking into the rules and regulations about lawyers dating their client's exes," said Dave, his chest puffed up and his face red.

"And I'll be happy to find you've signed the last of the documents so I can move on to a new case," said Colin.

"Fine," said Dave. "But this isn't over."

"But it is, Dave. I've signed the documents," said Melissa.

"We'll see about that."

The look on Samantha's face made Melissa bite her cheek to keep from giggling. As they brushed past them and out into the chilly night air, Melissa held her breath until they were around the corner. Then she burst into laughter with a mix of tears.

"You okay?" asked Colin.

"You were brilliant!" said Melissa, pulling her coat around her as they hurried down the crowded street.

"Was I, though? He knows we're dating. Could be a serious problem," said Colin.

"I know what a cheapskate he is. This is not something he wants to draw out," said Melissa.

"Even if he thinks he can get his hands on the house in Scotland?" asked Colin, his forehead wrinkling in worry.

"Cheapskate to the core. He'll drop it so you don't bill him for that ... that ... whatever that was."

"Let's hope so."

* * *

WHEN COLIN DROPPED Melissa off at Caitlin's house, there was an awkward air of longing and regret.

"Thank you for taking me on our first date."

"Sorry it ended with a confrontation with … my client." Colin grimaced as he spoke.

"I'm sorry our first date ended with a confrontation with my ex."

"Stop apologizing, Melissa," said Colin softly as he stood next to Melissa on the steps, their breath visible in the cold air.

"Did you want to come in and have a cup of tea?" Melissa asked, uncertain where this was leading, but certain she didn't want to be away from Colin just yet.

"I would love to," He looked at her longingly. She leaned in and kissed him.

As he held her close and kissed her back, Melissa was filled with hope and optimism for the future. Whatever happened, this feeling between them was real. She hadn't felt like this in ages. Now, it was here, and she didn't think the warm glow inside her was going to go away.

Then Colin's phone buzzed. He ignored it, but a moment later, it buzzed again. And again. Reluctantly, he reached into his pocket and looked at it while Melissa studied his face, which soon grew serious.

"It's Dave. He …" Colin's eyes met Melissa's, his expression filled with a mix of regret and hesitation. "There's an attorney-client privilege."

"Oh."

"And I can't …" his voice trailed off as he thought. "But if I get to work right now, I can finalize everything before I need to check my email Monday morning. Then I won't have to take action on what he, um …"

"Right," said Melissa. As Colin put the phone back in his pocket, it dawned on Melissa. "He wants to stall so he can get the Scotland house," she said.

"Attorney-client privilege. But suffice it to say, I've got to get to work. Trust me?"

"Absolutely," said Melissa.

Colin kissed her again, gently but longingly.

"Caitlin's taking me to the airport Friday," Melissa said, her voice tinged with regret.

"He may well have orchestrated this to keep us apart," said Colin, gently running a hand down her cheek.

"I'm not sure he's that clever," said Melissa.

Colin laughed as he took her hands.

"This isn't goodbye," said Melissa.

"Of course not."

"I think I want to stay."

"I want you to stay. But believe me, you'd be much better off to have me get to work and not stop until those papers are finalized. That's all I can say."

"Goodnight, then," Melissa said.

"See you soon," said Colin, pressing one last kiss onto her lips.

"Absolutely. Goodnight."

Melissa stood on the porch and waved as Colin drove away. As she turned to go inside, she was struck by the fact that Dave had won either way. Either he'd get what he wanted or disrupt their happiness. Or both.

CHAPTER 7

Melissa spent the next day in a flurry of boxes, packing tape, and wrapping as she sorted through keepsakes and decided what was worth shipping overseas and what was going to be donated.

That evening, Melissa sipped a glass of wine in a window seat overlooking Jamaica Pond, feeling the relief that comes with lightning your load—quite literally—down to the bare necessities.

Snowflakes drifted gently down, and people strolled by, walking their dogs. She missed her border collie puppy, Jingles, terribly. Though she was relieved that her little dog was staying with Colin's father—who had trained Jingles and all of his ancestors—she longed for Jingles' unconditional cuddles and playful energy. Caitlin's large orange-and-white cat ambled over, stretched his paws, and gazed up at her.

"Sure, come on up, Ollie," said Melissa, patting her leg. Sure enough, the cat leapt up and nestled into her lap.

Caitlin came in with the bottle of wine, some cheese and crackers, and fruit. "Now he's got you just where he wants you!" she laughed.

"Trapped!" Melissa laughed as she scratched Ollie behind his ear.

Caitlin refilled Melissa's glass and offered her the plate of snacks. As she reached for a piece of cheese, Melissa groaned.

"I've got muscles aching that I never knew I had," Melissa said ruefully.

"You and me both," said Caitlin.

"Thanks for your help with all those boxes. I never could've moved all that without you and Emma," said Melissa.

"How are you ever going to unload the packages once they arrive in Inverness?"

"Colin's dad has a dolly. We'll figure it out. He and Lindsay know everyone in town, and it's a really strong community. Fortunately, I've got so much room in Greenhill House."

Just then, her phone buzzed an email alert: *New forms available via DocuSign.* Melissa clicked on the link and took a deep breath.

"Everything okay?" asked Caitlin.

"More than okay. Colin has officially finalized the divorce documents!"

"That calls for another glass of wine! Or should I find some celebration music so we can dance the night away?"

Melissa laughed. "All of the above. Maybe I should do this on a computer so I can see what I'm doing," she said.

Melissa opened her computer and found the link. She clicked and soon was engrossed in the legalese that would divide up everything she and Dave had owned together, although somehow he was keeping the Boston house. *Whatever. It didn't matter. She and Dave were officially over. She and Colin had a new beginning.*

Colin came over with a box of pizza from their favorite spot in the North End. They gathered around the fireplace, savoring the crispy, thin-crust slices generously topped with gooey cheese and spicy pepperoni. The aroma of fresh basil and melted mozzarella filled the room, and their cheeks were flushed from the never-ending glasses of wine Caitlin poured, until Colin finally covered his glass.

"No more for me. I'm on my way to being well and truly blootered," said Colin.

"Blootered, eh?" said Caitlin with a laugh. "I'll try that one out on Angus."

"Too bad he can't be here."

"The work of a pub owner's never done," said Caitlin. "Neither rain, nor snow, nor well and truly blootered … something."

Colin laughed, and he and Melissa began to clear the table.

"So all those things you can't tell me about … they're going to be okay?" asked Melissa as Colin ripped the pizza boxes in half for recycling.

"I can't discuss any work with my client. But, as your boyfriend, what I can tell you is that I'm not reading any work emails until Monday morning, because I was so busy finalizing the paperwork after that confrontation—which will be billed—on the weekend," said Colin, planting a kiss on her cheek.

Melissa sighed contentedly, while she tried to push aside thoughts about flying back to Scotland … alone.

RIDING in Caitlin's car toward Logan airport, Melissa was feeling all the feels as she watched the major landmarks of Boston pass by. Fenway. The Citgo sign. The Prudential Building. But as much as Boston was home, she was filled with nervous excitement at the prospect that she was heading *home*. Her real home. Her own home.

As Caitlin turned into the busy airport and followed the signs for departures, Melissa felt like the bottom of her stomach was dropping out. She started to hyperventilate a bit, and Caitlin glanced over at her.

"You okay?"

Melissa took a deep breath. "Think so?"

"What's up?"

"On my way here I felt like I was coming home. And now that you're taking me back to the airport, I'm realizing I'm actually *going* home. It's just ... a new feeling."

"I bet. You've got this, though, Mel."

Caitlin maneuvered the car into a spot at the curb and beamed at Melissa, her eyes sparkling with excitement. "It's an adventure, and one hundred percent meant for you."

Melissa hopped out. Caitlin popped the trunk, and Melissa grabbed her bag and hugged her friend. "Please come visit again."

"Angus comes out several times a year, so I will too."

THANKFULLY, the check-in and security lines moved quickly, giving Melissa enough time to get herself a sweet treat before boarding. At the gate, Melissa sipped her coffee and watched the people reading, playing games, and staring into space, and she realized it was only about six weeks ago that she'd sat at this same gate, waiting for a flight that would change her life forever. She took a deep breath and a long sip of her mocha. *She was on her way to greener pastures.*

CHAPTER 8

Melissa walked out of the Inverness airport, the cool, Scottish air a welcome change from the plane's confines. She hailed a taxi and gave the driver her address. A mix of anticipation and nostalgia settled in as the familiar scenery of the Highlands began to unfold through the window.

With each mile closer, she found the tension rolling off her shoulders and her breath calming. The landscape, a comforting blend of rolling hills and scattered cottages, felt unchanged by time. She was grateful to be able to return. As they approached the snowy banks of Loch Ness and turned onto the narrow road, she felt a tug in her heart. The taxi pulled into the driveway of a large stone home with a front gate. She was home. This was Greenhill House, an ancestral MacKenzie home that Melissa had inherited from a long-lost relative.

Opening the front door, she couldn't wait to see Jingles, her puppy. "Hello! Lindsay? Jingles?" Soon she heard the jingling bells of her adorable little dog, followed by the soft footsteps of her friend, Lindsay.

"Welcome back," said Lindsay.

And her new life was open to all possibilities.

* * *

THE NEXT FEW days were a blur of grocery shopping, picking up mail—not much there, just the first bills—catching up with her new friends, who felt a little like old friends, and working as the interior designer at the new MacAlister Inn where Lindsay would be the chef. The very idea of divorce, which caused her such incredible pain just a few months ago, ended up being the spark she needed to dramatically change her life for the better. Today was the best of all. She was going to finalize the paperwork on her home. She could barely believe it. Greenhill House, the lovely stone cottage on the banks of Loch Ness, was going to be 100% hers. Her own home in the highlands of Scotland, where she could cozy up in the library—her favorite room by far—with a cup of tea and watch the snow fall with Jingles at her side.

The chilly Scottish air nipped at Melissa's cheeks as she ascended the worn stone steps of the real estate office, her heart pounding with anticipation. She opened the large wooden door, and her jaw dropped. The building felt like something out of an old movie—old woodwork, a beautiful oak banister, and intricate carvings. Even her hometown of Boston's quaint old office buildings didn't have this kind of charm. She climbed the stairs up to a second floor office where she greeted Margaret Douglas. The kind-hearted real estate agent, with laughter lines etched deep in her face, was about to make Melissa's dreams a reality.

Margaret greeted her with a warm embrace. "Today's the day!" She handed Melissa a pen and a stack of papers. "Once it's signed, Greenhill House is officially all yours!"

"So exciting!" Melissa sat in the cushioned chair and picked up the pen. She flipped through, scanned the documents, signed here, added initials there—and then, just like that, it was done.

"Congratulations, Melissa!" said Margaret. "You're going to love your home."

"I absolutely am! You'll have to come out for dinner sometime soon."

"I'll bring the wine!" said Margaret. "But I'll wait until you're more settled in. Speaking of waiting, when is that new inn in town going to be finished? I know you've been working on the decor."

"Nearly done! We just have some finishing touches left, and the chef is working on menus. It's going to be so much fun when they open!"

"Sounds grand."

"Thank you so much for all your help, Margaret."

"It was my pleasure, really. Enjoy!"

As she descended the stairs into the main lobby and out the door, Melissa felt more accomplished than she'd felt in years. She tried to remember the last time she'd felt so strong and independent. Probably college graduation. But even then, she'd been under Dave's wing or standing in his shadow or ... what was the right metaphor for being in a bad relationship and not realizing it?

As she hopped into her little red car—a color she'd chosen on her own—and drove down the winding road toward her home, she sang along with the radio. Dave had always hated when she sang. Or had any fun, to be honest. What a jerk. Dave could keep the squirrel-infested house they had lived in back in Boston. Melissa laughed to herself as she remembered her parting act. Dave had always hated squirrels, so she'd left the hideous nut basket centerpiece his girlfriend had gifted her in the wide-open doorway as she left. *He might not deserve a piano falling on his head, but squirrels? Absolutely!* Melissa still enjoyed imagining scores of squirrels streaming into the home, eating the nuts, leaving a chaotic mess, and Dave coming home to find it.

Melissa sang loudly to Sinead O'Connor's "This is the Last Day of Our Acquaintance" as she steered the little red car along the lochside road. She reached a stone wall and a little gate and turned into the driveway. She felt a sense of relief and satisfaction as she knew now the home was officially hers and nothing could take that away. She loved everything about it. On one hand, it was stately enough to have a gate and a name, but really, it was a perfect cozy stone cottage. Far too big for one person, but a great place for parties.

She walked up the stone pathway which had recently been cleared of snow. As she opened the door, she could hear the cheerful bells of her border collie puppy, Jingles, racing toward the door to greet her. As she pet him, she felt a surge of love, hope, and optimism that she hadn't felt in ages.

* * *

MELISSA PULLED her car up in front of the newly renovated MacAlister Inn, a grand building situated along the tranquil River Ness in Inverness, Scotland. She grabbed her lookbook filled with inspiring decorating ideas and headed inside toward the kitchen.

Lindsay, Colin's sister and Melissa's friend, was busy chopping onions, leeks, and potatoes for dinner. "Hey there, how's it going, Chef?" asked Melissa.

"Living the dream," Lindsay replied, pausing to hug her friend.

"I can't wait to show Sydney and Elspeth all of my decorating plans," said Melissa.

Just then, Sydney, the manager of the new inn, strode in. "Can't wait to see them," she said as she placed a box of vegetables on the counter. "Smells delicious, Lindsay."

"It's just some cock-a-leekie soup and Balmoral chicken. Drew wanted to test the menu this afternoon."

"Sounds great. And I wanted to catch you two because I had a thought," Sydney began.

"Yes?" said Lindsay as she continued chopping.

"Well, of course we still have a lot of work to do to get the inn itself up and running," Sydney began.

Melissa nodded, "I have a lookbook right here."

"I can't wait to see it. The dining room looks great—they're almost done refinishing the floors, and the tables and chairs are good. All the painting on the first floor is done."

"It's just the upstairs and the guest rooms that are left," Melissa added.

"So I was thinking … a lot of new establishments have a 'soft opening' where they open the doors to a smaller crowd, a trial run of sorts. What if we held a Burns Night event, just to whet the appetite and give the locals a little introduction to what we have to offer?" said Sydney.

"Brilliant," said Lindsay. "But … wait. That's coming right up."

"January 25th." Sydney studied Lindsay, who appeared to be quickly calculating.

"Well, we'd need to hire some waitstaff," Lindsay began. "And I'd have to train them. And hire some line cooks. And dishwashers and the like."

"I've already posted some ads, but the great news is that Drew says his inn just doesn't get the traffic in Drumnadrochit that we'd be getting in Inverness, so he's willing to send some staff over to help cover."

"Really? He wouldn't be short staffed?"

Sydney shook her head. "You know Drew. He doesn't want anyone out of a job, so he's had a lot of staff on the payroll just to keep them afloat during the winter months. That's part of the reason he wanted to get involved with the inn at Inverness. It would actually be more cost-effective if the waitstaff doesn't mind making the drive."

"What's Burns Night?" asked Melissa.

Lindsay and Sydney looked at Melissa in surprise. "You've never heard of it?"

Melissa shook her head. "Nope."

"Well, it's a uniquely Scottish holiday to honor the poet Robert Burns," said Lindsay.

"Something like our President's Day?" asked Melissa.

They looked at Melissa blankly.

"We get the day off. Some people go to events—historical talks, that kind of thing. Most people go skiing," said Melissa.

Lindsay shook her head. "No. This is a proper holiday—no offense—but it's a little like Thanksgiving to a certain extent. There's a focus on the meal. It's called a Burns Supper. There's a set menu, set events. It's all about celebrating the poet by reading his poems."

"They really read them? It's not just 'Happy Burns Day, let's have the day off'?"

"Most people go to work, but at night there are celebratory dinners and people read his poems. Really. It's a thing," said Lindsay.

"The most important readings that everyone always does are *The Selkirk Grace* and *Address to a Haggis*. But they can read any of his poems. The diners sit at tables, and we 'pipe in the Haggis.' That means a bagpiper plays as someone ceremoniously carries in the haggis on a tray," said Sydney.

"The meal is usually served family-style," Lindsay continued. "First course is either Cullen Skink or cock-a-leekie soup, then haggis, neeps and tatties, and that's when someone reads Burns' famous poem, *Address to a Haggis*. Then there might be dancing —remember those sword dancers we saw back before Christmas at the Highland Games, Melissa?"

Melissa nodded.

"They dress in traditional outfits and perform that dance,

then various guests read poems by Robert Burns. We drink Scotch, listen to the poems, and enjoy the meal," said Lindsay.

"That sounds amazing. What a lovely holiday!" said Melissa.

"It really is. And it's not just the sort of people who read poetry or the book group types. Most Scots enjoy the holiday. It's good food, good company, and a nice way to keep the holiday spirit going through the January blahs," said Sydney.

"That sounds great. I'm happy to help however I can!" said Melissa.

"Well, great! Today's ... what? January 15th. We've got ten days. The menu is a no-brainer: cullen skink, haggis, neeps and tatties, plenty of Scotch, and probably cranachan," said Lindsay.

"And I'll hire a piper, some dancers, and someone to read the poems," said Sydney.

"I can't wait!" said Melissa.

"Pure dead brilliant," said Lindsay.

* * *

LINDSAY WATCHED onions sizzle in a pan and stirred them as she phoned her father, Alexander "Sandy" MacGregor. She knew if she texted, he wouldn't see it right away, but he'd always answer a phone call.

"Hello, Da!"

"Hello! How are things going at the restaurant?"

"We're working out the menu. A lot of the items will be the same as at the MacAlister Inn's other location, but I am trying out some new ideas as well. I wonder if you'd like to come over tonight and sample some dishes?"

"Absolutely," he said cheerfully.

CHAPTER 9

Melissa took Sydney up the decorative wooden staircase to the guest rooms. "I'm thinking we've got to get rid of the wallpaper," Melissa began.

"Definitely," said Sydney.

"Then we can brighten everything up. What people love is the woodwork, the charm. But we don't need this dated carpeting. Now, as far as the furniture, here are my ideas: We keep the stuff that looks antique or classic. But what do you think of getting rid of all this art deco stuff?"

"What would we put in? Anything too modern will look out of place," said Sydney.

"Exactly. So we go with minimalism," began Melissa as she looked around the space. "Simple, classic wood. Dark cherry will be fine—anything too light will look out of place with the trim and all the woodwork in the hallways. We put in oversized, ultra-comfortable beds with amazingly soft sheets—maybe bamboo—and we go for a really minimalist design. White. Navy. Some plaid throw pillows and nice tartan throw blankets. A modern classic tartan chair in the corner. And then all the updated amenities for coffee, phone charging, streaming television, and really strong wifi."

"That's exactly it," said Sydney, excited.

"And really sleek, modern-yet-classic bathrooms—maybe some nice blue and white tile."

"I love it. Perfect. And you can keep the costs down?"

"Absolutely," said Melissa. "I found a discount vendor for the basics, and I've been in touch with the gallery down the street. What about local artists' work hanging on the walls?"

"Great idea! And maybe maps and photographs."

"Stags, Highland cows, sheep, sights that people can see in the area."

"Lovely," said Sydney.

"This is so much fun. Thank you for having me. I'm so grateful for the opportunity," said Melissa.

"We're glad to have you. You'll join us for the menu tasting this afternoon, won't you?"

"I'd be honored," said Melissa.

* * *

LINDSAY'S FATHER, Sandy, parked his car in front of the snowy sidewalk outside the MacAlister Inn just as Melissa was coming outside to feed the parking meter. A golden retriever on a long leash, walking ahead of a woman about Sandy's age, walked past them.

Melissa took off her gloves to pet the dog.

"Hey there," said Melissa. "What a good dog."

"Oh! Wait! Stop!" said the woman as she caught up with them.

Melissa was surprised to see Margaret Douglas, the realtor who had helped her file the paperwork for her home.

"Margaret! Hello!" said Melissa.

Just then, the dog grabbed Melissa's glove.

"Oh, I'm too late," said Margaret, exasperated. "I'm so sorry."

"What? There's no trouble, and that's a fine dog," said Sandy.

"I would've warned you, but—"

"But I'm fine. She didn't bite," said Melissa, showing her hands.

"Bella doesn't bite, but she is a menace."

Sandy was completely baffled.

"What in blazes is the problem?" he finally asked.

"The glove," Margaret said. "I'm afraid once that dog has got someone's glove, that's the end."

"Nonsense," said Sandy, looking down at the dog's innocent brown eyes and wagging tail.

"No, it's true. She's partial to gloves. I don't understand why, but she takes them everywhere like a security blanket or a stuffed animal. I can't get them away from her."

"Aye ma auntie," said Sandy.

"What?" inquired Melissa curiously.

Margaret's face lit up with a smile. "It's just another way of saying *nonsense,* but I can assure you that dog will not let go of that glove."

Margaret reached for the glove, and the happy-go-lucky golden retriever suddenly growled. "See?" said Margaret.

"It's like a two-year-old with a toy they won't give back. You just trade them for something they'll want more," Melissa suggested. "Maybe a stick, or a bone?"

Margaret shook her head. "Tried it."

"What about a treat?" Melissa asked.

"You'll spoil the little devil," said Margaret.

Sandy squatted down, meeting the dog's gaze. "You like that glove, huh?" he said with a chuckle.

The dog's tail wagged enthusiastically.

"That's Melissa's glove," Sandy continued, holding the dog's gaze. "She'd like it back, please."

The dog stared back, unblinking.

Sandy reached into his pocket and pulled out a dog treat. "May I?" he asked, glancing at Margaret.

Margaret sighed and shrugged, looking amused.

Sandy placed the treat on the sidewalk and waited. The dog quickly snatched up the treat, then, with surprising speed and skill, managed to get the glove back into her mouth.

Sandy laughed, shaking his head in disbelief.

"I'm so sorry. Maybe when we get to the car I can get it," said Margaret.

Sandy handed the woman his business card.

"I mean no offense, but I'm an experienced dog trainer …" he began.

Margaret covered her mouth in embarrassment. "Digging myself deeper and deeper. How embarrassing!"

"Not at all. This dog can be trained with the best of 'em. Seeing as it's my friend Melissa's glove, I'll let the two of you handle that, but I'd be happy to help you with the training."

She looked at the card. "Sandy MacGregor."

He doffed his tweed hat and nodded. "And you might be …"

"Margaret. Margaret Douglas."

"Lovely to meet you," said Sandy.

Melissa immediately noticed a spark between them and tried to hide her smile.

"Why don't you stop by my croft one afternoon this week … if you're interested," he added quickly.

"I'm very interested. I mean, my dog definitely needs training," Margaret said, her rosy cheeks reddening.

"I'm sure she'll take to it just fine. She's got a lovely mum," said Sandy.

AS THEY STEPPED inside the inn, Sandy marveled at the spacious entryway and new carpets.

"Melissa, it's grand. How you've been able to make so many changes in such a short time is just astonishing," he said.

"Well, I just make the decisions. We're fortunate to have found some excellent workers who've painted, refinished, and hung curtains and decorations," said Melissa.

"It's stunning. What's for dinner?" asked Sandy.

"Lindsay's working on the menu, but I think she's starting with some classics for a Burns Supper."

"Wonderful."

He pulled out a chair for Melissa, and she sat. Sydney came out and filled glasses with water and set out a plate of oatcakes and butter. "Can I start you with a drink?"

Melissa and Sandy nodded.

"Here's the drinks menu. I think it'll evolve into a Scotch, mixed drinks, and wine list. But for now ..."

"No worries at all!" said Melissa. "We're just honored to be among the first to try the menu. And I hope you and Elspeth will be joining us?"

"Elspeth is in Fort William shopping for the rooms upstairs," said Sydney. "But I'll join if you'll have me?"

"Of course!"

Sydney sat down, and they munched on oatcakes.

"So, Mr. MacGregor, you're Melissa's ...?"

"Oh, no. We're no relation, although he's like my adopted father. He's actually Lindsay's father," said Melissa.

"And Colin's," added Sandy.

Lindsay brought out salads and set them down.

"We'll start with a pomegranate and quinoa edamame salad with a light lemon-pomegranate vinaigrette."

"That looks incredible," said Melissa.

"Thank you," said Lindsay. "And what can I bring you to drink? We have whisky, red and white wine, and the like, but I'd love for you to try some of our specialty mixed drinks."

"Don't tell me my brother, Angus, shared his top-secret recipes?" asked Sydney.

"Aye, your brother has a fantastic talent for mixology ..." said Lindsay. " ... and secrets. So, these are my own inventions."

"Grand. What are the choices?" asked Sydney.

"We have an Auld Fashioned—our spin on a classic bourbon Old Fashioned, but made with Scotch whisky, bitters, and sugar. We have a Talisker Negroni, with Talisker, Campari, and Antica Formula. And we have our Bobby Burns, which is Scotch whisky, sweet vermouth, and Benedictine."

"Well, seeing as I need to know more about him, I'll try the Bobby Burns," said Melissa.

"I'll stick with a Talisker Skye, neat," said Sandy.

"I'll try the Auld Fashioned," said Sydney.

"Lovely," said Lindsay, and she turned toward the bar.

"It's strange to have a friend waiting on me. I feel like we're playing restaurant," said Melissa.

"Aye, she and Colin used to love to play restaurant as bairns," said Sandy.

They ate their salads, and soon it was time for the mains.

"We have Balmoral chicken, which is chicken stuffed with haggis and wrapped in bacon; a roasted partridge with elderberry sauce; the Haggis supper with neeps and tatties; or venison with whisky sauce."

"What if we had all four and shared?" asked Melissa.

"Yes, I had thought about a sampler plate, since it's a tasting event. What do you think, Sydney?" replied Lindsay

"Absolutely! Let's do that with the dessert round as well," Sydney said.

They sipped their drinks and watched the sun set over the river. It was a beautiful evening. "It almost feels like spring," said Melissa.

"Aye. Almost is the keyword there. We're nay out of the woods yet," said Sandy.

"When does spring arrive?"

"According to the Irish, Imbolc is the first day of spring. That's the 1st of February. But around here, I'd say don't put away your parka until at least April," said Sandy.

"Maybe even May," said Sydney.

"That's like Boston. We can have a sixty or seventy degree day in January, then get six inches of snow a few days later," said Melissa.

Soon Lindsay served the meal and sat down at the table with them to enjoy it, just as Drew breezed into the room.

"How's my favorite chef?" asked Drew as he greeted Lindsay with a friendly peck on the cheek.

"You're lucky I'm the chef so I can reheat your dinner!" said Lindsay.

"You sit. I'll reheat," said Drew.

"You lovebirds should both sit. I'm capable of running a microwave if Lindsay isn't offended," said Melissa.

Lindsay pretended to look appalled but then nodded. "Thanks, Mel."

"Drew, nice to see you," said Sandy. "My daughter has made an amazing meal."

Drew slid into a chair next to Lindsay. "Looks delicious."

"Thank you," said Lindsay, passing him oat cakes and salad. "What can I get you to drink?"

"I'll stick with water because I need to drive back to Drumnadrochit tonight," said Drew.

"Really? Can't you stay?" Lindsay asked.

He put his arm around Lindsay. "I suppose I could stick around till morning."

Melissa got Drew a plate of food, and they shared laughs and lighthearted banter. As the evening wore on, it became clear to everyone that the new MacAlister Inn was destined for success.

* * *

Burns Night couldn't come soon enough. Melissa needed to keep her mind off of all the issues with Dave, and her worries about Colin, and her home, and ... she needed to keep busy.

At the inn, the painters were finishing, the woodwork was done, and the HVAC was in. So she surrounded herself with samples of upholstery, curtains, and bedding. The last touches were more local art for the upstairs guest rooms.

Melissa wandered through the galleries in Inverness. There were watercolors of Highland landscapes, oil paintings of the battle of Culloden, Mary Queen of Scots, Highland Coos, sheep, Inverness Castle, photographs of the Fairy Pools, Fairy Glen, the Old Man of Storr, puffins ... She finally plunked down her company credit card and bought them all. It felt good to support artists and, in turn, encourage more tourism. Not that Scotland didn't have tourists. In the summer they'd be overrun, Drew had assured her. But it seemed like a good way to help the local economy. Seeing these sights in the winter was a whole different experience, and Melissa wondered if there was a way to encourage tourism during the colder months. And that led her back to Burns Night—a unique holiday that many foreigners hadn't even heard of. She'd make it spectacular.

Excited, she returned to the inn and began unloading frames and tartan pillows and little stuffed Highland Coos and sheep. She hauled several loads up the stairs before Sydney found her and insisted on helping. Soon everything was upstairs, and Melissa was humming to herself as she hung paintings, placed pillows on chairs, and laid soft mohair blankets in each of the rooms. She looked around and decided she should consider looking for some antique mirrors to go in some rooms—maybe a collection of hand mirrors hung on the walls. She also thought about adding some vintage books on travel or by Scottish authors, maybe on a desk in each room or next to the fireplace.

CHAPTER 10

Early Monday morning, Colin was dotting the i's and crossing the t's on the divorce papers. Everything was in order, so he gave them to his assistant to submit. He took a sip of coffee and looked out at the dark clouds over the Charles. Another stormy day lay ahead.

At 8:05, there was a commotion outside his office door. Colin took a deep breath as he anticipated—and confirmed—that it was Melissa's ex, Dave.

"Hello, David," said Colin. "Per our unplanned meeting over the weekend, I went ahead and sped things up. You'll be happy to know that I've completed all the documents on both sides of the divorce, and everything's in order, so—"

"I had an idea," said Dave.

Colin set down his cup of coffee. "All right. Have a seat. What can I do for you?" asked Colin.

"As you know, I've requested half. That includes that house in Scotland I've been hearing about," said Dave.

Colin took a deep breath. "The house wasn't part of—" began Colin.

Dave interrupted, "No, half means half—Cut down the middle: 50% for me, 50% for her."

Colin nodded. "Well, that's a good idea, but unfortunately the divorce has been finalized."

"Then why don't I have the notarized final copies of the divorce in my hands?"

"They're on their way. It was finalized per your request over the weekend, and I just need to—"

"No, you don't need to. You're my lawyer, and I'm telling you to stop everything until I can sort this house thing out."

Colin froze. "I can't do that."

"You can, and you will."

"It's already done," said Colin boldly, hoping that his lawyerly tone would resonate with Dave.

"But it's not. The papers have to be notarized, and final copies get sent to both parties. I don't have those notarized final copies."

"They're already in process," said Colin. "I mean, they're being finalized right now." Colin peeked through his office door and could see his assistant furiously printing the papers so she could notarize them.

And just then, the power went out.

Colin closed his eyes. *Ice storm strikes again. Why couldn't it have prevented Dave from coming over?*

He glanced through the door with raised eyebrows. *We got it?*

His assistant shook her head and mouthed, "not yet."

"So yeah, I wanna put that Scotland house on the market. Like I told you, me and my girlfriend wanna sell the place and get a condo in Vegas," said Dave.

"I understand," said Colin through gritted teeth. "Unfortunately, David, it's a done deal. You and Melissa have both signed the divorce papers."

"Yeah, but the thing is … they're not in my hand. And better yet, they're not in Melissa's hands. Not notarized copies, at least.

Which means there's nothing to stop me from putting that house on the market today." He checked his watch. "And since it's morning, it's still business hours. Looks like Melissa's lost this one."

The power flashed back on, and the printer whirred and hissed, spitting out the hard copies of the divorce documents. Colin collected them and handed them to Dave, along with a pen.

"Here you go, David. As you can see, Melissa has signed, and you have signed. One final signature with the date should seal the deal."

Dave scowled and looked at the calendar. A twisted grimace flashed across his face as he quickly signed and dated the documents.

Colin wondered what had changed, but he was grateful.

"Good day, then, MacGregor. Looking forward to selling that estate."

"You'll need the owner's signature in order to sell it," said Colin evenly.

"I'm the owner. We're still married," Dave repeated like a broken record.

Colin took a deep breath. *Why did he have to keep repeating this to this numpty?*

"You and Melissa both signed the documents dissolving the marriage. You just now signed the final, notarized—"

"I gave myself some wiggle room. I dated those documents February 1st, and you didn't even notice. What a sham lawyer you turned out to be, but it's all in my favor now. I've got several more weeks of domestic bliss that says I get half of that house when it sells. But considering my own lawyer is dating my wife, I may be able to get the whole thing."

And with that, Dave walked out, slamming the door behind him.

* * *

THAT NIGHT COLIN sat at his desk in his condo with a cup of tea, staring at the computer screen. He opened a new tab and scrolled through some flights to Scotland. Then he clicked back to his work.

His cell phone rang.

"Colin MacGregor," he answered.

"Colin?" It was his boss, Derek. "I hate to do this over the phone, but I wanted to talk to you right away," he said.

Colin sat up and set down his tea. "How can I help?"

"There's no good way to phrase this ..."

Colin winced. He could guess what was coming.

"Are you dating a client?" Derek asked.

Ever the lawyer, Colin couldn't help but notice the error in his boss's phrasing.

"Um ... no. But since you asked, I will disclose that I have been dating the soon-to-be-ex-wife of one of my clients."

Silence on the phone.

"Colin, you're the best lawyer I've ever worked with, and you're honest to a fault."

"Thank you?" responded Colin.

"You know why I phrased my question the way I did," he continued.

"Yes, but I also knew what you were asking," said Colin. "Did Dave call you?"

"He's furious. He also really wants that house in Scotland," said Derek.

"I know."

There was an awkward silence.

"He wants me to let you go," said Derek.

Colin nodded and sipped his tea. He flipped back to the tab with flights to Scotland and took a deep breath.

His boss continued, "I said he'd have to simply dissolve your contract and find another lawyer because you have several other cases you're working on for me."

"But I haven't started them yet."

"You've been in the office every day, early, reading through—"

"It's time, Derek. I think this is the wake-up call I needed."

"What are you saying?"

"I'm saying I'm in love with Melissa, I miss my home, and my family needs me. It's time for me to leave Boston."

"If I were to lay you off, you could collect—"

"It's been a pleasure, Derek. Thank you for the opportunity."

"Colin!"

Colin hung up the phone and took a deep breath. *What's done is done,* he thought. He looked around his condo. He had a minimalist style, so there were just the basics: a couch, a large chair, bar stools in the kitchen, a simple bedspread. He could probably rent it out until he was fully ready to sell.

In fact ... He snapped a few photos with his phone and sat down at his computer. He created an account on a rental website. Soon he had a listing.

He went back to the computer to continue searching for a plane ticket. Excitement flowed through him as he scrolled through the options. *Fly to London first? Straight to Edinburgh? Train? Rent a car? What if he had Melissa meet him in Dublin, and then they could drive up to Northern Ireland, see the Giant's Causeway, and then take a ferry—*

Wait. He'd just quit his job.

He had to move to another country where a woman who he hadn't known for long had settled. Would she even want him there? Of course she would. She would, wouldn't she?

What would he do for work?

His dad certainly needed help on the croft, with the sheep and the dogs he trained, but that wasn't going to pay the bills. He wasn't licensed to practice law in Scotland anymore. Gah. What had he been thinking? This wasn't like him at all. He wasn't impulsive. He was reliable, steadfast ... Oh hell. He was gonna get on a plane and go to Scotland and start his new life.

CHAPTER 11

Stepping outside the Inverness airport, Colin felt the crisp Highland breeze greet him like an old friend. Quickly catching a taxi, Colin watched the rolling hills and heather-clad moors pass by, each bend in the road stirring memories of his childhood. And as the MacGregor croft appeared, Colin felt a lump in his throat; he was finally back where he belonged.

Colin paid the driver and rolled his luggage up to the front door. He thought about knocking, but it was really his home as much as his father's. And he knew with his father's arthritis, it would be easier if he didn't have to get up out of his chair. Colin opened the door and was about to shout *hello* when he saw two people entwined on the couch. The woman quickly shifted away from his father, who straightened his shirt and looked in shocked surprise at his son standing in the doorway.

"Colin!"

"Uh, surprise?" said Colin. He wasn't sure what else to say. He sat down his bags tentatively.

"Margaret, I'd like you to meet my son, Colin. He lives in the

States," Sandy said pointedly. Colin looked down at his shoes. "Colin, meet Margaret Douglas. She and I …"

"He's training my dog," Margaret said quietly, with a sparkle in her eyes.

Colin looked down at the golden retriever sitting on the floor by the fire. "What a good dog," he said. He slipped off his gloves to pet the dog.

"Wait! Don't!" yelled Margaret. But it was too late. The dog took Colin's glove in her mouth and wasn't going to let go.

Sandy winked at Colin, who was completely perplexed.

"The dog likes gloves," explained Sandy, amused.

"You haven't progressed very far in your training, I see," said Colin. Normally, banter like this with his father was fair game, but with this woman there, he wasn't sure.

"Yes, well, we're just getting started. Preliminary …" mumbled Sandy awkwardly as Margaret picked up her purse.

"That's me off," said Margaret. "I'll get the messages and stop back for Bella … in an hour?"

"Sounds good," said Sandy automatically.

Margaret and Sandy both studied Colin. He had two large bags and had arrived unannounced. "Maybe two hours?" asked Margaret.

"Perfect," said Sandy, and Margaret was out the door.

Sandy looked at his son.

"So," he said. "We've both had some changes in our lives."

"Aye," said Colin.

"Margaret just made tea. The kettle's still hot," said Sandy.

"Thanks," replied Colin as he went into the kitchen and poured himself some Earl Gray.

He returned, sipping the tea as he walked, and his father chuckled. "Walking with your tea. You've really become an American."

"Yeah, well, I think that chapter is closing," said Colin.

"Oh?"

"I mean, I slammed it shut."

Sandy studied his son's face. "Do you want to talk about it?"

Colin sat beside his father and began to talk.

* * *

MELISSA TIDIED the living room as she glanced at the antique clock on the wall. It was almost eleven a.m. It had been a few hours since Colin had sent her a mysterious text:

I have news.

She had no patience whatsoever, and wondering about his news was making Melissa completely stir-crazy. She'd already scrubbed the kitchen, re-organized the pantry, and put all the books away in the library. She needed to keep busy to keep from bursting at the seams. *What could it be? News about the divorce settlement? News about the inn? Something about his father? Could he be sick? Could it be bad news? Bad news?! That hadn't even occurred to her.*

A small gray car turned into her driveway. Her heart raced. *Could Colin have decided on an impromptu holiday? What a wonderful surprise!* She looked in the mirror and saw that her brown hair was relatively tamed—it wasn't raining—and her blue eyes sparkled. Brimming with joy, Melissa slipped on her boots and walked out to greet her visitor. But when she got within sight of the driver, her stomach twisted in knots. She would recognize that balding, miserable being anywhere. It was Dave.

Melissa just stared as Dave parked the car and got out, looking around in wonder at the spectacular stone home that was hers. *Hers,* she stressed as she watched him appraising the brass fixtures, the stone fence, and the grounds.

"What are you doing here?" Melissa pressed her lips together and looked at Dave. She couldn't believe she'd been married to him, let alone for two whole years.

"I had to fly to see this house you've been hiding from me. It looks like it's worth quite a lot," said Dave smugly.

"It's mine," Melissa asserted, her voice laced with determination.

"It's ours, dear," he said. His tone carried an undercurrent of malice that made the words all the more chilling. He'd never been abusive before, and Melissa had never seen him this way. She mustered up all her courage and faced him.

"It was a Mackenzie inheritance, and you're not a Mackenzie."

"I'm married to one, darling. And as the man of the house, I'm putting it on the market immediately."

"No, you're not," said Melissa bravely, while frantically wondering what she could do. "We're officially divorced," she added, as if that would stop this lunatic.

What could she do? Could she sell the house to Colin? Lindsay? Rent it out as an Airbnb? She remembered ruefully that she'd once talked about putting the home in Jingles' name. As she looked at the fierce determination in Dave's eyes, she knew she'd have to do something.

"Can I have a tour?"

"No."

"I'll call my lawyer," said Dave with a smirk on his face.

"You do that," she said. She went inside and slammed the door shut behind her.

Inside, she looked around at her beautiful house. The first thing she'd ever owned all by herself. It was perfect. Spacious, yet cozy. Old-fashioned, yet modern. Full of stone and wood and Mackenzie history. It meant so much to her. There was no way she'd let Dave get control of it or sell it. She'd gone through too much.

Melissa called Lindsay as she watched Dave scout the grounds.

"Dave's here," she whispered.

"What?! Where?"

"Walking around outside my house!"

"No!"

"Yes. He wants to sell it. Have you heard from Colin? I can't reach him. When I call, there's just a recording."

Lindsay paused. "That's strange."

"Maybe he got a new phone?"

"Is Dave still there? What's he doing?"

Melissa snuck another look out the window. Dave was walking toward the back yard, peering into the well—the beautiful, historic wishing well that held ancient healing waters and legendary powers. The well that had made her own wishes come true. Her blood boiled thinking of him trying to take this place away from her.

"Walking around like he owns the place. He's so pompous and awful."

"You should set Jingles on him," said Lindsay.

"I don't want Jingles anywhere near him."

Melissa drew in her breath as she looked out the front window. Another car was turning into the driveway.

"Someone else is here," she whispered. "Maybe he got a real estate agent? Or a new lawyer?"

"I can call Drew and have him come over and pretend to be a—"

Melissa gasped as the car door opened and Colin got out. "It's Colin!"

"He's there? At your house?"

"Yep."

"They're both there," said Lindsay. "Egads!"

"Yep."

"Well, that should be interesting. I'll bring over some popcorn."

"Not funny."

"You're right. I'm sorry," said Lindsay.

Melissa pondered the situation for a moment. "Actually, it is *kind* of funny." She never thought her ex-husband and current boyfriend would be in the same place at the same time, not to mention the whole divorce lawyer and client connection.

"What's happening now?" asked Lindsay.

Melissa peered out the window again. "I think the shit show's about to begin."

* * *

MELISSA STOOD at the window wondering what to do. *Text Colin a quick warning that Dave was there? He must know, right? Maybe it was a coincidence.* She cracked open the door just as Colin slammed the car door shut. Dave turned.

Colin's face lit up as he saw Melissa standing in the doorway, but as she nodded her head toward Dave, his happiness vanished.

Dave walked over toward the front walkway, and Melissa stood her ground, while Colin tried to brace himself for the inevitable.

"What kind of a lawyer do you think you are? What kind of MAN do you think you are? What gives you the right to go stalking after my wife when I hired you to represent me?" said Dave.

Colin held up his hands. "It was all a coincidence that we met. I was in line beside Melissa at the airport on her way here, and we got to chatting. She was on my flight, then she was on my train—we were both traveling to the same town. We became good friends. And now I am here to—"

"Not to represent me."

"That's correct. I'm here to start my life over in the place I belong with the woman I love, if she'll have me."

Melissa caught her breath.

"Well, I hope you don't plan on living here, because I've met with an enthusiastic realtor who's ready to get things in motion."

"You'll need the owner's signature in order to sell it," said Colin evenly.

"As I mentioned, I post-dated my signature on the divorce papers, so I'm still half-owner," said Dave.

He went to his car and tried to maneuver around Colin's. "Get your pathetic excuse for a vehicle out of my way," he yelled. "I'm out of here!"

Colin and Melissa stood watching as Dave backed away and then nearly crashed into another car as he drove on the wrong side of the road.

"Maybe Darwin will take care of this problem for us?" said Colin, hugging Melissa close.

Melissa tightly embraced Colin, then pulled back. "So … you said you had news?"

"Loads to tell you. I think we should sit."

Melissa led Colin into the cozy den area, where she had a fire going and a warm pot of tea sitting on the coffee table. "Tea or something stronger?"

"At this point, I'd rather keep my wits about me," said Colin.

Melissa poured them each a cup, and they sipped their tea quietly for a moment.

Melissa took a deep breath and broke the silence. "So … Hello! Welcome! What's going on?"

"Well, as you can see, Dave's found out about the house. As you know, the divorce was finalized, but he seems to think he's created a little loophole."

"Something about post-dating the papers. Would that hold up?"

"I don't think so, but it might. I'm so sorry. I was in such a hurry to close the deal, it didn't occur to me that he might write the wrong date."

"Who would? I didn't notice either."

JUST THEN, Melissa's phone rang. "Yes? … No, it's not … Well, he's not the owner. We're divorced."

Colin motioned for Melissa to turn on the speaker phone, so she did. "... to take interior photos for the listing," said the voice on the other end of the line.

Melissa's face flushed red. "It's not for sale," she said firmly, then hung up.

"How can so many things change so fast?" Melissa got up. "Excuse me, I just need a moment." She left the room and headed down the hallway to the bathroom to blow her nose.

Melissa returned a few minutes later, red-eyed and frazzled, but she managed a weak grin. "What doesn't kill us makes us stronger, right?" she said, sniffling and sitting down in a chair across from Colin. "Speaking of hasty decisions, what brings you here?"

"I wanted to see you?" said Colin with a shrug and a look in his eye that said there was much more to his arrival. He beckoned for Melissa to sit beside him, and he tucked her against him when she sat down.

* * *

COLIN SLOUCHED beside the crackling fire, his expression serious, while Melissa, lost in thought, fixated on the dancing flames. Embers popped and hissed, sending occasional sparks spiraling into the dimly lit room as the hypnotic play of light and shadow mesmerized the silent pair.

Finally Melissa giggled. First a little, then more. Colin

looked over at her, certain she was beginning to lose it, but the giggles turned into full blown laughter until she was in tears.

"What on earth could be so funny?" he asked.

She finally took a deep breath and tried to center herself.

"He wants to buy a condo in Vegas. He'll only get half the price of Greenhill, so he'll still need to sell our home. And our home is infested with squirrels."

"A condo doesn't need to cost—"

"Yeah, but the condo he wants and the lifestyle he wants ... and I know Samantha only rents. They'll need to sell that squirrel-infested house come hell or high water, and it's not going to be easy."

Melissa grinned. "I think it might be time to pour a wee dram," she said.

Colin nodded. "We deserve it."

Melissa went to the cupboard and pulled out a bottle of Talisker Skye and poured two drams, neat, and handed one to Colin.

"*Sláinte*," she said, lifting her glass.

"*Sláinte*," he said. His eyes, reflecting a gentle warmth, met hers, creating a moment of quiet connection between them.

Melissa felt a warm glow flush across her cheeks as she clinked glasses and took a sip.

"You said you had news," she said, embarrassed that so much of the afternoon had been about her.

"Aye. I do. I'm ... coming to Scotland," he said with a chuckle.

"Great! Can't wait to see you!" Melissa laughed. "How long are you staying?" she asked, sipping her dram, her tone more serious now.

He stared into the fire, unsure what to stay. "As long as you stay," he said, finally looking up into her blue-green eyes.

Melissa was stunned. Now the tears returned, but this time

they really were tears of joy. *But was it really real?* "But what about your job?"

"I quit."

Melissa's eyes widened. "You quit? Just like that?"

"Maybe with a little help and inspiration from my last client, but yes, I quit. And it was my decision. My boss was more than willing to work with me, but I realized I'm just not living the life I want to lead, so I decided to make a change." A determined furrow settled on Colin's brow.

"What about your friends, condo, furniture, your car …"

"I'll rent out the condo, and the rest is not important. I need to be here," he said. "With the people I love," he added.

"And if I didn't live here …?"

"I'd be searching for you. There's been something missing for a long time. My spark. The zest of life. It sounds rubbish, but it's true, Melissa. You've reminded me how to enjoy life, and I want to do that … with you."

Melissa drew in her breath as Colin reached out to gently caress her cheek.

"I know we've only been seeing each other for a few months. And you had no idea I was going to live here. It'll take some time to process everything. But … let's at least start dating. Can we do that?"

Melissa threw her arms around Colin. He held her close and gently kissed her neck, cheek, and finally her lips.

* * *

"FANCY A TREAT?" asked Sandy as he held a treat out for Bella, the beautiful golden retriever with an unhealthy fascination with gloves.

Bella tilted her head to the side, gazing intently at the treat.

Sandy set the treat down. Just as before, Bella bent her head down, let the glove go for a nanosecond, then wolfed down the treat. But this time, Sandy snagged the glove and quickly stuffed it into his pocket. Bella looked at him, bewildered.

"Where'd that glove go, Bella?" he said with a chuckle. "I think it's time we go outside and try the whistle."

Steadying himself with his cane, Sandy slowly made his way across the living room to the front door. He slipped on his jacket, stepped into his boots, and opened the front door. Bella dashed out as if she'd never had any training at all. He chuckled. *One step at a time.*

CHAPTER 12

To keep her mind off of her troubles, Melissa spent as much time as she could at the inn. She hung the artwork in the dining room, entryway, and upstairs hallways and guest rooms. She hung lovely blue tartan curtains in each window. A small wooden cutout of a sheep and a Highland cow sat on the front desk where guests checked in.

Lindsay had finalized the menu, and Elspeth had taken it to the printers. Sydney was putting the final touches on the seating arrangements for the big opening night. She tapped Melissa on the shoulder. "Melissa, I have a man who says he knows you and wants to sit at your table?"

"Colin MacGregor?"

"No, it's a Dave something—"

"No!" Melissa spat out the word so fast that Elspeth, used to Melissa's sunny demeanor, was taken aback.

"Please, no. He's my ex-husband, and he … he shouldn't be here."

"Enough said."

But it wasn't enough said for Lindsay. "How dare he try to follow you around, haunt the places where you'll be?"

"He's just trying to get a rise out of me."

"Definitely don't let him come, Elspeth. This is a soft opening for locals only. That means people we know."

"And like," added Melissa.

Elspeth nodded. "Got it. Oh, hey. I got the new banner advertising our grand opening. What do you think?"

The banner showed a picture of the Inn, with its new landscaping, fresh paint, and the *MacAlister Inn* sign on a blue-and-white tartan background with the words *OPENING 7-2.*

"That looks fabulous!" said Lindsay.

Melissa squinted at it. "I thought we were opening next month."

"We are. February 7th," said Elspeth.

"But the banner says July 2nd," said Melissa.

Now Elspeth and Lindsay were confused. "It says February 7th."

Melissa thought for a moment. "Oh, right. Over here you put the day first and then the month. We usually do it the opposite way in the US."

"Ah."

* * *

JANUARY 25TH FINALLY ARRIVED—BURNS Night! There were thirty guests, and the dining room looked spectacular. Melissa had placed some of the art meant for the upstairs in the dining room; Sydney had put together a great playlist to play until the *ceilidh* band arrived; and Drew had set out several collections of Robert Burns' works on tables throughout the dining room.

Sandy and Margaret were among the first to arrive. Melissa gave them both a hug, then took Margaret's jacket. "Thanks so much for coming," said Melissa.

"Wouldn't miss this for the world," said Sandy. "Been brushing up on my Robert Burns."

As people began to arrive, Sydney and Elspeth acted as hostesses, checking coats and showing guests to their tables.

The fireplace in the corner crackled, and snow fell lightly on the windows. The music played classic Scottish songs and pop music by Scottish bands, and the smell of haggis wafted from the kitchen.

Melissa hovered near the door until Elspeth finally shooed her away. "You've got a seat with Lindsay's father. Go sit. I'll bring Colin when he gets here."

Melissa moved over near the water pitchers, but the waitstaff shooed her away from there as well. Finally, she plopped herself into a seat next to Sandy and Margaret.

Margaret sipped her water and admired the dining room. "You know, I used to work here when I was in uni, and it made me so sad to see this place fall into disrepair. I'm so glad you all have been able to restore this back to what it once was ... or even better."

"Drew was the mastermind, but we all did our parts. You're going to love the food Lindsay's preparing for tonight."

"Can't wait," said Sandy.

Just then, Colin arrived. Melissa waved him over, and he settled into his seat next to her after greeting his father and Margaret.

"Can you tell me more about Burns Night?" asked Melissa.

"Well, it started back in the 1800s, not long after Robert Burns died. Some of his friends wanted to honor his life and his works. They chose his birthday. One of his most famous poems is *Address to a Haggis*, so the menu was pretty clear from day one. And you can't have haggis and Burns poems without infusing the water of life, so whisky is, of course, part of the tradition," said Sandy.

"Sometimes the piper greets the guests; other times, they wait to pipe in the haggis," said Margaret.

The room was nearly full now. The wait staff brought out

drams of whisky, and the scent of peat and smoke wafted through the room. The first course was soup: a choice of cullen skink or scotch broth. As Melissa reached for her spoon, Colin shook his head slightly. Once everyone was served, Drew came into the dining room.

"Welcome, folks, and thank you for being the very first to attend what I hope will be the first of many Burns Suppers here at the MacAlister Inn. We're here to appreciate our national treasure, the Bard himself, on his birthday, so let's raise a glass to our favorite poet, Robert Burns!"

They raised glasses. "*Sláinte!*"

"And since he wrote *The Selkirk Grace,* we'll be starting out with that," said Drew.

"Some hae meat an canna eat,
And some wad eat that want it;
But we hae meat, and we can eat,
And sae the Lord be thankit."

Everyone raised their drams again with a "*Sláinte.*" Then they started the soup course.

"So, Melissa, what's your favorite Robert Burns poem?" asked Margaret.

Melissa felt caught off guard, but she thought about it. "I think I probably read *My Love Is Like a Red, Red Rose* somewhere along the line. Probably high school?"

Margaret nodded kindly, and Melissa was relieved that she had gotten the correct writer.

"What are your favorites?" Melissa asked quickly to pull herself away from the center of attention.

"I always liked *To a Mouse,*" said Margaret. "How about you, Sandy?"

Sandy coughed, and Colin suppressed a grin.

Margaret looked from one to the other. "One of the more bawdy poems, then?" she asked.

Sandy said nothing but took a long sip of his dram. "Burns had quite a wit."

"I look forward to hearing you read, then," she said.

As they finished their soup course, Lindsay popped out of the kitchen for a minute.

"This is just amazing!" said Melissa.

Lindsay blushed and looked excited. "Really?"

Sandy stood and hugged his daughter. "So proud of you."

"Not bad," said Colin, punching her lightly on the arm.

"Thank you so much. I've got to dash back, but thank you!" Lindsay flushed and hurried back into the kitchen just as a piper appeared in the room.

The piper was a young dark-haired man dressed in a red, black, and white Inverness tartan kilt, with a dark gray vest and jacket and a black sporran.

"He's going to pipe in the haggis," said Colin.

"That makes it sound like he'll be frosting a cake," said Melissa.

"Nope, this is part of the tradition."

Soon the pipes began to drone, and everyone stood. The piper played a tune that Melissa didn't recognize at all. The program on the table listed it as *A Man's a Man for A' That,* a song written by Robert Burns.

Drew, also dressed in his finest kilt—a slightly different red-and-black plaid—carried the haggis on a silver tray. He lifted it high, at shoulder level. He walked solemnly and ceremoniously, following the piper around the room so that everyone had a chance to see the haggis.

Melissa had half expected to see an entire sheep on the plate, displayed the way some chefs served the whole fish or roast suckling pig. Instead, this was a smallish cylinder, a little bigger than a large baked potato. On the outside was the gray casing. Inside, Melissa knew the haggis contained sheep's heart, liver, and lungs, some spices, and oats.

Melissa stood at attention like the rest of the room, but her thoughts raced. She was surprised at what a solemn affair this was, and how seriously everyone was taking it. She thought it was amazing. *Chocolates and books on Christmas eve like the Scandinavians, and now celebrating a poet as part of a national holiday.* Melissa tried to think of any other writers or creators who had sparked a holiday. *There was May the Fourth, the informal holiday for geeks who loved Star Wars. Some people celebrated Festivus, the holiday from the television show Seinfeld. Others had toast, jelly beans, and popcorn on Thanksgiving in honor of Charlie Brown's Friendsgiving. But nothing like this.*

When the piper finished playing and Drew had displayed the haggis for all to see, he set it down on the table in the middle of the room.

Melissa's eyes widened as Colin coughed and stood. Without a book, without a scrap of paper, he began to recite from memory Robert Burns' *Address to a Haggis*.

"Fair fa' your honest, sonsie face,
Great Chieftain o' the Puddin-race!
Aboon them a' ye tak your place,
Painch, tripe, or thairm:
Weel are ye wordy of a grace
As lang 's my arm ..."

Melissa was in awe. She could barely understand him, but it didn't matter. In his gorgeous Scots—which she had never heard him speak—he recited the poem as if he were composing it on the spot.

When he reached the part about the knife, Colin picked up the huge kitchen knife that sat beside the haggis and brandished it like he was a Shakespearean actor. He then plunged it deep into the poor, unsuspecting haggis as he read the lines:

"... His knife see Rustic-labour dight,
An' cut ye up wi' ready slight,
Trenching your gushing entrails bright,
Like onie ditch;
And then, O what a glorious sight,
Warm-reekin, rich! ..."

BOTH GROSSED OUT AND FASCINATED, Melissa pulled out her phone and began to record the amazing performance.

The whole audience was entranced. By the time he reached the last line, he roared like Alan Cumming in a one-man-show of *Macbeth*.

"... But, if ye wish her gratefu' prayer,
Gie her a Haggis!"

THE ROOM ERUPTED into thunderous applause. Colin, always rather reserved, flushed and returned to his seat.

"Good on you," said Sandy.

"Outstanding," said Margaret.

"You are incredible!" Melissa gushed. "I can't believe ... I mean, of course, I know ... but wow!"

"Courtroom experience helps with poetry recitation," said Colin humbly.

They clinked glasses and downed more whisky. Waitstaff brought plates of haggis, neeps, and tatties with whisky sauce to the tables. The food was served family style as everyone chatted.

Now that the main course was served, Drew set up the microphone and a podium. And as the meal began to wind down, Drew took the mic.

"It's time for some readings and a toast to the lassies and laddies."

Sandy stood and unfolded a piece of paper from his pocket. He read a rich, wonderful rhyming poem—both soulful and hilarious—talking about everything from his daughter, his wife, his mother, and ending with Margaret. There were tears in his eyes as he finally raised his glass and ended with "Let us toast … to the lassies!"

Drew raised a glass and said "Now which brave lassie wants to give a toast to the laddies?"

Melissa was nervous just thinking about speaking, but Margaret stepped up and grabbed the microphone and belted out a savage, bawdy, hilarious poem that shot back at Sandy's little digs. It was feminist and funny and wonderful. "You've met your match!" shouted a member of the audience to Sandy, who chuckled and nodded.

The kitchen doors opened, and waitstaff emerged with pudding. There were trays with a variety of choices for each table. As their waiter appeared, Melissa was awestruck.

"Tonight we have a choice of desserts and small plates for all to share. This one is cranachan, a raspberry whipped cream dessert; this caramel covered cookie is millionaire's shortbread; this is sticky toffee pudding; and finally, we have a heather-honey specialty ice cream made in-house. Bon appetit!"

As they sampled the incredible desserts, guests took turns approaching the mic and reading Burns poetry. *To a Mouse* was followed by *To a Louse,* and then Drew stood. Someone brought Lindsay out, and she looked around at the crowd finishing their desserts. Everyone was relaxed and happy, and Lindsay's cheeks flushed with pride.

The dancing was next. Despite his arthritis, Sandy somehow managed to whisk Margaret off her feet. Melissa and Colin soon joined, along with Drew and Lindsay, and Sydney and Elspeth. It reminded Melissa of the square dancing required in elementary school, combined with the country line dancing she'd done at weddings. Breathless, she circled, twirled, and raced down the line and back again while the rest of the crowd joined in.

When it was all over, they gathered and crossed arms—it reminded Melissa of the Girl Scouts' closing ceremony, where they held hands and passed a hand squeeze around the circle. They sang *Old Lang Syne,* mostly in Scots. Melissa was grateful to have the lyrics written out on a little card on the table. She hadn't realized it was originally written by Robert Burns. *What a guy!*

Afterwards, as friends stood and said their goodbyes, Melissa hugged Lindsay. "That was incredible! This place is going to be such a success!" Then she hugged Elspeth and Sydney. "It was great! Thank you!"

"I think we're off to a cracking good start. Thank you, Lindsay, for your incredible skills!" said Sydney.

CHAPTER 13

The road was lined with tall trees, their branches reaching up to the sky. In the distance, Greenhill House stood, a dark silhouette against the colorful sky. As they drove closer, Melissa couldn't help but notice the bright green hue that seemed to intensify as they got closer. "Are those the Northern Lights?" she asked in awe.

Colin squinted out the window and confirmed her suspicions. "Yes, it appears so."

Melissa couldn't believe her luck, living in a place where such otherworldly beauty was a regular occurrence. "It's incredible," she remarked.

Colin nodded in agreement, adding, "It's been a while since I've seen them. We'll have to take a walk and admire them when we get to your place."

After parking in the driveway, they walked out toward the loch. The Northern Lights danced above them, swirling in mesmerizing patterns of green, turquoise, and purple.

"It's just amazing," said Melissa.

As they stood there, Colin gently put his arm around Melissa's shoulders. She leaned into him, feeling a warm sense of comfort and closeness. They stayed like that for a while, standing by the edge of the loch, watching the lights twirl and dance in hypnotizing patterns above them. The greenish glow reflected off the water, creating a magical atmosphere.

"I can't think of a better ending to such a perfect evening," said Melissa, breaking the silence.

"Aye?" said Colin, a glint in his eye.

Melissa raised an eyebrow in response, curious about what he was thinking.

Colin took a deep breath and turned toward her, his expression serious yet playful. "Well, there's one thought I'd had ..."

"And what would that be?" she asked coyly.

Without hesitation, Colin leaned in and kissed her. Their lips met in a tender yet passionate embrace, and Melissa felt herself swept away by the whirlwind of emotions that flooded through her body. She wrapped her arms around him and melted into his embrace, feeling like she was exactly where she was meant to be.

After what felt like both an eternity and only a few seconds, they pulled away from each other, their faces flushed with excitement and desire. They gazed into each other's eyes for a moment before Colin spoke up again.

"I've been wanting to do that all night," he admitted sheepishly.

Melissa chuckled and gave him another quick kiss. "I'm glad you finally did," she replied.

They stood there a while longer before the wind picked up. Melissa shivered, and Colin put his arm around her. "Let's get you inside by the fire!"

* * *

INSIDE, Melissa put on a kettle, while Colin started the fire. As she got two mugs out and fixed hot chocolate, she realized how long it had been since they were truly alone. Perhaps this was the first time since she was officially divorced. She certainly hadn't intended to find someone new so quickly. *Well, she hadn't intended to get a divorce at all.* She was amazed to think how long her life had been the same old predictable pattern of work, groceries, dinner, sleep, coffee, work, gym, sleep … and now to break free of these patterns and live a new life.

She knew she was stalling.

She brought the mugs of steaming hot chocolate into the living room where Colin was coaxing the fire. Jingles followed Melissa from the kitchen and sat down on the rug by the hearth.

"This night just gets better and better," said Melissa.

"That it does," said Colin as Melissa snuggled next to him.

"Was Burns Night our second date?" asked Colin.

"You know, I think New Year's—I mean, Hogmanay—probably counted as a date."

"So we're into third date territory?"

Melissa and Colin sat close to each other, their faces lit by the warm glow of the fire. Melissa's hand grazed Colin's as she reached for her cup of hot chocolate, the rich aroma filling her senses. As they sipped from their mugs, the warmth spread through their bodies. Colin's hand tenderly stroked Melissa's cheek before he leaned in for a kiss.

Melissa's heart fluttered as Colin's lips met hers. The kiss was gentle at first, but gradually grew in intensity as they melted into each other. Jingles watched them curiously, his tail thumping against the rug.

When they finally pulled apart, Melissa's eyes twinkled with joy. "I think that definitely counts as a third date," she said breathlessly.

Colin chuckled and leaned back against the couch, pulling Melissa closer to him. They sat in comfortable silence for a while, just enjoying each other's company and the crackling of the fire.

. . .

"CAN I ASK YOU SOMETHING?" Melissa finally broke the silence, her fingers tracing patterns on Colin's arm.

"Of course," Colin replied, turning to face her.

"Do you really think you could live here full time? What made you leave?"

Colin took a deep breath. "Well, I loved the croft, but I was young, and I wanted something more. I wanted to see the world, big cities with skyscrapers and subways and art museums. Certainly there's London and Edinburgh, but I wanted to … I needed to escape."

"And now? There aren't any skyscrapers and subways around here."

"I no longer feel a need to escape. I am right where I want to be."

Melissa's heart filled with warmth, and she blushed before changing the subject. They talked about their childhoods, their dreams and goals, and everything in between until the fire started to die down.

Melissa tried to stifle her yawn, but Colin spotted it.

"Same here."

"We should probably head to bed soon," Melissa said regretfully, looking at her watch.

Melissa didn't want this magical night to end just yet. Then she realized she'd said *we*.

Colin waited, watching as Melissa replayed the words in her head. She hadn't meant to say it out loud, but now that it was out there, she couldn't take it back.

"Sorry, I didn't mean … I mean, we don't have to …" she stumbled over her words.

"I'd like that," said Colin.

Melissa's heart skipped a beat. She couldn't believe how comfortable and open she felt with Colin after such a short time. But then again, these past few weeks had been nothing short of magical.

Flushed with excitement and nervousness, Melissa led Colin up the staircase toward her bedroom.

Just as Colin leaned in and kissed Melissa hungrily, his phone buzzed. Melissa paused, but he shook his head and continued kissing her.

The phone buzzed again.

And again.

Colin sighed and looked at it.

"It's Lindsay."

"She wouldn't call at this hour if it wasn't important."

Colin answered. "Aye, Lindsay, what's the—" He listened, his expression growing more grave by the second. "I'll be right there."

He hung up and shook his head. "Melissa, I'm so sorry. There's been an accident."

He was already starting down the stairs with Melissa right behind him.

"Is it Lindsay? Is she okay?" Melissa's voice trembled.

"My dad and his friend … Margaret. They took a cab home, but there was ice—"

"I'm coming with you."

"You don't have to."

"But I want to," Melissa said firmly.

They slipped on their coats and raced outside to Colin's car.

CHAPTER 14

Colin drove carefully down the icy driveway. As they approached the main road toward Inverness, the car nearly spun out on the slick surface.

"Are you okay?" Colin asked, his grip tightening on the steering wheel.

Melissa nodded, taking a deep breath as she looked out at the snowy landscape passing by. They stayed silent, Colin clearly worried about his father and Melissa worried for Colin.

Melissa and Colin burst through the doors of the hospital, their hearts racing with worry. They quickly scanned the waiting room until they spotted Lindsay, still dressed in her chef's gear, sitting with Drew.

"How's your father doing?" Melissa asked as she rushed over to them.

Lindsay shook her head tearfully. "I don't know. They're still running tests."

Melissa hugged her friend tightly, and Colin, ever the lawyer, had questions. "How did the car accident happen? I mean, he took a taxi ... he should've been safe."

Lindsay let out a heavy sigh before explaining what had

happened. "Apparently, the taxi driver lost control on the ice and crashed into another vehicle. Both drivers are fine, but Margaret has some glass in her arm, and Da hit his head during the impact. He's having some memory loss and confusion."

Melissa felt her heart sink at the news.

"Is there anything we can do?" asked Melissa, who had been standing quietly by Lindsay's side.

Lindsay shook her head again. "No, but thanks for being here."

As they waited for more updates on Sandy's condition, Melissa couldn't help but feel grateful that they were all able to be here together to support Lindsay and Colin. Eventually, after what seemed like hours of waiting, Margaret emerged with a bandage on her arm and shared the good news that Sandy would be okay with some rest and observation time in the hospital.

"Thank you all for coming," Margaret said. "He's asleep, but if you want to see him—"

"We'd better let him rest," said Colin.

"You all should try to rest, as well,," said Margaret. "Get some sleep and come back in the morning. I expect they'll release him then."

Colin and Lindsay shared a knowing look. Margaret was new in the picture, but everything she said and did suggested that her relationship with Sandy was much more than dog trainer and client.

Lindsay hugged Margaret. "I'm glad you were there for him. I mean, I'm not glad you were there, but—"

"I know what you meant, lass." Margaret planted a soft kiss on Lindsay's forehead.

Melissa watched her friend carefully, worrying it would be too much, but Lindsay softened. She hadn't had a mother figure in her life for a long time, and it looked like, even though

Lindsay was certainly an adult, Margaret might be well suited for the role.

"Shall I drive you back to Greenhill?" asked Colin, stifling a yawn.

"Yes, but you need to promise to get some rest," said Melissa.

Colin sighed but nodded his head. "Aye, I'm pure done in."

* * *

As they drove back in the early morning light, Melissa began to realize this was the new normal.

"Colin!"

"What?!" said Colin, scanning the road for ice or sheep. Seeing nothing, he turned to Melissa. "What?" he repeated.

"It's just dawning on me. This isn't goodbye. You don't have to go back to the States. We both live here now!"

"Aye … Though technically I don't live anywhere at the moment. I was certain the croft would be a fine place to set up camp until I got myself sorted, but it looks like Da and Margaret may be … nesting?"

"I think that's a pretty safe guess. Do you like her? Did you know her before?"

"No, I didn't know her, which is unusual in a town this size and with my Da's reputation for knowing everyone in town. But she seems …" Colin was at a loss for words.

"Pure dead brilliant?" Melissa suggested.

"I think a phrase like that is better suited for someone like yourself," he replied with a lopsided grin that made Melissa's heart flutter.

As he turned into the Greenhill House driveway and Melissa opened the car to get out, she turned back to him.

"You look exhausted," she said sympathetically. "Physically and emotionally. You need a place to rest."

"I don't know, Melissa," Colin replied wearily.

"You should come inside," she urged, extending her hand toward him. "I have plenty of space and all the time in the world."

Colin followed her inside, looking forward to catching up on some much-needed sleep.

* * *

FIVE HOURS LATER, Colin awoke to sunlight streaming through the window and the smell of bacon wafting up from the kitchen. He threw on some clothes and hurried downstairs to find Melissa flipping pancakes on the stove. She handed him a mug of coffee and soon sat a plate of steaming pancakes, sizzling bacon, and a bottle of Vermont maple syrup on the table in front of him. Colin, taking a big sip of coffee, eyed the syrup and raised an eyebrow in question.

"I wrapped it in bubble wrap and carried it in my checked luggage. That's one of the few things you don't seem to have here," she said.

"We have something similar made from birch trees, or there's golden syrup ... but yeah, the Vermont stuff is the real thing."

"I suppose you probably could ship it from Canada easily, since it's part of the commonwealth?" asked Melissa.

"Yeah, probably." said Colin, drizzling the fluffy pancakes with syrup and taking a large bite.

Melissa's phone buzzed. She looked down at it, and Colin watched her expression morph from relaxed joy into something that looked a lot like fear.

"What is it?"

"I have two texts. The first is Lindsay, saying your dad is home. The second is Dave."

"What now?"

"He wants to have a showing of the house."

"We've got to put a stop to this. What was the date he put on the bloody divorce documents?"

"February 1st."

"He thinks he can find a buyer that quickly? Who wants to move in the dead of winter?"

"I don't have to let them in, do I?"

"No. It's your house."

Melissa texted Dave back:

Not happening.

She stared at her phone, waiting for the three dots to appear, indicating he was responding, but all it said was *delivered*.

"Well, we've got time to think this through," she said, determination in her voice. "February 1st is coming right up. After that, even his lies won't save him."

* * *

THEY DROVE to Colin's father's house, where Margaret greeted them with warm hugs, and Sandy waved ruefully from his comfortable chair by the fire.

"You gave us quite a scare," said Melissa, hugging Sandy.

"Best laid plans, right, Colin?" said Sandy.

"I'm glad you're okay, Da" said Colin.

Margaret filled bowls with steaming hot potato leek soup and freshly baked bread.

"To your places, with clean hands and faces!" said Sandy.

As Melissa put her phone in her purse, the three dots appeared. Dave's new text read:

They don't need a tour; that was a courtesy. This is a large corporation who wants to buy the house, and they're willing to pay top dollar sight unseen.

Margaret watched as Melissa's face grew ashen. "What's wrong, dear?"

"Just my ex … but I'd rather not talk about it," said Melissa, not wanting to ruin the evening.

The soup was warm and comforting, and Melissa tried to focus on that.

* * *

THAT NIGHT MELISSA tossed and turned. She hated that the happiest time of her life was invaded by fears and worries from someone who had already hurt her so much. She hated that she'd worked so hard to keep this house from Dave, but he never seemed to give up.

Frustrated, she finally slipped out of bed and padded into her study where her computer was set up. Maybe she could finish ordering the designs for the inn.

Checking the MacAlister Inn website, Melissa admired the work that had been done over the past few months to make the inn ready to open. She looked again at the banner featuring opening night, *7-2.* She noticed that, once again, her brain immediately translated that as July 2nd. However, in the UK, that was February 7th, right around the corner.

That's it! she thought.

She opened her email and found the file with the finalized divorce papers, then quickly scrolled through to the final page. Dave had signed and dated his signature *2-1.* He meant that to read February 1st, but in the UK, Melissa realized that 2-1 meant January 2nd. "We've been officially divorced for weeks!" sang Melissa.

With that, Melissa plotted her plan of attack.

* * *

MELISSA'S CAR was coated in a thin layer of frost as she climbed in. She turned on the heater to defrost the windows, her breath creating little clouds in the cold air. She arrived at Margaret's now-familiar office just after they opened. In her arms, Melissa carried a variety of pastries, each one decorated with mouth-watering frosting and toppings. The smell of freshly brewed coffee wafted out of the open door as she entered the building, her heels clicking against the hardwood floor. Melissa was filled with an optimism she hadn't felt in days.

"Good morning, Margaret. I brought breakfast and fantastic news," said Melissa as she walked through the door of her office.

"That's just what the doctor ordered," replied Margaret. She took a lemon scone from the box that Melissa offered her and took a bite. "What is it?"

"I have an easy way to shut down my ex-husband, Dave," said Melissa triumphantly.

Margaret's eyebrows shot up in surprise. "Delicious! On both counts. Fill me in."

Melissa sat down at the desk and opened her laptop, pulling up an email she had received early that morning from her legal team. As she explained the situation to Margaret, the two women sipped their coffee and laid out their plans.

CHAPTER 15

Dave texted Melissa mid-morning, and relief washed over her, knowing that she could stop him. His text read:

> Got a buyer. It's a company that wants to tear it down and build a hotel. Boo hoo.

Margaret stood poised and confident behind Melissa, her eyes fiery and ready for battle when she saw the text. She made a quick call, and soon a handsome and sharp-witted barrister appeared, ready to take down the enemy with legal prowess and a flair for dramatic revenge.

"I'm told you've got baked goods and a good revenge plot," he said. "How can I be of service? I'm Andrew Douglas, Margaret's brother."

"And the best barrister north of Edinburgh," said Margaret proudly.

"Maybe this side of Inverness?" said Andrew.

"Don't sell yourself short, baby brother," said Margaret.

"Lovely to meet you. And perfect timing," said Melissa.

Melissa handed Andrew the divorce papers and pointed out

the 2-1 date that Dave had scribbled at the bottom. "He post-dated this so he could try to scam his way into co-owning and selling my newly inherited home."

Andrew looked over the papers and raised an eyebrow. "Well, that's certainly not playing nice. Fortunately, I have some tricks up my sleeve," he said.

Andrew read through the documents, then looked at the text Dave had sent Melissa.

"Hmmmm ... Yes ... Well ..." Andrew paused, his index finger tapping thoughtfully against his chin. "I hate to ask, but I have to." He turned toward Melissa and raised an eyebrow inquisitively. "Does this man play poker?"

Melissa let out a small sigh before answering. "Excuse me?"

Andrew leaned forward, his eyes narrowing as he drilled into her with his stare. "Is he cunning? Can he read people? Is he ..." He paused, searching for the right word.

"He's a *glaikit bampot eejit,*" said Margaret matter-of-factly.

Melissa, who had been silent up until this point, looked puzzled at the unfamiliar words. "*Eejit,* yes. The rest of that I didn't really get."

Andrew threw back his head and let out a hearty laugh. "I think we're all set then." He turned to face Melissa. "Now here's the situation." He gestured with his hands as he spoke. "In the US, what he did was sly, but the date holds up. In the UK, you're right—that's not how we handle dates." He glanced back at Margaret for confirmation before continuing. "However, it's not like we don't understand American dates. But for the good of the cause, I'll be happy to play the strict and to-the-letter barrister who has a stick up his arse." His voice dripped with sarcasm as he emphasized the last few words. "I think we can scare him away so he'll never come back to bother you again." He turned back to Melissa with a mischievous glint in his eye. "What do you think?"

Melissa's face lit up with excitement as she answered. "Unleash the kraken!"

"Here's how it's going to play out," said Andrew, and the three began to conspire.

* * *

DAVE'S REALTOR'S office was a bustling hub of activity, filled with the sounds of ringing phones and clicking keyboards. Colin was already waiting inside when Melissa, Margaret, and Andrew arrived. Dressed in a sharp, polished gray suit, Colin's eyes twinkled as they fell upon Melissa entering the room. Despite his obvious admiration for her, he maintained a professional demeanor and didn't show any signs of recognizing her team.

MELISSA EXUDED confidence and elegance in her favorite Mackenzie tartan dress, complete with matching shoes and her clan pin proudly displayed on her lapel—her version of a power suit. As she took in the scene around her, Melissa couldn't help but feel a sense of importance and determination wash over her. Margaret and Andrew stood by her side, fierce protectors, guarding her back. She breathed a sigh of relief, grateful to have their unwavering support. Though she avoided making eye contact with Colin, she was secretly thankful to have him as her secret weapon in this situation.

Dave sauntered into the office a few minutes later, coffee in hand and sporting a rumpled navy suit and scuffed black shoes. With him were a stern-looking corporate businessman and a high-end realtor, both clearly well-versed in the art of negotiation and deal-making.

As Dave and Melissa stood in the office, a sense of tension hung thick in the air.

"All right. Wasn't sure you'd show up or be able to find the place, but here you are," he chuckled, a hint of smugness in his voice.

"It was easy," said Melissa.

Dave's cronies snickered, but she didn't let his teasing faze her. She knew her worth and capabilities, despite what Dave may think. Her attention quickly turned to the matter at hand as Dave continued speaking.

"So, my buyer is ready to close and would like to take possession in the next two weeks."

"I'm afraid that won't be possible," Melissa interjected innocently.

"I've already made the agreement, Mel. Your opinion doesn't matter here," Dave stated firmly.

But before Dave could continue, Andrew spoke up with a mischievous twinkle in his eye. "About that ..." he began, drawing out each word for effect. "It seems that you are no longer married to Melissa."

Dave's confidence faltered for a moment before he regained his composure. "Nope," he proclaimed proudly. "We're still married until February 1st." He tapped on his phone screen and turned it toward Andrew to show him the paperwork.

Andrew put on a show of examining the documents, furrowing his brow and making thoughtful noises. Finally, he looked up at Dave and shook his head slowly. "I'm sorry," he said with mock concern. "I don't see anything here about February. You've clearly dated this January 2nd." He gestured toward the date on the document.

Dave's expression turned to confusion as he checked the date himself. "January 2nd? That can't be right." He studied his phone, trying to understand Andrew's statement.

"In the UK, we put the day before the month," Melissa explained triumphantly.

Dave's face fell as he realized his mistake.

"We don't accept post-dated documents, or whatever this is *meant* to be," Andrew stated firmly, looking pointedly at Dave. "Your divorce was finalized weeks ago when Melissa signed her papers. She wasn't even in possession of Greenhill House at that time."

Andrew paused for effect, then added with a flourish, "It wasn't until mid-January, I believe."

Dave's face contorted into a scowl. "This is absolute bull-shit!" he exclaimed, his voice rising in anger.

"Colin, you're my divorce lawyer. Tell them," Dave pleaded, turning to his former attorney with desperation in his eyes.

But Colin simply shook his head, a sad expression crossing his face. "Actually, Dave, I'm not your lawyer anymore. Your constant interference and accusations regarding my relation-ship with Melissa caused me to be let go from the firm."

"What's more, your name is not on the deed to Greenhill House," said Margaret with a grin.

"We're not married; you're not on the deed ... You can see where this is going, right, Dave?" said Melissa.

Dave's cheeks went pale, and he stared at Colin, his mouth agape in shock. "You ... you can't do this to me," he stammered.

"I'm sorry, Dave. But it's been years since I've had a license to practice law in the UK, and even if I did, I wouldn't want to represent someone who doesn't trust me," Colin replied calmly but firmly.

Dave opened and closed his mouth several times, but no words came out. Finally, he turned to Melissa with a pleading look. "Melissa ... please ... baby ... isn't there anything we can do?"

But Melissa stood tall and unwavering, her voice lacking any hint of hesitation or doubt. "I'm sorry about the misunderstand-ing, Dave. But Colin is right. I'm sure you fellows can find another property that suits your needs," said Melissa in the most confident and steady tone she'd ever used in her life.

Melissa savored the sweet feeling of satisfaction as she watched Dave's expression of defeat. Justice had been served, and she couldn't be happier.

Melissa confidently collected her purse. "Well then, I'll be off now. Good luck, Dave. See you around the pubs, then."

Dave retorted with a hint of sarcasm, "I'm going back to America where they actually speak English!"

He stormed out the door, his two cronies following meekly behind him.

When it was all over, Melissa looked at Margaret, and the two of them burst into laughter. Andrew and Colin joined them.

"Tonight, we're all going to Greenhill to celebrate!" said Melissa.

MELISSA COULDN'T WIPE the smile off her face as she drove back toward Greenhill House. The sun was finally beginning to burst through the clouds, filling the sky with a warm golden glow. Ice glimmered on the trees, and the landscape looked like something out of a fairy tale.

As she turned into the gates, Melissa was struck by how beautiful this gorgeous stone home was, with its rolling hills, tall pine trees, and the magical Loch Ness in the background. And it was all hers, forever. A Mackenzie legacy that had been in the family for generations. As Melissa parked her car, she noticed Colin arrive behind her. He emerged from his car carrying a large box.

"I've ordered loads of catering from Lindsay. You didn't need to bring anything, Colin!"

Colin shook his head. "It's a present I've been saving for this moment, and the time has come."

He set the giant box down on the steps, and Melissa opened it. It was a large Mackenzie clan shield with their motto: *Luceo, non uro.* Melissa's eyes filled with tears as she translated the Latin aloud, "I shine, not burn."

"Whereas, he who shall not be named will probably always fly too close to the sun, you sparkle, my dear Melissa. And you were just brilliant today, inside and out."

He kissed her and took her hand as they walked into her home.

* * *

LATER THAT EVENING, the house smelled like fresh bread, cozy fire, and pine. Sunlight streamed through the windows, and the view of the snowy hillside and the old wishing well made Melissa's heart sing. Lindsay, Elspeth, and Sydney brought in trays of food, while Drew set up a playlist of lively music. Sandy arrived looking dapper and flushed, with Margaret on his arm. Caitlin and Angus joined the party via FaceTime, their faces beaming with happiness.

They ate, drank, bantered, and told funny stories, and Melissa added log after log to the crackling fire. As Sandy stood and hugged Melissa goodbye, tears filled her eyes. "Thank you so much for coming."

"I'm so happy for you, Melissa. You deserve all this and more," Sandy said, his eyes drifting toward Colin.

Melissa flushed and hugged him again. "Drive safely!"

"I've got my personal chauffeur here," he said, a twinkle in his eye as he took Margaret's arm. "Margaret, thank you. I don't know what I'd do without you."

"I guess you're stuck with me then," said Margaret.

"Maybe we'll have to do something about that," said Sandy.

Melissa's eyes sparkled as she noticed Colin and Lindsay exchange a knowing glance, a touch of amusement flickering between them.

Melissa hugged Lindsay tightly, not wanting the evening to

end. Her best friend had been by her side through all her struggles, and now she had finally achieved her dream.

"Thank you for everything, Lindsay," said Melissa as they pulled away from each other.

"I'm just happy to see you happy, Mel," replied Lindsay warmly,

Melissa nodded, knowing that she could always count on Lindsay.

"Looks like we're the last ones here," said Colin, who was standing by the fireplace, the amber liquid in his glass casting a warm glow on his face. She moved toward him, her heart pounding in her chest, her breath hitching in her throat.

He turned to her, and she could see the desire in his eyes, mirroring her own. Without a word, he set his glass down on the mantelpiece, and reached for her, pulling her against him. His lips found hers, and she moaned softly at the feel of his mouth on hers. His kiss was demanding and urgent, and she responded eagerly, her tongue dancing with his. He tasted like whisky and smoke, and she found herself wanting more.

They broke apart for a moment, both breathless, and Melissa could see the heat in Colin's eyes. He ran his thumb over her bottom lip, and she shivered at the sensation.

"You're so beautiful," he murmured, before capturing her lips again. This time, his kiss was softer, more tender, and she melted into him, feeling safe and desired.

They kissed for what felt like hours, lost in each other's embrace, until finally they broke apart, both panting and flushed. Melissa sighed and looked up at Colin, feeling a deep sense of satisfaction and excitement at what was to come.

And with that, they disappeared upstairs.

CHAPTER 16

Opening night at the MacAlister Inn was the talk of the town. After their soft opening for Burns Night, the small, well-chosen crowd of locals who'd attended had spread the word about the wonderful food, updated interiors, and all the promise of events to come.

Melissa stopped in early to find the inn buzzing with excitement. Elspeth and Sydney had hung a giant *Grand Opening* banner in the entryway. Lindsay had created a gorgeous selection of appetizers and mixed drinks that waiters, circulating around the room, served on trays as guests arrived. The white tablecloths were adorned with lovely heather and thistle bouquets and candles. A fire crackled in the hearth, and the delicious scents of pine, haggis, and scotch filled the air.

Melissa made her way to her table with Colin. They savored their drinks and dug into tiny meat pies, croquettes, oatcakes, and an assortment of cheeses. Melissa felt a warm glow around her as she realized this was exactly where she belonged.

Just then, Sandy and Margaret arrived. Hand in hand, they looked like they were ready to celebrate a 60th anniversary rather than six weeks or so of dating.

Sandy pulled the chair out for Margaret, who greeted Colin and Melissa with little cheek kisses before sitting down. Sandy gave Melissa a gentle kiss on the cheek, feeling like a father figure to her. She couldn't help but hope for something more in the future, but she knew she was getting ahead of herself.

Once all the guests arrived and the main courses were served, Lindsay was able to slip in and join the table.

"You've done it again, Lindsay!" said Sandy, raising a glass to his daughter.

"Incredible. I'd ask for the recipes, but I'm sure it's a trade secret," said Margaret.

"Oh, these are just traditional Scottish recipes that I've made my own. I learned it all from my mother." As Lindsay spoke, she couldn't help but feel a pang of sadness in her chest. Her mother was no longer here to taste her creations and offer her words of praise.

Sandy, sensing Lindsay's change in mood, reached out and gave her a gentle squeeze on the shoulder. "And your mother would be right proud of you. I guarantee it."

"If you'll excuse me, I'm going to go see the new tiles in the loo," said Margaret.

As Lindsay watched Margaret walk gracefully through the dining room, Sandy watched Lindsay, understanding the bitter-sweet emotions that must be running through her mind.

"It's all right, Lindsay," Sandy reassured her. "She understands."

"She's a wonderful woman, Da. Truly," said Lindsay, her eyes glistening as she looked at her father.

"I'm glad you feel that way," Sandy said mischievously. "How did the desserts turn out?" he asked, almost in a whisper.

"I think everything's in order," Lindsay responded with a grin..

Margaret returned, and soon the waiters had cleared the tables and brought out a selection of deserts.

"This looks incredible!" said Melissa, "But how do we decide between cheesecake, raspberry cranachan, shortbread, and rice pudding?"

"A little bit of everything!" said Colin, taking a knife and beginning to divide and conquer. Sandy subtly took the knife from Colin and gave him a knowing look.

"Allow me, son."

Sandy began carefully cutting each slice into four small pieces, then passed around the plates.

"What's your favorite, Margaret?"

"You know I'm always partial to cranachan," she said.

Sandy nodded. He scooped a large dollop of cranachan onto her plate and handed it to her. Margaret dug her spoon into it. "I love the mix of raspberry, whisky, whipping cream, and—" Margaret stopped abruptly as she found something on her spoon that was not any of those things.

Colin's brow furrowed in concern as he asked, "Is everything alright?" But Lindsay's eyes sparkled with joy and excitement, and Sandy stood and moved closer to Margaret.

"Let me help you with that, Margaret," said Sandy. As it became evident to Margaret just what was going on, her face flushed pink, and her eyes sparkled as she looked lovingly into Sandy's eyes.

"Margaret Douglas. You've got a bloody stubborn little bampot of a dog. And I love every stolen glove and other act of disobedience that creature has ever committed, because otherwise, we might not have ever met. I thought I was just fine living on my croft alone with my own dogs, tending the sheep and meeting friends at the pub. I had no idea what I was missing out on. And now that I know, I never want to be without it ever again. And I know this may seem awfully soon, but at our age, there's no time like the present. So, Margaret Douglas ... will you marry me?"

Margaret's eyes shimmered with tears of joy. "Sandy, you are so incredibly sweet," she said, her gaze fixed on the ring that was now resting on her spoon, topped with a small dollop of whipped cream.

"Does that mean *yes*?" Sandy asked eagerly.

"Yes. Without a doubt and completely," Margaret replied joyfully. Sandy burst into a little happy dance and leaned in to kiss Margaret tenderly. The other diners in the restaurant paused their conversations to witness this heartfelt moment between the two lovers.

Lindsay stood and made a toast.

"Thank you all for coming to our grand opening here at the MacAlister Inn. Thanks to Drew for his vision that made all this happen, thanks to Sydney and Elspeth for their organization, and thanks to Margaret, who has just made my father the happiest man in the world!"

"A round of drinks on me," said Sandy.

They all raised their glasses to toast the happy couple. The clinking of glasses echoed through the restaurant, followed by cheers and well wishes from the guests.

EPILOGUE

A FEW MONTHS LATER

Rows of white chairs and tartan bows lined the backyard of the MacGregor croft, and guests dressed in their finest milled in to take their seats.

Sandy stood beside a gazebo dressed in his Highland formal—his red and green plaid MacGregor kilt, white fur sporran, a white kilt shirt, his Prince Charlie jacket, kilt hose, flashes, ghillie brogues, and a fly plaid.

Lindsay, dressed in a dark green bridesmaid gown with a MacGregor tartan sash, walked down the aisle arm in arm with Drew; while Melissa, dressed in the same gown and sash, followed behind them on Colin's arm.

A string quartet began playing *Pachabel's Canon in D,* and guests turned to Margaret. Her white hair was adorned with heather and thistle, and she wore a silky ivory gown—simple yet elegant, with long sleeves and a slight ruffle down the middle that added a delicate touch.

Though she started out walking down the aisle on her own, after a few steps, she nodded to the beaming Sandy, who reached into his pocket and pulled out a dog whistle. With a quick tweet, Bella, Margaret's golden retriever—matchmaker extraordinaire—trotted down the aisle with a MacGregor tartan plaid scarf around her neck. In her mouth, Bella proudly carried a delicate tartan glove, with their wedding rings securely tied to it.

As the two reached Sandy and the minister, Sandy handed the dog a treat, gently took the glove from the now-compliant dog, and handed the glove and rings to Colin for safe keeping, then beamed at his bride-to-be.

As the sun began to set on the horizon, the minister began the wedding ceremony. Margaret and Sandy stood side by side, their hands clasped together as they exchanged loving glances. The minister spoke about love and commitment and how the joining of two souls in marriage was a sacred bond. In the distance, a bagpiper played a traditional Scottish tune, adding to the magic of the moment.

After exchanging heartfelt vows and rings, Margaret and Sandy were declared husband and wife. They sealed their union with a kiss, surrounded by their loved ones, who cheered and clapped joyously.

As Margaret and Sandy walked back down the flower-petal-strewn aisle as Mr. and Mrs. MacGregor, Lindsay and Drew followed, arm in arm.

Behind them, Melissa clutched Colin's hand tightly, her eyes shining with unshed tears. As they passed by rows of happy guests, Colin leaned in and whispered, "Walking down the aisle is easier than I had expected."

Melissa's heart skipped a beat at his words. She squeezed his hand in response, feeling hopeful for their future together.

AFTERWORD

Thank you so much for reading the *Highlands Christmas Trilogy!* Did this arm-chair trip to Scotland make you want to try your hand at making traditional Scottish foods? Whether it's oatcakes, cranachan or something more savory like rumbledethumps, I've got you covered.

Head over to my website and grab a free copy of my *Highlands Christmas Cookbook.* Or start planning your Scottish adventure now and enjoy a free blank-book travel journal to document your travel memories. You can find them at www.amyquickparrish.com

Reviews are one of the greatest ways to support authors, and I would be incredibly grateful if you could share your honest thoughts on GoodReads, BookBub, or any of your favorite book sites.

Thank you so much for your support following Melissa's adventures in Scotland. It means the world to me!

ACKNOWLEDGMENTS

Highlands Christmas

Editor: Gary Smailes/BubbleCow, Jaime Cody

Cover Design by the author, titles by Cover Fixer

Illustrations from CanvaPro: Sketchify, Jan Natsicha

Highlands New Year

Editor: Jaime Cody

Cover Design by the author, titles by Cover Fixer

Illustrations from CanvaPro: Chonnieartwork, Jan Natsicha, Drawcee

Highlands Homecoming

Editors: Danielle Dresser, Jaime Cody

Cover Design: Cover Fixer

Illustrations from CanvaPro: HL12Studio, VOVA and Dee@strelitziastudio

Highlands Trilogy

Cover Design by the author, titles by CoverFixer.

Illustrations from CanvaPro: Nimas exacti, Drawcee, Yucalora, Mspoint, UnfoldX

ABOUT THE AUTHOR

Amy Quick Parrish is the bestselling author of young adult novels *Into Dust, Into the Storm,* and *The Frequency,* as well as her debut holiday book, *Highlands Christmas.* Born and raised in Michigan, she now lives in the Boston area with a wonderful husband and son and a lovely gray cat. When she's not busy crafting compelling screenplays or novels, you can find her watching Michigan football or on a quest to find the perfect taco.

ALSO BY AMY QUICK PARRISH

Into Dust - The Thunderbird Chronicles

Into the Storm - The Thunderbird Chronicles Book 2

The Frequency - False Flag

Highlands Christmas - Wishes Come True

www.ingramcontent.com/pod-product-compliance
Lightning Source LLC
Chambersburg PA
CBHW060539310726
48982CB00009B/1309/J

* 9 7 9 8 9 9 1 6 8 7 3 2 4 *